Copyright

Bibliographical Note

This Dover edition, first published by Dover Publications, Inc., in 2010, is an unabridged, slightly corrected republication of the work first published by Herbert S. Stone & Co., Chicago, in 1899, plus literary analysis and perspectives from *MAXnotes® for The Awakening,* published in 1996 by Research and Education Association, Inc., Piscataway, New Jersey.

Library of Congress Cataloging-in-Publication Data

Chopin, Kate, 1850–1904.
The awakening / Kate Chopin
p. cm. — (Dover thrift study edition)
"This Dover edition… is an unabridged, slightly corrected republication of the work first published by Herbert S. Stone & Co., Chicago, in 1899, plus literary analysis and perspectives from MAXnotes® for The awakening, published in 1996 by Research & Education Association, Inc., Piscataway, New Jersey"—T.p. verso.
ISBN-13: 978-0-486-47566-0
ISBN-10: 0-486-47566-2
1. Women—Louisiana—Fiction. 2. Adultery—Fiction. 3. New Orleans (La.)—Fiction. 4. Chopin, Kate, 1850–1904. Awakening. 5. Psychological fiction. I. Title.

PS1294.C63A64 2010
813'.4—dc22

2010003069

Manufactured in the United States by Courier Corporation
47566202
www.doverpublications.com

[illegible]

Dover Thrift Study Edition

The Awakening

KATE CHOPIN

DOVER PUBLICATIONS, INC.
Mineola, New York

At Dover Publications we're committed to producing books in an earth-friendly manner and to helping our customers make greener choices.

Manufacturing books in the United States ensures compliance with strict environmental laws and eliminates the need for international freight shipping, a major contributor to global air pollution. And printing on recycled paper helps minimize our consumption of trees, water and fossil fuels.

The text of this book was printed on paper made with 10% post-consumer waste and the cover was printed on paper made with 10% post-consumer waste. At Dover, we use Environmental Defense's Paper Calculator to measure the benefits of these choices, including: the number of trees saved, gallons of water conserved, as well as air emissions and solid waste eliminated.

Please visit the product page for *The Awakening Thrift Study Edition* at www.doverpublications.com to see a detailed account of the environmental savings we've achieved over the life of this book.

Copyright

Bibliographical Note

This Dover edition, first published by Dover Publications, Inc., in 2010, is an unabridged, slightly corrected republication of the work first published by Herbert S. Stone & Co., Chicago, in 1899, plus literary analysis and perspectives from *MAXnotes® for The Awakening,* published in 1996 by Research and Education Association, Inc., Piscataway, New Jersey.

Library of Congress Cataloging-in-Publication Data

Chopin, Kate, 1850–1904.
The awakening / Kate Chopin
p. cm. — (Dover thrift study edition)
"This Dover edition… is an unabridged, slightly corrected republication of the work first published by Herbert S. Stone & Co., Chicago, in 1899, plus literary analysis and perspectives from MAXnotes® for The awakening, published in 1996 by Research & Education Association, Inc., Piscataway, New Jersey"—T.p. verso.
ISBN-13: 978-0-486-47566-0
ISBN-10: 0-486-47566-2
1. Women—Louisiana—Fiction. 2. Adultery—Fiction. 3. New Orleans (La.)—Fiction. 4. Chopin, Kate, 1850–1904. Awakening. 5. Psychological fiction. I. Title.

PS1294.C63A64 2010
813'.4—dc22

2010003069

Manufactured in the United States by Courier Corporation
47566202
www.doverpublications.com

Publisher's Note

Combining the complete text of a classic novel or drama with a comprehensive study guide, Dover Thrift Study Editions are the most effective way to gain a thorough understanding of the major works of world literature.

The study guide features up-to-date and expert analysis of every chapter or section from the source work. Questions and fully explained answers follow, allowing readers to analyze the material critically. Character lists, author bios, and discussions of the work's historical context are also provided.

Each Dover Thrift Study Edition includes everything a student needs to prepare for homework, discussions, reports, and exams.

Contents

The Awakening v

Study Guide 117

The Awakening

KATE CHOPIN

The Awakening

I

A GREEN AND YELLOW parrot, which hung in a cage outside the door, kept repeating over and over:

"*Allez vous-en! Allez vous-en! Sapristi!*[1] That's all right!"

He could speak a little Spanish, and also a language which nobody understood, unless it was the mocking-bird that hung on the other side of the door, whistling his fluty notes out upon the breeze with maddening persistence.

Mr. Pontellier, unable to read his newspaper with any degree of comfort, arose with an expression and an exclamation of disgust. He walked down the gallery and across the narrow "bridges" which connected the Lebrun cottages one with the other. He had been seated before the door of the main house. The parrot and the mocking-bird were the property of Madame Lebrun, and they had the right to make all the noise they wished. Mr. Pontellier had the privilege of quitting their society when they ceased to be entertaining.

He stopped before the door of his own cottage, which was the fourth one from the main building and next to the last. Seating himself in a wicker rocker which was there, he once more applied himself to the task of reading the newspaper. The day was Sunday; the paper was a day old. The Sunday papers had not yet reached Grand Isle. He was already acquainted with the market reports, and he glanced restlessly over the editorials and bits of news which he had not had time to read before quitting New Orleans the day before.

Mr. Pontellier wore eye-glasses. He was a man of forty, of medium height and rather slender build; he stooped a little. His hair was brown and straight, parted on one side. His beard was neatly and closely trimmed.

[1] ["Go away! Go away! For heaven's sake!"]

Once in a while he withdrew his glance from the newspaper and looked about him. There was more noise than ever over at the house. The main building was called "the house," to distinguish it from the cottages. The chattering and whistling birds were still at it. Two young girls, the Farival twins, were playing a duet from "Zampa" upon the piano. Madame Lebrun was bustling in and out, giving orders in a high key to a yard-boy whenever she got inside the house, and directions in an equally high voice to a dining-room servant whenever she got outside. She was a fresh, pretty woman, clad always in white with elbow sleeves. Her starched skirts crinkled as she came and went. Farther down, before one of the cottages, a lady in black was walking demurely up and down, telling her beads. A good many persons of the *pension* had gone over to the *Chênière Caminada* in Beaudelet's lugger to hear mass. Some young people were out under the water-oaks playing croquet. Mr. Pontellier's two children were there—sturdy little fellows of four and five. A quadroon nurse followed them about with a far-away, meditative air.

Mr. Pontellier finally lit a cigar and began to smoke, letting the paper drag idly from his hand. He fixed his gaze upon a white sunshade that was advancing at snail's pace from the beach. He could see it plainly between the gaunt trunks of the water-oaks and across the stretch of yellow camomile. The gulf looked far away, melting hazily into the blue of the horizon. The sunshade continued to approach slowly. Beneath its pink-lined shelter were his wife, Mrs. Pontellier, and young Robert Lebrun. When they reached the cottage, the two seated themselves with some appearance of fatigue upon the upper step of the porch, facing each other, each leaning against a supporting post.

"What folly! to bathe at such an hour in such heat!" exclaimed Mr. Pontellier. He himself had taken a plunge at daylight. That was why the morning seemed long to him.

"You are burnt beyond recognition," he added, looking at his wife as one looks at a valuable piece of personal property which has suffered some damage. She held up her hands, strong, shapely hands, and surveyed them critically, drawing up her lawn sleeves above the wrists. Looking at them reminded her of her rings, which she had given to her husband before leaving for the beach. She silently reached out to him, and he, understanding, took the rings from his vest pocket and dropped them into her open palm. She slipped them upon her fingers; then clasping her knees, she looked across at Robert and began to laugh. The rings sparkled upon her fingers. He sent back an answering smile.

"What is it?" asked Pontellier, looking lazily and amused from one to the other. It was some utter nonsense; some adventure out there in the water, and they both tried to relate it at once. It did not seem half so amusing when told. They realized this, and so did Mr. Pontellier. He yawned and stretched himself. Then he got up, saying he had half a mind to go over to Klein's hotel and play a game of billiards.

"Come go along, Lebrun," he proposed to Robert. But Robert admitted quite frankly that he preferred to stay where he was and talk to Mrs. Pontellier.

"Well, send him about his business when he bores you, Edna," instructed her husband as he prepared to leave.

"Here, take the umbrella," she exclaimed, holding it out to him. He accepted the sunshade, and lifting it over his head descended the steps and walked away.

"Coming back to dinner?" his wife called after him. He halted a moment and shrugged his shoulders. He felt in his vest pocket; there was a ten-dollar bill there. He did not know; perhaps he would return for the early dinner and perhaps he would not. It all depended upon the company which he found over at Klein's and the size of "the game." He did not say this, but she understood it, and laughed, nodding good-by to him.

Both children wanted to follow their father when they saw him starting out. He kissed them and promised to bring them back bonbons and peanuts.

II

Mrs. Pontellier's eyes were quick and bright; they were a yellowish brown, about the color of her hair. She had a way of turning them swiftly upon an object and holding them there as if lost in some inward maze of contemplation or thought.

Her eyebrows were a shade darker than her hair. They were thick and almost horizontal, emphasizing the depth of her eyes. She was rather handsome than beautiful. Her face was captivating by reason of a certain frankness of expression and a contradictory subtle play of features. Her manner was engaging.

Robert rolled a cigarette. He smoked cigarettes because he could not afford cigars, he said. He had a cigar in his pocket which Mr. Pontellier had presented him with, and he was saving it for his after-dinner smoke.

This seemed quite proper and natural on his part. In coloring he was not unlike his companion. A clean-shaved face made the resemblance more pronounced than it would otherwise have been. There rested no shadow of care upon his open countenance. His eyes gathered in and reflected the light and languor of the summer day.

Mrs. Pontellier reached over for a palm-leaf fan that lay on the porch and began to fan herself, while Robert sent between his lips light puffs from his cigarette. They chatted incessantly: about the things around them; their amusing adventure out in the water—it had again assumed its entertaining aspect; about the wind, the trees, the people who had gone to the *Chênière*; about the children playing croquet under the oaks, and the Farival twins, who were now performing the overture to "The Poet and the Peasant."

Robert talked a good deal about himself. He was very young, and did not know any better. Mrs. Pontellier talked a little about herself for the same reason. Each was interested in what the other said. Robert spoke of his intention to go to Mexico in the autumn, where fortune awaited him. He was always intending to go to Mexico, but some way never got there. Meanwhile he held on to his modest position in a mercantile house in New Orleans, where an equal familiarity with English, French and Spanish gave him no small value as a clerk and correspondent.

He was spending his summer vacation, as he always did, with his mother at Grand Isle. In former times, before Robert could remember, "the house" had been a summer luxury of the Lebruns. Now, flanked by its dozen or more cottages, which were always filled with exclusive visitors from the "*Quartier Français*," it enabled Madame Lebrun to maintain the easy and comfortable existence which appeared to be her birthright.

Mrs. Pontellier talked about her father's Mississippi plantation and her girlhood home in the old Kentucky blue-grass country. She was an American woman, with a small infusion of French which seemed to have been lost in dilution. She read a letter from her sister, who was away in the East, and who had engaged herself to be married. Robert was interested, and wanted to know what manner of girls the sisters were, what the father was like, and how long the mother had been dead.

When Mrs. Pontellier folded the letter it was time for her to dress for the early dinner.

"I see Léonce isn't coming back," she said, with a glance in the direction whence her husband had disappeared. Robert supposed he was not, as there were a good many New Orleans club men over at Klein's.

When Mrs. Pontellier left him to enter her room, the young man descended the steps and strolled over toward the croquet players, where, during the half-hour before dinner, he amused himself with the little Pontellier children, who were very fond of him.

III

IT WAS ELEVEN o'clock that night when Mr. Pontellier returned from Klein's hotel. He was in an excellent humor, in high spirits, and very talkative. His entrance awoke his wife, who was in bed and fast asleep when he came in. He talked to her while he undressed, telling her anecdotes and bits of news and gossip that he had gathered during the day. From his trousers pockets he took a fistful of crumpled bank notes and a good deal of silver coin, which he piled on the bureau indiscriminately with keys, knife, handkerchief, and whatever else happened to be in his pockets. She was overcome with sleep, and answered him with little half utterances.

He thought it very discouraging that his wife, who was the sole object of his existence, evinced so little interest in things which concerned him, and valued so little his conversation.

Mr. Pontellier had forgotten the bonbons and peanuts for the boys. Notwithstanding he loved them very much, and went into the adjoining room where they slept to take a look at them and make sure that they were resting comfortably. The result of his investigation was far from satisfactory. He turned and shifted the youngsters about in bed. One of them began to kick and talk about a basket full of crabs.

Mr. Pontellier returned to his wife with the information that Raoul had a high fever and needed looking after. Then he lit a cigar and went and sat near the open door to smoke it.

Mrs. Pontellier was quite sure Raoul had no fever. He had gone to bed perfectly well, she said, and nothing had ailed him all day. Mr. Pontellier was too well acquainted with fever symptoms to be mistaken. He assured her the child was consuming at that moment in the next room.

He reproached his wife with her inattention, her habitual neglect of the children. If it was not a mother's place to look after children, whose on earth was it? He himself had his hands full with his brokerage business. He could not be in two places at once; making a living for his family on the street, and staying at home to see that no harm befell them. He talked in a monotonous, insistent way.

Mrs. Pontellier sprang out of bed and went into the next room. She soon came back and sat on the edge of the bed, leaning her head down on the pillow. She said nothing, and refused to answer her husband when he questioned her. When his cigar was smoked out he went to bed, and in half a minute he was fast asleep.

Mrs. Pontellier was by that time thoroughly awake. She began to cry a little, and wiped her eyes on the sleeve of her *peignoir*. Blowing out the candle, which her husband had left burning, she slipped her bare feet into a pair of satin *mules* at the foot of the bed and went out on the porch, where she sat down in the wicker chair and began to rock gently to and fro.

It was then past midnight. The cottages were all dark. A single faint light gleamed out from the hallway of the house. There was no sound abroad except the hooting of an old owl in the top of a water-oak, and the everlasting voice of the sea, that was not uplifted at that soft hour. It broke like a mournful lullaby upon the night.

The tears came so fast to Mrs. Pontellier's eyes that the damp sleeve of her *peignoir* no longer served to dry them. She was holding the back of her chair with one hand; her loose sleeve had slipped almost to the shoulder of her uplifted arm. Turning, she thrust her face, steaming and wet, into the bend of her arm, and she went on crying there, not caring any longer to dry her face, her eyes, her arms. She could not have told why she was crying. Such experiences as the foregoing were not uncommon in her married life. They seemed never before to have weighed much against the abundance of her husband's kindness and a uniform devotion which had come to be tacit and self-understood.

An indescribable oppression, which seemed to generate in some unfamiliar part of her consciousness, filled her whole being with a vague anguish. It was like a shadow, like a mist passing across her soul's summer day. It was strange and unfamiliar; it was a mood. She did not sit there inwardly upbraiding her husband, lamenting at Fate, which had directed her footsteps to the path which they had taken. She was just having a good cry all to herself. The mosquitoes made merry over her, biting her firm, round arms and nipping at her bare insteps.

The little stinging, buzzing imps succeeded in dispelling a mood which might have held her there in the darkness half a night longer.

The following morning Mr. Pontellier was up in good time to take the rockaway which was to convey him to the steamer at the wharf. He was returning to the city to his business, and they would not see him again at the Island till the coming Saturday. He had regained his composure, which seemed to have been somewhat impaired the night before. He was eager to be gone, as he looked forward to a lively week in Carondelet Street.

Mr. Pontellier gave his wife half of the money which he had brought away from Klein's hotel the evening before. She liked money as well as most women, and accepted it with no little satisfaction.

"It will buy a handsome wedding present for Sister Janet!" she exclaimed, smoothing out the bills as she counted them one by one.

"Oh! we'll treat Sister Janet better than that, my dear," he laughed, as he prepared to kiss her good-by.

The boys were tumbling about, clinging to his legs, imploring that numerous things be brought back to them. Mr. Pontellier was a great favorite, and ladies, men, children, even nurses, were always on hand to say good-by to him. His wife stood smiling and waving, the boys shouting, as he disappeared in the old rockaway down the sandy road.

A few days later a box arrived for Mrs. Pontellier from New Orleans. It was from her husband. It was filled with *friandises*, with luscious and toothsome bits—the finest of fruits, *patés*, a rare bottle or two, delicious syrups, and bonbons in abundance.

Mrs. Pontellier was always very generous with the contents of such a box; she was quite used to receiving them when away from home. The *patés* and fruit were brought to the dining-room; the bonbons were passed around. And the ladies, selecting with dainty and discriminating fingers and a little greedily, all declared that Mr. Pontellier was the best husband in the world. Mrs. Pontellier was forced to admit that she knew of none better.

IV

It would have been a difficult matter for Mr. Pontellier to define to his own satisfaction or any one else's wherein his wife failed in her duty toward their children. It was something which he felt rather than perceived, and he never voiced the feeling without subsequent regret and ample atonement.

If one of the little Pontellier boys took a tumble whilst at play, he was not apt to rush crying to his mother's arms for comfort; he would more likely pick himself up, wipe the water out of his eyes and the sand out of his mouth, and go on playing. Tots as they were, they pulled together and stood their ground in childish battles with doubled fists and uplifted voices, which usually prevailed against the other mother-tots. The quadroon nurse was looked upon as a huge encumbrance, only good to button up waists and panties and to brush and part hair; since it seemed to be a law of society that hair must be parted and brushed.

In short, Mrs. Pontellier was not a mother-woman. The mother-women seemed to prevail that summer at Grand Isle. It was easy to know them, fluttering about with extended, protecting wings when any harm, real or imaginary, threatened their precious brood. They were women who idolized their children, worshiped their husbands, and esteemed it a holy privilege to efface themselves as individuals and grow wings as ministering angels.

Many of them were delicious in the rôle; one of them was the embodiment of every womanly grace and charm. If her husband did not adore her, he was a brute, deserving of death by slow torture. Her name was Adèle Ratignolle. There are no words to describe her save the old ones that have served so often to picture the bygone heroine of romance and the fair lady of our dreams. There was nothing subtle or hidden about her charms; her beauty was all there, flaming and apparent: the spun-gold hair that comb nor confining pin could restrain; the blue eyes that were like nothing but sapphires; two lips that pouted, that were so red one could only think of cherries or some other delicious crimson fruit in looking at them. She was growing a little stout, but it did not seem to detract an iota from the grace of every step, pose, gesture. One would not have wanted her white neck a mite less full or her beautiful arms more slender. Never were hands more exquisite than hers, and it was a joy to look at them when she threaded her needle or adjusted her gold thimble to her taper middle finger as she sewed away on the little night-drawers or fashioned a bodice or a bib.

Madame Ratignolle was very fond of Mrs. Pontellier, and often she took her sewing and went over to sit with her in the afternoons. She was sitting there the afternoon of the day the box arrived from New Orleans. She had possession of the rocker, and she was busily engaged in sewing upon a diminutive pair of night-drawers.

She had brought the pattern of the drawers for Mrs. Pontellier to cut out—a marvel of construction, fashioned to enclose a baby's body so effectually that only two small eyes might look out from the garment, like an Eskimo's. They were designed for winter wear, when treacherous drafts came down chimneys and insidious currents of deadly cold found their way through key-holes.

Mrs. Pontellier's mind was quite at rest concerning the present material needs of her children, and she could not see the use of anticipating and making winter night garments the subject of her summer meditations. But she did not want to appear unamiable and uninterested, so she had brought forth newspapers, which she spread upon the floor of the gallery, and under Madame Ratignolle's directions she had cut a pattern of the impervious garment.

Robert was there, seated as he had been the Sunday before, and Mrs. Pontellier also occupied her former position on the upper step, leaning listlessly against the post. Beside her was a box of bonbons, which she held out at intervals to Madame Ratignolle.

That lady seemed at a loss to make a selection, but finally settled upon a stick of nugat, wondering if it were not too rich; whether it could possibly hurt her. Madame Ratignolle had been married seven years. About every two years she had a baby. At that time she had three babies, and was beginning to think of a fourth one. She was always talking about her "condition." Her "condition" was in no way apparent, and no one would have known a thing about it but for her persistence in making it the subject of conversation.

Robert started to reassure her, asserting that he had known a lady who had subsisted upon nugat during the entire—but seeing the color mount into Mrs. Pontellier's face he checked himself and changed the subject.

Mrs. Pontellier, though she had married a Creole, was not thoroughly at home in the society of Creoles; never before had she been thrown so intimately among them. There were only Creoles that summer at Lebrun's. They all knew each other, and felt like one large family, among whom existed the most amicable relations. A characteristic which distinguished them and which impressed Mrs. Pontellier most forcibly was their entire absence of prudery. Their freedom of expression was at first incomprehensible to her, though she had no difficulty in reconciling it with a lofty chastity which in the Creole woman seems to be inborn and unmistakable.

Never would Edna Pontellier forget the shock with which she heard Madame Ratignolle relating to old Monsieur Farival the harrowing story of one of her *accouchements*,[1] withholding no intimate detail. She was growing accustomed to like shocks, but she could not keep the mounting color back from her cheeks. Oftener than once her coming had interrupted the droll story with which Robert was entertaining some amused group of married women.

A book had gone the rounds of the *pension*. When it came her turn to read it, she did so with profound astonishment. She felt moved to read the book in secret and solitude, though none of the others had done so—to hide it from view at the sound of approaching footsteps. It was openly

[1] [Parturitions.]

criticised and freely discussed at table. Mrs. Pontellier gave over being astonished, and concluded that wonders would never cease.

V

THEY FORMED A congenial group sitting there that summer afternoon—Madame Ratignolle sewing away, often stopping to relate a story or incident with much expressive gesture of her perfect hands; Robert and Mrs. Pontellier sitting idle, exchanging occasional words, glances or smiles which indicated a certain advanced stage of intimacy and *camaraderie.*

He had lived in her shadow during the past month. No one thought anything of it. Many had predicted that Robert would devote himself to Mrs. Pontellier when he arrived. Since the age of fifteen, which was eleven years before, Robert each summer at Grand Isle had constituted himself the devoted attendant of some fair dame or damsel. Sometimes it was a young girl, again a widow; but as often as not it was some interesting married woman.

For two consecutive seasons he lived in the sunlight of Mademoiselle Duvigné's presence. But she died between summers; then Robert posed as an inconsolable, prostrating himself at the feet of Madame Ratignolle for whatever crumbs of sympathy and comfort she might be pleased to vouchsafe.

Mrs. Pontellier liked to sit and gaze at her fair companion as she might look upon a faultless Madonna.

"Could any one fathom the cruelty beneath that fair exterior?" murmured Robert. "She knew that I adored her once, and she let me adore her. It was 'Robert, come; go; stand up; sit down; do this; do that; see if the baby sleeps; my thimble, please, that I left God knows where. Come and read Daudet to me while I sew.' "

"*Par exemple!*[1] I never had to ask. You were always there under my feet, like a troublesome cat."

"You mean like an adoring dog. And just as soon as Ratignolle appeared on the scene, then it *was* like a dog. '*Passez! Adieu! Allez vous-en!*' "[2]

"Perhaps I feared to make Alphonse jealous," she interjoined, with

1 ["Well!"]

2 [" 'Leave! Goodbye! Go away!' "]

excessive naïveté. That made them all laugh. The right hand jealous of the left! The heart jealous of the soul! But for that matter, the Creole husband is never jealous; with him the gangrene passion is one which has become dwarfed by disuse.

Meanwhile Robert, addressing Mrs. Pontellier, continued to tell of his one time hopeless passion for Madame Ratignolle; of sleepless nights, of consuming flames till the very sea sizzled when he took his daily plunge. While the lady at the needle kept up a little running, contemptuous comment:

"*Blagueur—farceur—gros bête, va!*"[1]

He never assumed this serio-comic tone when alone with Mrs. Pontellier. She never knew precisely what to make of it; at that moment it was impossible for her to guess how much of it was jest and what proportion was earnest. It was understood that he had often spoken words of love to Madame Ratignolle, without any thought of being taken seriously. Mrs. Pontellier was glad he had not assumed a similar rôle toward herself. It would have been unacceptable and annoying.

Mrs. Pontellier had brought her sketching materials, which she sometimes dabbled with in an unprofessional way. She liked the dabbling. She felt in it satisfaction of a kind which no other employment afforded her.

She had long wished to try herself on Madame Ratignolle. Never had that lady seemed a more tempting subject than at that moment, seated there like some sensuous Madonna, with the gleam of the fading day enriching her splendid color.

Robert crossed over and seated himself upon the step below Mrs. Pontellier, that he might watch her work. She handled her brushes with a certain ease and freedom which came, not from long and close acquaintance with them, but from a natural aptitude. Robert followed her work with close attention, giving forth little ejaculatory expressions of appreciation in French, which he addressed to Madame Ratignolle.

"*Mais ce n'est pas mal! Elle s'y connait, elle a de la force, oui.*"[2]

During his oblivious attention he once quietly rested his head against Mrs. Pontellier's arm. As gently she repulsed him. Once again he repeated the offense. She could not but believe it to be thoughtlessness on his part; yet that was no reason she should submit to it. She did not remonstrate, except again to repulse him quietly but firmly. He offered no apology.

The picture completed bore no resemblance to Madame Ratignolle.

[1] ["Joker—clown—big fool, get on with you!"]

[2] ["Why, it's not bad! She knows what she's doing, she has skill, indeed."]

She was greatly disappointed to find that it did not look like her. But it was a fair enough piece of work, and in many respects satisfying.

Mrs. Pontellier evidently did not think so. After surveying the sketch critically she drew a broad smudge of paint across its surface, and crumpled the paper between her hands.

The youngsters came tumbling up the steps, the quadroon following at the respectful distance which they required her to observe. Mrs. Pontellier made them carry her paints and things into the house. She sought to detain them for a little talk and some pleasantry. But they were greatly in earnest. They had only come to investigate the contents of the bonbon box. They accepted without murmuring what she chose to give them, each holding out two chubby hands scoop-like, in the vain hope that they might be filled; and then away they went.

The sun was low in the west, and the breeze soft and languorous that came up from the south, charged with the seductive odor of the sea. Children, freshly befurbelowed, were gathering for their games under the oaks. Their voices were high and penetrating.

Madame Ratignolle folded her sewing, placing thimble, scissors and thread all neatly together in the roll, which she pinned securely. She complained of faintness. Mrs. Pontellier flew for the cologne water and a fan. She bathed Madame Ratignolle's face with cologne, while Robert plied the fan with unnecessary vigor.

The spell was soon over, and Mrs. Pontellier could not help wondering if there were not a little imagination responsible for its origin, for the rose tint had never faded from her friend's face.

She stood watching the fair woman walk down the long line of galleries with the grace and majesty which queens are sometimes supposed to possess. Her little ones ran to meet her. Two of them clung about her white skirts, the third she took from its nurse and with a thousand endearments bore it along in her own fond, encircling arms. Though, as everybody well knew, the doctor had forbidden her to lift so much as a pin!

"Are you going bathing?" asked Robert of Mrs. Pontellier. It was not so much a question as a reminder.

"Oh, no," she answered, with a tone of indecision. "I'm tired; I think not." Her glance wandered from his face away toward the Gulf, whose sonorous murmur reached her like a loving but imperative entreaty.

"Oh, come!" he insisted. "You mustn't miss your bath. Come on. The water must be delicious; it will not hurt you. Come."

He reached up for her big, rough straw hat that hung on a peg outside the door, and put it on her head. They descended the steps, and walked away together toward the beach. The sun was low in the west and the breeze was soft and warm.

VI

EDNA PONTELLIER COULD not have told why, wishing to go to the beach with Robert, she should in the first place have declined, and in the second place have followed in obedience to one of the two contradictory impulses which impelled her.

A certain light was beginning to dawn dimly within her,—the light which, showing the way, forbids it.

At that early period it served but to bewilder her. It moved her to dreams, to thoughtfulness, to the shadowy anguish which had overcome her the midnight when she had abandoned herself to tears.

In short, Mrs. Pontellier was beginning to realize her position in the universe as a human being, and to recognize her relations as an individual to the world within and about her. This may seem like a ponderous weight of wisdom to descend upon the soul of a young woman of twenty-eight—perhaps more wisdom than the Holy Ghost is usually pleased to vouchsafe to any woman.

But the beginning of things, of a world especially, is necessarily vague, tangled, chaotic, and exceedingly disturbing. How few of us ever emerge from such beginning! How many souls perish in its tumult!

The voice of the sea is seductive; never ceasing, whispering, clamoring, murmuring, inviting the soul to wander for a spell in abysses of solitude; to lose itself in mazes of inward contemplation.

The voice of the sea speaks to the soul. The touch of the sea is sensuous, enfolding the body in its soft, close embrace.

VII

MRS. PONTELLIER WAS not a woman given to confidences, a characteristic hitherto contrary to her nature. Even as a child she had lived her own small life all within herself. At a very early period she had apprehended instinctively the dual life—that outward existence which conforms, the inward life which questions.

That summer at Grand Isle she began to loosen a little the mantle of reserve that had always enveloped her. There may have been—there must have been—influences, both subtle and apparent, working in their several ways to induce her to do this; but the most obvious was the influence of Adèle Ratignolle. The excessive physical charm of the Creole had first attracted her, for Edna had a sensuous susceptibility to beauty. Then the candor of the woman's whole existence, which every one might read, and which formed so striking a contrast to her own habitual reserve—this might have furnished a link. Who can tell what metals the gods use in forging the subtle bond which we call sympathy, which we might as well call love.

The two women went away one morning to the beach together, arm in arm, under the huge white sunshade. Edna had prevailed upon Madame Ratignolle to leave the children behind, though she could not induce her to relinquish a diminutive roll of needlework, which Adèle begged to be allowed to slip into the depths of her pocket. In some unaccountable way they had escaped from Robert.

The walk to the beach was no inconsiderable one, consisting as it did of a long, sandy path, upon which a sporadic and tangled growth that bordered it on either side made frequent and unexpected inroads. There were acres of yellow camomile reaching out on either hand. Further away still, vegetable gardens abounded, with frequent small plantations of orange or lemon trees intervening. The dark green clusters glistened from afar in the sun.

The women were both of goodly height, Madame Ratignolle possessing the more feminine and matronly figure. The charm of Edna Pontellier's physique stole insensibly upon you. The lines of her body were long, clean and symmetrical; it was a body which occasionally fell into splendid poses; there was no suggestion of the trim, stereotyped fashion-plate about it. A casual and indiscriminating observer, in passing, might not cast a second glance upon the figure. But with more feeling and discernment he would have recognized the noble beauty of its modeling, and the graceful severity of poise and movement, which made Edna Pontellier different from the crowd.

She wore a cool muslin that morning—white, with a waving vertical line of brown running through it; also a white linen collar and the big straw hat which she had taken from the peg outside the door. The hat rested any way on her yellow-brown hair, that waved a little, was heavy, and clung close to her head.

Madame Ratignolle, more careful of her complexion, had twined a gauze veil about her head. She wore dogskin gloves, with gauntlets that protected her wrists. She was dressed in pure white, with a fluffiness of ruffles that became her. The draperies and fluttering things which she wore suited her rich, luxuriant beauty as a greater severity of line could not have done.

There were a number of bath-houses along the beach, of rough but solid construction, built with small, protecting galleries facing the water. Each house consisted of two compartments, and each family at Lebrun's possessed a compartment for itself, fitted out with all the essential paraphernalia of the bath and whatever other conveniences the owners might desire. The two women had no intention of bathing; they had just strolled down to the beach for a walk and to be alone and near the water. The Pontellier and Ratignolle compartments adjoined one another under the same roof.

Mrs. Pontellier had brought down her key through force of habit. Unlocking the door of her bath-room she went inside, and soon emerged, bringing a rug, which she spread upon the floor of the gallery, and two huge hair pillows covered with crash, which she placed against the front of the building.

The two seated themselves there in the shade of the porch, side by side, with their backs against the pillows and their feet extended. Madame Ratignolle removed her veil, wiped her face with a rather delicate handkerchief, and fanned herself with the fan which she always carried suspended somewhere about her person by a long, narrow ribbon. Edna removed her collar and opened her dress at the throat. She took the fan from Madame Ratignolle and began to fan both herself and her companion. It was very warm, and for a while they did nothing but exchange remarks about the heat, the sun, the glare. But there was a breeze blowing, a choppy, stiff wind that whipped the water into froth. It fluttered the skirts of the two women and kept them for a while engaged in adjusting, readjusting, tucking in, securing hair-pins and hat-pins. A few persons were sporting some distance away in the water. The beach was very still of human sound at that hour. The lady in black was reading her morning devotions on the porch of a neighboring bath-house. Two young lovers were exchanging their hearts' yearnings beneath the children's tent, which they had found unoccupied.

Edna Pontellier, casting her eyes about, had finally kept them at rest upon the sea. The day was clear and carried the gaze out as far as the blue sky went; there were a few white clouds suspended idly over the horizon. A lateen sail was visible in the direction of Cat Island, and others to the south seemed almost motionless in the far distance.

"Of whom—of what are you thinking?" asked Adèle of her companion, whose countenance she had been watching with a little amused attention, arrested by the absorbed expression which seemed to have seized and fixed every feature into a statuesque repose.

"Nothing," returned Mrs. Pontellier, with a start, adding at once: "How stupid! But it seems to me it is the reply we make instinctively to such a question. Let me see," she went on, throwing back her head and narrowing her fine eyes till they shone like two vivid points of light. "Let me see. I was really not conscious of thinking of anything; but perhaps I can retrace my thoughts."

"Oh! never mind!" laughed Madame Ratignolle. "I am not quite so exacting. I will let you off this time. It is really too hot to think, especially to think about thinking."

"But for the fun of it," persisted Edna. "First of all, the sight of the water stretching so far away, those motionless sails against the blue sky, made a delicious picture that I just wanted to sit and look at. The hot wind beating in my face made me think—without any connection that I can trace—of a summer day in Kentucky, of a meadow that seemed as big as the ocean to the very little girl walking through the grass, which was higher than her waist. She threw out her arms as if swimming when she walked, beating the tall grass as one strikes out in the water. Oh, I see the connection now!"

"Where were you going that day in Kentucky, walking through the grass?"

"I don't remember now. I was just walking diagonally across a big field. My sun-bonnet obstructed the view. I could see only the stretch of green before me, and I felt as if I must walk on forever, without coming to the end of it. I don't remember whether I was frightened or pleased. I must have been entertained.

"Likely as not it was Sunday," she laughed; "and I was running away from prayers, from the Presbyterian service, read in a spirit of gloom by my father that chills me yet to think of."

"And have you been running away from prayers ever since, *ma chère?*" asked Madame Ratignolle, amused.

"No! oh, no!" Edna hastened to say. "I was a little unthinking child in those days, just following a misleading impulse without question. On the contrary, during one period of my life religion took a firm hold upon me; after I was twelve and until—until—why, I suppose until now, though I never thought much about it—just driven along by habit. But do you know," she broke off, turning her quick eyes upon Madame Ratignolle and leaning forward a little so as to bring her face quite close to that of her companion, "sometimes I feel this summer as if I were walking through the green meadow again; idly, aimlessly, unthinking and unguided."

Madame Ratignolle laid her hand over that of Mrs. Pontellier, which was near her. Seeing that the hand was not withdrawn, she clasped it firmly and warmly. She even stroked it a little, fondly, with the other hand, murmuring in an undertone, "*Pauvre chérie.*"

The action was at first a little confusing to Edna, but she soon lent herself readily to the Creole's gentle caress. She was not accustomed to an outward and spoken expression of affection, either in herself or in others. She and her younger sister, Janet, had quarreled a good deal through force of unfortunate habit. Her older sister, Margaret, was matronly and dignified, probably from having assumed matronly and house-wifely responsibilities too early in life, their mother having died when they were quite young. Margaret was not effusive; she was practical. Edna had had an occasional girl friend, but whether accidentally or not, they seemed to have been all of one type—the self-contained. She never realized that the reserve of her own character had much, perhaps everything, to do with this. Her most intimate friend at school had been one of rather exceptional intellectual gifts, who wrote fine-sounding essays, which Edna admired and strove to imitate; and with her she talked and glowed over the English classics, and sometimes held religious and political controversies.

Edna often wondered at one propensity which sometimes had inwardly disturbed her without causing any outward show or manifestation on her part. At a very early age—perhaps it was when she traversed the ocean of waving grass—she remembered that she had been passionately enamored of a dignified and sad-eyed cavalry officer who visited her father in Kentucky. She could not leave his presence when he was there, nor remove her eyes from his face, which was something like Napoleon's, with a lock of black hair falling across the forehead. But the cavalry officer melted imperceptibly out of her existence.

At another time her affections were deeply engaged by a young gentleman who visited a lady on a neighboring plantation. It was after they went to Mississippi to live. The young man was engaged to be married to the young lady, and they sometimes called upon Margaret, driving over of afternoons in a buggy. Edna was a little miss, just merging into her teens; and the realization that she herself was nothing, nothing, nothing to the engaged young man was a bitter affliction to her. But he, too, went the way of dreams.

She was a grown young woman when she was overtaken by what she supposed to be the climax of her fate. It was when the face and figure of a great tragedian began to haunt her imagination and stir her senses. The persistence of the infatuation lent it an aspect of genuineness. The hopelessness of it colored it with the lofty tones of a great passion.

The picture of the tragedian stood enframed upon her desk. Any one may possess the portrait of a tragedian without exciting suspicion or comment. (This was a sinister reflection which she cherished.) In the presence of others she expressed admiration for his exalted gifts, as she handed the photograph around and dwelt upon the fidelity of the likeness. When alone she sometimes picked it up and kissed the cold glass passionately.

Her marriage to Léonce Pontellier was purely an accident, in this respect resembling many other marriages which masquerade as the decrees of Fate. It was in the midst of her secret great passion that she met him. He fell in love, as men are in the habit of doing, and pressed his suit with an earnestness and an ardor which left nothing to be desired. He pleased her; his absolute devotion flattered her. She fancied there was a sympathy of thought and taste between them, in which fancy she was mistaken. Add to this the violent opposition of her father and her sister Margaret to her marriage with a Catholic, and we need seek no further for the motives which led her to accept Monsieur Pontellier for her husband.

The acme of bliss, which would have been a marriage with the tragedian, was not for her in this world. As the devoted wife of a man who worshiped her, she felt she would take her place with a certain dignity in the world of reality, closing the portals forever behind her upon the realm of romance and dreams.

But it was not long before the tragedian had gone to join the cavalry officer and the engaged young man and a few others; and Edna found herself face to face with the realities. She grew fond of her husband, realizing with some unaccountable satisfaction that no trace of passion or excessive and fictitious warmth colored her affection, thereby threatening its dissolution.

She was fond of her children in an uneven, impulsive way. She would sometimes gather them passionately to her heart; she would sometimes forget them. The year before they had spent part of the summer with their grandmother Pontellier in Iberville. Feeling secure regarding their happiness and welfare, she did not miss them except with an occasional intense longing. Their absence was a sort of relief, though she did not admit this, even to herself. It seemed to free her of a responsibility which she had blindly assumed and for which Fate had not fitted her.

Edna did not reveal so much as all this to Madame Ratignolle that summer day when they sat with faces turned to the sea. But a good part of it escaped her. She had put her head down on Madame Ratignolle's shoulder. She was flushed and felt intoxicated with the sound of her own voice and the unaccustomed taste of candor. It muddled her like wine, or like a first breath of freedom.

There was the sound of approaching voices. It was Robert, surrounded by a troop of children, searching for them. The two little Pontelliers were with him, and he carried Madame Ratignolle's little girl in his arms. There were other children beside, and two nurse-maids followed, looking disagreeable and resigned.

The women at once rose and began to shake out their draperies and relax their muscles. Mrs. Pontellier threw the cushions and rug into the bath-house. The children all scampered off to the awning, and they stood there in a line, gazing upon the intruding lovers, still exchanging their vows and sighs. The lovers got up, with only a silent protest, and walked slowly away somewhere else.

The children possessed themselves of the tent, and Mrs. Pontellier went over to join them.

Madame Ratignolle begged Robert to accompany her to the house; she complained of cramp in her limbs and stiffness of the joints. She leaned draggingly upon his arm as they walked.

VIII

"DO ME A favor, Robert," spoke the pretty woman at his side, almost as soon as she and Robert had started on their slow, homeward way. She looked up in his face, leaning on his arm beneath the encircling shadow of the umbrella which he had lifted.

"Granted; as many as you like," he returned, glancing down into her eyes that were full of thoughtfulness and some speculation.

"I only ask for one; let Mrs. Pontellier alone."

"*Tiens!*" he exclaimed, with a sudden, boyish laugh. "*Voilà que Madame Ratignolle est jalouse!*"[1]

"Nonsense! I'm in earnest; I mean what I say. Let Mrs. Pontellier alone."

"Why?" he asked; himself growing serious at his companion's solicitation.

"She is not one of us; she is not like us. She might make the unfortunate blunder of taking you seriously."

His face flushed with annoyance, and taking off his soft hat he began to

[1] ["What do you know? Madame Ratignolle is jealous!"]

beat it impatiently against his leg as he walked. "Why shouldn't she take me seriously?" he demanded sharply. "Am I a comedian, a clown, a jack-in-the-box? Why shouldn't she? You Creoles! I have no patience with you! Am I always to be regarded as a feature of an amusing programme? I hope Mrs. Pontellier does take me seriously. I hope she has discernment enough to find in me something besides the *blagueur*. If I thought there was any doubt—"

"Oh, enough, Robert!" she broke into his heated outburst. "You are not thinking of what you are saying. You speak with about as little reflection as we might expect from one of those children down there playing in the sand. If your attentions to any married women here were ever offered with any intention of being convincing, you would not be the gentleman we all know you to be, and you would be unfit to associate with the wives and daughters of the people who trust you."

Madame Ratignolle had spoken what she believed to be the law and the gospel. The young man shrugged his shoulders impatiently.

"Oh! well! That isn't it," slamming his hat down vehemently upon his head. "You ought to feel that such things are not flattering to say to a fellow."

"Should our whole intercourse consist of an exchange of compliments? *Ma foi!*"[1]

"It isn't pleasant to have a woman tell you—" he went on, unheedingly, but breaking off suddenly: "Now if I were like Arobin—you remember Alcée Arobin and that story of the consul's wife at Biloxi?" And he related the story of Alcée Arobin and the consul's wife; and another about the tenor of the French Opera, who received letters which should never have been written; and still other stories, grave and gay, till Mrs. Pontellier and her possible propensity for taking young men seriously was apparently forgotten.

Madame Ratignolle, when they had regained her cottage, went in to take the hour's rest which she considered helpful. Before leaving her, Robert begged her pardon for the impatience—he called it rudeness—with which he had received her well-meant caution.

"You made one mistake, Adèle," he said, with a light smile; "there is no earthly possibility of Mrs. Pontellier ever taking me seriously. You should have warned me against taking myself seriously. Your advice might then have carried some weight and given me subject for some reflection. *Au revoir*. But you look tired," he added, solicitously. "Would you like a cup of bouillon? Shall I stir you a toddy? Let me mix you a toddy with a drop of Angostura."

[1] ["Really!" (Literally, "My faith!")]

She acceded to the suggestion of bouillon, which was grateful and acceptable. He went himself to the kitchen, which was a building apart from the cottages and lying to the rear of the house. And he himself brought her the golden-brown bouillon, in a dainty Sèvres cup, with a flaky cracker or two on the saucer.

She thrust a bare, white arm from the curtain which shielded her open door, and received the cup from his hands. She told him he was a *bon garçon*, and she meant it. Robert thanked her and turned away toward "the house."

The lovers were just entering the grounds of the *pension*. They were leaning toward each other as the water-oaks bent from the sea. There was not a particle of earth beneath their feet. Their heads might have been turned upside-down, so absolutely did they tread upon blue ether. The lady in black, creeping behind them, looked a trifle paler and more jaded than usual. There was no sign of Mrs. Pontellier and the children. Robert scanned the distance for any such apparition. They would doubtless remain away till the dinner hour. The young man ascended to his mother's room. It was situated at the top of the house, made up of odd angles and a queer, sloping ceiling. Two broad dormer windows looked out toward the Gulf, and as far across it as a man's eye might reach. The furnishings of the room were light, cool, and practical.

Madame Lebrun was busily engaged at the sewing-machine. A little black girl sat on the floor, and with her hands worked the treadle of the machine. The Creole woman does not take any chances which may be avoided of imperiling her health.

Robert went over and seated himself on the broad sill of one of the dormer windows. He took a book from his pocket and began energetically to read it, judging by the precision and frequency with which he turned the leaves. The sewing-machine made a resounding clatter in the room; it was of a ponderous, by-gone make. In the lulls, Robert and his mother exchanged bits of desultory conversation.

"Where is Mrs. Pontellier?"

"Down at the beach with the children."

"I promised to lend her the Goncourt. Don't forget to take it down when you go; it's there on the bookshelf over the small table." Clatter, clatter, clatter, bang! for the next five or eight minutes.

"Where is Victor going with the rockaway?"

"The rockaway? Victor?"

"Yes; down there in front. He seems to be getting ready to drive away somewhere."

"Call him." Clatter, clatter!

Robert uttered a shrill, piercing whistle which might have been heard back at the wharf.

"He won't look up."

Madame Lebrun flew to the window. She called "Victor!" She waved a handkerchief and called again. The young fellow below got into the vehicle and started the horse off at a gallop.

Madame Lebrun went back to the machine, crimson with annoyance. Victor was the younger son and brother—a *tête montée*,[1] with a temper which invited violence and a will which no ax could break.

"Whenever you say the word I'm ready to thrash any amount of reason into him that he's able to hold."

"If your father had only lived!" Clatter, clatter, clatter, clatter, bang! It was a fixed belief with Madame Lebrun that the conduct of the universe and all things pertaining thereto would have been manifestly of a more intelligent and higher order had not Monsieur Lebrun been removed to other spheres during the early years of their married life.

"What do you hear from Montel?" Montel was a middle-aged gentleman whose vain ambition and desire for the past twenty years had been to fill the void which Monsieur Lebrun's taking off had left in the Lebrun household. Clatter, clatter, bang, clatter!

"I have a letter somewhere," looking in the machine drawer and finding the letter in the bottom of the work-basket. "He says to tell you he will be in Vera Cruz the beginning of next month"—clatter, clatter!—"and if you still have the intention of joining him"—bang! clatter, clatter, bang!

"Why didn't you tell me so before, mother? You know I wanted—" Clatter, clatter, clatter!

"Do you see Mrs. Pontellier starting back with the children? She will be in late to luncheon again. She never starts to get ready for luncheon till the last minute." Clatter, clatter! "Where are you going?"

"Where did you say the Goncourt was?"

IX

EVERY LIGHT IN the hall was ablaze; every lamp turned as high as it could be without smoking the chimney or threatening explosion. The lamps were fixed at intervals against the wall, encircling the whole room. Some

[1] [Hothead.]

one had gathered orange and lemon branches, and with these fashioned graceful festoons between. The dark green of the branches stood out and glistened against the white muslin curtains which draped the windows, and which puffed, floated, and flapped at the capricious will of a stiff breeze that swept up from the Gulf.

It was Saturday night a few weeks after the intimate conversation held between Robert and Madame Ratignolle on their way from the beach. An unusual number of husbands, fathers, and friends had come down to stay over Sunday; and they were being suitably entertained by their families, with the material help of Madame Lebrun. The dining tables had all been removed to one end of the hall, and the chairs ranged about in rows and in clusters. Each little family group had had its say and exchanged its domestic gossip earlier in the evening. There was now an apparent disposition to relax; to widen the circle of confidences and give a more general tone to the conversation.

Many of the children had been permitted to sit up beyond their usual bedtime. A small band of them were lying on their stomachs on the floor looking at the colored sheets of the comic papers which Mr. Pontellier had brought down. The little Pontellier boys were permitting them to do so, and making their authority felt.

Music, dancing, and a recitation or two were the entertainments furnished, or rather, offered. But there was nothing systematic about the programme, no appearance of prearrangement nor even premeditation.

At an early hour in the evening the Farival twins were prevailed upon to play the piano. They were girls of fourteen, always clad in the Virgin's colors, blue and white, having been dedicated to the Blessed Virgin at their baptism. They played a duet from "Zampa," and at the earnest solicitation of every one present followed it with the overture to "The Poet and the Peasant."

"*Allez vous-en! Sapristi!*" shrieked the parrot outside the door. He was the only being present who possessed sufficient candor to admit that he was not listening to these gracious performances for the first time that summer. Old Monsieur Farival, grandfather of the twins, grew indignant over the interruption, and insisted upon having the bird removed and consigned to regions of darkness. Victor Lebrun objected; and his decrees were as immutable as those of Fate. The parrot fortunately offered no further interruption to the entertainment, the whole venom of his nature apparently having been cherished up and hurled against the twins in that one impetuous outburst.

Later a young brother and sister gave recitations, which every one present had heard many times at winter evening entertainments in the city.

A little girl performed a skirt dance in the center of the floor. The mother played her accompaniments and at the same time watched her daughter with greedy admiration and nervous apprehension. She need have had no apprehension. The child was mistress of the situation. She had been properly dressed for the occasion in black tulle and black silk tights. Her little neck and arms were bare, and her hair, artificially crimped, stood out like fluffy black plumes over her head. Her poses were full of grace, and her little black-shod toes twinkled as they shot out and upward with a rapidity and suddenness which were bewildering.

But there was no reason why every one should not dance. Madame Ratignolle could not, so it was she who gaily consented to play for the others. She played very well, keeping excellent waltz time and infusing an expression into the strains which was indeed inspiring. She was keeping up her music on account of the children, she said; because she and her husband both considered it a means of brightening the home and making it attractive.

Almost every one danced but the twins, who could not be induced to separate during the brief period when one or the other should be whirling around the room in the arms of a man. They might have danced together, but they did not think of it.

The children were sent to bed. Some went submissively; others with shrieks and protests as they were dragged away. They had been permitted to sit up till after the ice-cream, which naturally marked the limit of human indulgence.

The ice-cream was passed around with cake—gold and silver cake arranged on platters in alternate slices; it had been made and frozen during the afternoon back of the kitchen by two black women, under the supervision of Victor. It was pronounced a great success—excellent if it had only contained a little less vanilla or a little more sugar, if it had been frozen a degree harder, and if the salt might have been kept out of portions of it. Victor was proud of his achievement, and went about recommending it and urging every one to partake of it to excess.

After Mrs. Pontellier had danced twice with her husband, once with Robert, and once with Monsieur Ratignolle, who was thin and tall and swayed like a reed in the wind when he danced, she went out on the gallery and seated herself on the low window-sill, where she commanded a view of all that went on in the hall and could look out toward the Gulf. There was a soft effulgence in the east. The moon was coming up, and its mystic shimmer was casting a million lights across the distant, restless water.

"Would you like to hear Mademoiselle Reisz play?" asked Robert, coming out on the porch where she was. Of course Edna would like to hear Mademoiselle Reisz play; but she feared it would be useless to entreat her.

"I'll ask her," he said. "I'll tell her that you want to hear her. She likes you. She will come." He turned and hurried away to one of the far cottages, where Mademoiselle Reisz was shuffling away. She was dragging a chair in and out of her room, and at intervals objecting to the crying of a baby, which a nurse in the adjoining cottage was endeavoring to put to sleep. She was a disagreeable little woman, no longer young, who had quarreled with almost every one, owing to a temper which was self-assertive and a disposition to trample upon the rights of others. Robert prevailed upon her without any too great difficulty.

She entered the hall with him during a lull in the dance. She made an awkward, imperious little bow as she went in. She was a homely woman, with a small weazened face and body and eyes that glowed. She had absolutely no taste in dress, and wore a batch of rusty black lace with a bunch of artificial violets pinned to the side of her hair.

"Ask Mrs. Pontellier what she would like to hear me play," she requested of Robert. She sat perfectly still before the piano, not touching the keys, while Robert carried her message to Edna at the window. A general air of surprise and genuine satisfaction fell upon every one as they saw the pianist enter. There was a settling down, and a prevailing air of expectancy everywhere. Edna was a trifle embarrassed at being thus signaled out for the imperious little woman's favor. She would not dare to choose, and begged that Mademoiselle Reisz would please herself in her selections.

Edna was what she herself called very fond of music. Musical strains, well rendered, had a way of evoking pictures in her mind. She sometimes liked to sit in the room of mornings when Madame Ratignolle played or practiced. One piece which that lady played Edna had entitled "Solitude." It was a short, plaintive, minor strain. The name of the piece was something else, but she called it "Solitude." When she heard it there came before her imagination the figure of a man standing beside a desolate rock on the seashore. He was naked. His attitude was one of hopeless resignation as he looked toward a distant bird winging its flight away from him.

Another piece called to her mind a dainty young woman clad in an Empire gown, taking mincing dancing steps as she came down a long avenue between tall hedges. Again, another reminded her of children at play, and still another of nothing on earth but a demure lady stroking a cat.

The very first chords which Mademoiselle Reisz struck upon the piano sent a keen tremor down Mrs. Pontellier's spinal column. It was not the first time she had heard an artist at the piano. Perhaps it was the first time she was ready, perhaps the first time her being was tempered to take an impress of the abiding truth.

She waited for the material pictures which she thought would gather and blaze before her imagination. She waited in vain. She saw no pictures of solitude, of hope, of longing, or of despair. But the very passions themselves were aroused within her soul, swaying it, lashing it, as the waves daily beat upon her splendid body. She trembled, she was choking, and the tears blinded her.

Mademoiselle had finished. She arose, and bowing her stiff, lofty bow, she went away, stopping for neither thanks nor applause. As she passed along the gallery she patted Edna upon the shoulder.

"Well, how did you like my music?" she asked. The young woman was unable to answer; she pressed the hand of the pianist convulsively. Mademoiselle Reisz perceived her agitation and even her tears. She patted her again upon the shoulder as she said:

"You are the only one worth playing for. Those others? Bah!" and she went shuffling and sidling on down the gallery toward her room.

But she was mistaken about "those others." Her playing had aroused a fever of enthusiasm. "What passion!" "What an artist!" "I have always said no one could play Chopin like Mademoiselle Reisz!" "That last prelude! Bon Dieu! It shakes a man!"

It was growing late, and there was a general disposition to disband. But some one, perhaps it was Robert, thought of a bath at that mystic hour and under that mystic moon.

X

AT ALL EVENTS Robert proposed it, and there was not a dissenting voice. There was not one but was ready to follow when he led the way. He did not lead the way, however, he directed the way; and he himself loitered behind with the lovers, who had betrayed a disposition to linger and hold themselves apart. He walked between them, whether with malicious or mischievous intent was not wholly clear, even to himself.

The Pontelliers and Ratignolles walked ahead; the women leaning upon the arms of their husbands. Edna could hear Robert's voice behind them, and could sometimes hear what he said. She wondered why he did not join them. It was unlike him not to. Of late he had sometimes held away from her for an entire day, redoubling his devotion upon the next and the next, as though to make up for hours that had been lost. She missed him the days when some pretext served to take him away from her, just as one misses the sun on a cloudy day without having thought much about the sun when it was shining.

The people walked in little groups toward the beach. They talked and laughed; some of them sang. There was a band playing down at Klein's hotel, and the strains reached them faintly, tempered by the distance. There were strange, rare odors abroad—a tangle of the sea smell and of weeds and damp, new-plowed earth, mingled with the heavy perfume of a field of white blossoms somewhere near. But the night sat lightly upon the sea and the land. There was no weight of darkness; there were no shadows. The white light of the moon had fallen upon the world like the mystery and the softness of sleep.

Most of them walked into the water as though into a native element. The sea was quiet now, and swelled lazily in broad billows that melted into one another and did not break except upon the beach in little foamy crests that coiled back like slow, white serpents.

Edna had attempted all summer to learn to swim. She had received instructions from both the men and women; in some instances from the children. Robert had pursued a system of lessons almost daily; and he was nearly at the point of discouragement in realizing the futility of his efforts. A certain ungovernable dread hung about her when in the water, unless there was a hand near by that might reach out and reassure her.

But that night she was like the little tottering, stumbling, clutching child, who of a sudden realizes its powers, and walks for the first time alone, boldly and with over-confidence. She could have shouted for joy. She did shout for joy, as with a sweeping stroke or two she lifted her body to the surface of the water.

A feeling of exultation overtook her, as if some power of significant import had been given her to control the working of her body and her soul. She grew daring and reckless, overestimating her strength. She wanted to swim far out, where no woman had swum before.

Her unlooked for achievement was the subject of wonder, applause, and admiration. Each one congratulated himself that his special teachings had accomplished this desired end.

"How easy it is!" she thought. "It is nothing," she said aloud; "why did I not discover before that it was nothing. Think of the time I have lost splashing about like a baby!" She would not join the groups in their sports and bouts, but intoxicated with her newly conquered power, she swam out alone.

She turned her face seaward to gather in an impression of space and solitude, which the vast expanse of water, meeting and melting with the moonlit sky, conveyed to her excited fancy. As she swam she seemed to be reaching out for the unlimited in which to lose herself.

Once she turned and looked toward the shore, toward the people she had left there. She had not gone any great distance—that is, what would have been a great distance for an experienced swimmer. But to her unaccustomed vision the stretch of water behind her assumed the aspect of a barrier which her unaided strength would never be able to overcome.

A quick vision of death smote her soul, and for a second of time appalled and enfeebled her senses. But by an effort she rallied her staggering faculties and managed to regain the land.

She made no mention of her encounter with death and her flash of terror, except to say to her husband, "I thought I should have perished out there alone."

"You were not so very far, my dear; I was watching you," he told her.

Edna went at once to the bath-house, and she had put on her dry clothes and was ready to return home before the others had left the water. She started to walk away alone. They all called to her and shouted to her. She waved a dissenting hand, and went on, paying no further heed to their renewed cries which sought to detain her.

"Sometimes I am tempted to think that Mrs. Pontellier is capricious," said Madame Lebrun, who was amusing herself immensely and feared that Edna's abrupt departure might put an end to the pleasure.

"I know she is," assented Mr. Pontellier; "sometimes, not often."

Edna had not traversed a quarter of the distance on her way home before she was overtaken by Robert.

"Did you think I was afraid?" she asked him, without a shade of annoyance.

"No; I knew you weren't afraid."

"Then why did you come? Why didn't you stay out there with the others?"

"I never thought of it."

"Thought of what?"

"Of anything. What difference does it make?"

"I'm very tired," she uttered, complainingly.

"I know you are."

"You don't know anything about it. Why should you know? I never was so exhausted in my life. But it isn't unpleasant. A thousand emotions have swept through me to-night. I don't comprehend half of them. Don't mind what I'm saying; I am just thinking aloud. I wonder if I shall ever be stirred again as Mademoiselle Reisz's playing moved me to-night. I wonder if any night on earth will ever again be like this one. It is like a night in a dream. The people about me are like some uncanny, half-human beings. There must be spirits abroad to-night."

"There are," whispered Robert. "Didn't you know this was the twenty-eighth of August?"

"The twenty-eighth of August?"

"Yes. On the twenty-eighth of August, at the hour of midnight, and if the moon is shining—the moon must be shining—a spirit that has haunted these shores for ages rises up from the Gulf. With its own penetrating vision the spirit seeks some one mortal worthy to hold him company, worthy of being exalted for a few hours into realms of the semi-celestials. His search has always hitherto been fruitless, and he has sunk back, disheartened, into the sea. But to-night he found Mrs. Pontellier. Perhaps he will never wholly release her from the spell. Perhaps she will never again suffer a poor, unworthy earthling to walk in the shadow of her divine presence."

"Don't banter me," she said, wounded at what appeared to be his flippancy. He did not mind the entreaty, but the tone with its delicate note of pathos was like a reproach. He could not explain; he could not tell her that he had penetrated her mood and understood. He said nothing except to offer her his arm, for, by her own admission, she was exhausted. She had been walking alone with her arms hanging limp, letting her white skirts trail along the dewy path. She took his arm, but she did not lean upon it. She let her hand lie listlessly, as though her thoughts were elsewhere—somewhere in advance of her body, and she was striving to overtake them.

Robert assisted her into the hammock which swung from the post before her door out to the trunk of a tree.

"Will you stay out here and wait for Mr. Pontellier?" he asked.

"I'll stay out here. Good-night."

"Shall I get you a pillow?"

"There's one here," she said, feeling about, for they were in the shadow.

"It must be soiled; the children have been tumbling it about."

"No matter." And having discovered the pillow, she adjusted it beneath her head. She extended herself in the hammock with a deep breath of relief. She was not a supercilious or an over-dainty woman. She was not much given to reclining in the hammock, and when she did so it was with no cat-like suggestion of voluptuous ease, but with a beneficent repose which seemed to invade her whole body.

"Shall I stay with you till Mr. Pontellier comes?" asked Robert, seating himself on the outer edge of one of the steps and taking hold of the hammock rope which was fastened to the post.

"If you wish. Don't swing the hammock. Will you get my white shawl which I left on the window-sill over at the house?"

"Are you chilly?"

"No; but I shall be presently."

"Presently?" he laughed. "Do you know what time it is? How long are you going to stay out here?"

"I don't know. Will you get the shawl?"

"Of course I will," he said, rising. He went over to the house, walking along the grass. She watched his figure pass in and out of the strips of moonlight. It was past midnight. It was very quiet.

When he returned with the shawl she took it and kept it in her hand. She did not put it around her.

"Did you say I should stay till Mr. Pontellier came back?"

"I said you might if you wished to."

He seated himself again and rolled a cigarette, which he smoked in silence. Neither did Mrs. Pontellier speak. No multitude of words could have been more significant than those moments of silence, or more pregnant with the first-felt throbbings of desire.

When the voices of the bathers were heard approaching, Robert said good-night. She did not answer him. He thought she was asleep. Again she watched his figure pass in and out of the strips of moonlight as he walked away.

XI

"WHAT ARE YOU doing out here, Edna? I thought I should find you in bed," said her husband, when he discovered her lying there. He had walked up with Madame Lebrun and left her at the house. His wife did not reply.

"Are you asleep?" he asked, bending down close to look at her.

"No." Her eyes gleamed bright and intense, with no sleepy shadows, as they looked into his.

"Do you know it is past one o'clock? Come on," and he mounted the steps and went into their room.

"Edna!" called Mr. Pontellier from within, after a few moments had gone by.

"Don't wait for me," she answered. He thrust his head through the door.

"You will take cold out there," he said, irritably. "What folly is this? Why don't you come in?"

"It isn't cold; I have my shawl."

"The mosquitoes will devour you."

"There are no mosquitoes."

She heard him moving about the room; every sound indicating impatience and irritation. Another time she would have gone in at his request. She would, through habit, have yielded to his desire; not with any sense of submission or obedience to his compelling wishes, but unthinkingly, as we walk, move, sit, stand, go through the daily treadmill of the life which has been portioned out to us.

"Edna, dear, are you not coming in soon?" he asked again, this time fondly, with a note of entreaty.

"No; I am going to stay out here."

"This is more than folly," he blurted out. "I can't permit you to stay out there all night. You must come in the house instantly."

With a writhing motion she settled herself more securely in the hammock. She perceived that her will had blazed up, stubborn and resistant. She could not at that moment have done other than denied and resisted. She wondered if her husband had ever spoken to her like that before, and if she had submitted to his command. Of course she had; she remembered that she had. But she could not realize why or how she should have yielded, feeling as she then did.

"Léonce, go to bed," she said. "I mean to stay out here. I don't wish to go in, and I don't intend to. Don't speak to me like that again; I shall not answer you."

Mr. Pontellier had prepared for bed, but he slipped on an extra garment. He opened a bottle of wine, of which he kept a small and select supply in a buffet of his own. He drank a glass of the wine and went out on the gallery and offered a glass to his wife. She did not wish any. He drew up the rocker, hoisted his slippered feet on the rail, and proceeded to smoke a cigar. He smoked two cigars; then he went inside and drank another glass of wine. Mrs. Pontellier again declined to accept a glass when it was offered to her. Mr. Pontellier once more seated himself with elevated feet, and after a reasonable interval of time smoked some more cigars.

Edna began to feel like one who awakens gradually out of a dream, a delicious, grotesque, impossible dream, to feel again the realities pressing into her soul. The physical need for sleep began to overtake her; the exuberance which had sustained and exalted her spirit left her helpless and yielding to the conditions which crowded her in.

The stillest hour of the night had come, the hour before dawn, when the world seems to hold its breath. The moon hung low, and had turned from silver to copper in the sleeping sky. The old owl no longer hooted, and the water-oaks had ceased to moan as they bent their heads.

Edna arose, cramped from lying so long and still in the hammock. She tottered up the steps, clutching feebly at the post before passing into the house.

"Are you coming in, Léonce?" she asked, turning her face toward her husband.

"Yes, dear," he answered, with a glance following a misty puff of smoke. "Just as soon as I have finished my cigar."

XII

SHE SLEPT BUT a few hours. They were troubled and feverish hours, disturbed with dreams that were intangible, that eluded her, leaving only an impression upon her half-awakened senses of something unattainable. She was up and dressed in the cool of the early morning. The air was invigorating and steadied somewhat her faculties. However, she was not seeking refreshment or help from any source, either external or from within. She was blindly following whatever impulse moved her, as if she had placed herself in alien hands for direction, and freed her soul of responsibility.

Most of the people at that early hour were still in bed and asleep. A few, who intended to go over to the *Chênière* for mass, were moving about. The lovers, who had laid their plans the night before, were already strolling toward the wharf. The lady in black, with her Sunday prayer-book, velvet and gold-clasped, and her Sunday silver beads, was following them at no great distance. Old Monsieur Farival was up, and was more than half inclined to do anything that suggested itself. He put on his big straw hat, and taking his umbrella from the stand in the hall, followed the lady in black, never overtaking her.

The little negro girl who worked Madame Lebrun's sewing-machine was sweeping the galleries with long, absent-minded strokes of the broom. Edna sent her up into the house to awaken Robert.

"Tell him I am going to the *Chênière*. The boat is ready; tell him to hurry."

He had soon joined her. She had never sent for him before. She had never asked for him. She had never seemed to want him before. She did not appear conscious that she had done anything unusual in commanding his presence. He was apparently equally unconscious of anything extraordinary in the situation. But his face was suffused with a quiet glow when he met her.

They went together back to the kitchen to drink coffee. There was no time to wait for any nicety of service. They stood outside the window and the cook passed them their coffee and a roll, which they drank and ate from the window-sill. Edna said it tasted good. She had not thought of coffee nor of anything. He told her he had often noticed that she lacked forethought.

"Wasn't it enough to think of going to the *Chênière* and waking you up?" she laughed. "Do I have to think of everything?—as Léonce says when he's in a bad humor. I don't blame him; he'd never be in a bad humor if it weren't for me."

They took a short cut across the sands. At a distance they could see the curious procession moving toward the wharf—the lovers, shoulder to shoulder, creeping; the lady in black, gaining steadily upon them; old Monsieur Farival, losing ground inch by inch, and a young barefooted Spanish girl, with a red kerchief on her head and a basket on her arm, bringing up the rear.

Robert knew the girl, and he talked to her a little in the boat. No one present understood what they said. Her name was Mariequita. She had a round, sly, piquant face and pretty black eyes. Her hands were small, and she kept them folded over the handle of her basket. Her feet were broad and coarse. She did not strive to hide them. Edna looked at her feet, and noticed the sand and slime between her brown toes.

Beaudelet grumbled because Mariequita was there, taking up so much room. In reality he was annoyed at having old Monsieur Farival, who considered himself the better sailor of the two. But he would not quarrel with so old a man as Monsieur Farival, so he quarreled with Mariequita. The girl was deprecatory at one moment, appealing to Robert. She was saucy the next, moving her head up and down, making "eyes" at Robert and making "mouths" at Beaudelet.

The lovers were all alone. They saw nothing, they heard nothing. The lady in black was counting her beads for the third time. Old Monsieur Farival talked incessantly of what he knew about handling a boat, and of what Beaudelet did not know on the same subject.

Edna liked it all. She looked Mariequita up and down, from her ugly brown toes to her pretty black eyes, and back again.

"Why does she look at me like that?" inquired the girl of Robert.

"Maybe she thinks you are pretty. Shall I ask her?"

"No. Is she your sweetheart?"

"She's a married lady, and has two children."

"Oh! well! Francisco ran away with Sylvano's wife, who had four children. They took all his money and one of the children and stole his boat."

"Shut up!"

"Does she understand?"

"Oh, hush!"

"Are those two married over there—leaning on each other?"

"Of course not," laughed Robert.

"Of course not," echoed Mariequita, with a serious, confirmatory bob of the head.

The sun was high up and beginning to bite. The swift breeze seemed to Edna to bury the sting of it into the pores of her face and hands. Robert held his umbrella over her.

As they went cutting sidewise through the water, the sails bellied taut, with the wind filling and overflowing them. Old Monsieur Farival laughed sardonically at something as he looked at the sails, and Beaudelet swore at the old man under his breath.

Sailing across the bay to the *Chênière Caminada*, Edna felt as if she were being borne away from some anchorage which had held her fast, whose chains had been loosening—had snapped the night before when the mystic spirit was abroad, leaving her free to drift whithersoever she chose to set her sails. Robert spoke to her incessantly; he no longer noticed Mariequita. The girl had shrimps in her bamboo basket. They were covered with Spanish moss. She beat the moss down impatiently, and muttered to herself sullenly.

"Let us go to Grande Terre to-morrow?" said Robert in a low voice.

"What shall we do there?"

"Climb up the hill to the old fort and look at the little wriggling gold snakes, and watch the lizards sun themselves."

She gazed away toward Grande Terre and thought she would like to be alone there with Robert, in the sun, listening to the ocean's roar and watching the slimy lizards writhe in and out among the ruins of the old fort.

"And the next day or the next we can sail to the Bayou Brulow," he went on.

"What shall we do there?"

"Anything—cast bait for fish."

"No; we'll go back to Grande Terre. Let the fish alone."

"We'll go wherever you like," he said. "I'll have Tonie come over and help me patch and trim my boat. We shall not need Beaudelet nor any one. Are you afraid of the pirogue?"

"Oh, no."

"Then I'll take you some night in the pirogue when the moon shines. Maybe your Gulf spirit will whisper to you in which of these islands the treasures are hidden—direct you to the very spot, perhaps."

"And in a day we should be rich!" she laughed. "I'd give it all to you, the pirate gold and every bit of treasure we could dig up. I think you would know how to spend it. Pirate gold isn't a thing to be hoarded or utilized. It is something to squander and throw to the four winds, for the fun of seeing the golden specks fly."

"We'd share it, and scatter it together," he said. His face flushed.

They all went together up to the quaint little Gothic church of Our Lady of Lourdes, gleaming all brown and yellow with paint in the sun's glare.

Only Beaudelet remained behind, tinkering at his boat, and Mariequita walked away with her basket of shrimps, casting a look of childish ill-humor and reproach at Robert from the corner of her eye.

XIII

A FEELING OF oppression and drowsiness overcame Edna during the service. Her head began to ache, and the lights on the altar swayed before her eyes. Another time she might have made an effort to regain her composure; but her one thought was to quit the stifling atmosphere of the church and reach the open air. She arose, climbing over Robert's feet with a muttered apology. Old Monsieur Farival, flurried, curious, stood up, but upon seeing that Robert had followed Mrs. Pontellier, he sank back into his seat. He whispered an anxious inquiry of the lady in black, who did not notice him or reply, but kept her eyes fastened upon the pages of her velvet prayer-book.

"I felt giddy and almost overcome," Edna said, lifting her hands instinctively to her head and pushing her straw hat up from her forehead. "I couldn't have stayed through the service." They were outside in the shadow of the church. Robert was full of solicitude.

"It was folly to have thought of going in the first place, let alone staying. Come over to Madame Antoine's; you can rest there." He took her arm and led her away, looking anxiously and continuously down into her face.

How still it was, with only the voice of the sea whispering through the reeds that grew in the salt-water pools! The long line of little gray, weather-beaten houses nestled peacefully among the orange trees. It must always have been God's day on that low, drowsy island, Edna thought. They stopped, leaning over a jagged fence made of sea-drift, to ask for water. A youth, a mild-faced Acadian, was drawing water from the cistern, which was nothing more than a rusty buoy, with an opening on one side, sunk in the ground. The water which the youth handed to them in a tin pail was not cold to taste, but it was cool to her heated face, and it greatly revived and refreshed her.

Madame Antoine's cot was at the far end of the village. She welcomed them with all the native hospitality, as she would have opened her door to let the sunlight in. She was fat, and walked heavily and clumsily across the floor. She could speak no English, but when Robert made her understand that the lady who accompanied him was ill and desired to rest, she was all eagerness to make Edna feel at home and to dispose of her comfortably.

The whole place was immaculately clean, and the big, four-posted bed, snow-white, invited one to repose. It stood in a small side room which looked out across a narrow grass plot toward the shed, where there was a disabled boat lying keel upward.

Madame Antoine had not gone to mass. Her son Tonie had, but she supposed he would soon be back, and she invited Robert to be seated and wait for him. But he went and sat outside the door and smoked. Madame Antoine busied herself in the large front room preparing dinner. She was boiling mullets over a few red coals in the huge fireplace.

Edna, left alone in the little side room, loosened her clothes, removing the greater part of them. She bathed her face, her neck and arms in the basin that stood between the windows. She took off her shoes and stockings and stretched herself in the very center of the high, white bed. How luxurious it felt to rest thus in a strange, quaint bed, with its sweet country odor of laurel lingering about the sheets and mattress! She stretched her strong limbs that ached a little. She ran her fingers through her loosened hair for a while. She looked at her round arms as she held them straight up and rubbed them one after the other, observing closely, as if it were something she saw for the first time, the fine, firm quality and texture of her flesh. She clasped her hands easily above her head, and it was thus she fell asleep.

She slept lightly at first, half awake and drowsily attentive to the things about her. She could hear Madame Antoine's heavy, scraping tread as she walked back and forth on the sanded floor. Some chickens were clucking outside the windows, scratching for bits of gravel in the grass. Later she half heard the voices of Robert and Tonie talking under the shed. She did not stir. Even her eyelids rested numb and heavily over her sleepy eyes. The voices went on—Tonie's slow, Acadian drawl, Robert's quick, soft, smooth French. She understood French imperfectly unless directly addressed, and the voices were only part of the other drowsy, muffled sounds lulling her senses.

When Edna awoke it was with the conviction that she had slept long and soundly. The voices were hushed under the shed. Madame Antoine's step was no longer to be heard in the adjoining room. Even the chickens had gone elsewhere to scratch and cluck. The mosquito bar was drawn over her; the old woman had come in while she slept and let down the bar. Edna arose quietly from the bed, and looking between the curtains of the window, she saw by the slanting rays of the sun that the afternoon was far advanced. Robert was out there under the shed, reclining in the shade against the sloping keel of the overturned boat. He was reading from a book. Tonie was no longer with him. She wondered what had become of the rest of the party. She peeped out at him two or three times as she stood washing herself in the little basin between the windows.

Madame Antoine had laid some coarse, clean towels upon a chair, and had placed a box of *poudre de riz* within easy reach. Edna dabbed the powder upon her nose and cheeks as she looked at herself closely in the little distorted mirror which hung on the wall above the basin. Her eyes were bright and wide awake and her face glowed.

When she had completed her toilet she walked into the adjoining room. She was very hungry. No one was there. But there was a cloth spread upon the table that stood against the wall, and a cover was laid for one, with a crusty brown loaf and a bottle of wine beside the plate. Edna bit a piece from the brown loaf, tearing it with her strong, white teeth. She poured some of the wine into the glass and drank it down. Then she went softly out of doors, and plucking an orange from the low-hanging bough of a tree, threw it at Robert, who did not know she was awake and up.

An illumination broke over his whole face when he saw her and joined her under the orange tree.

"How many years have I slept?" she inquired. "The whole island seems changed. A new race of beings must have sprung up, leaving only you and me as past relics. How many ages ago did Madame Antoine and

Tonie die? and when did our people from Grand Isle disappear from the earth?"

He familiarly adjusted a ruffle upon her shoulder.

"You have slept precisely one hundred years. I was left here to guard your slumbers; and for one hundred years I have been out under the shed reading a book. The only evil I couldn't prevent was to keep a broiled fowl from drying up."

"If it has turned to stone, still will I eat it," said Edna, moving with him into the house. "But really, what has become of Monsieur Farival and the others?"

"Gone hours ago. When they found that you were sleeping they thought it best not to awake you. Any way, I wouldn't have let them. What was I here for?"

"I wonder if Léonce will be uneasy!" she speculated, as she seated herself at table.

"Of course not; he knows you are with me," Robert replied, as he busied himself among sundry pans and covered dishes which had been left standing on the hearth.

"Where are Madame Antoine and her son?" asked Edna.

"Gone to Vespers, and to visit some friends, I believe. I am to take you back in Tonie's boat whenever you are ready to go."

He stirred the smoldering ashes till the broiled fowl began to sizzle afresh. He served her with no mean repast, dripping the coffee anew and sharing it with her. Madame Antoine had cooked little else than the mullets, but while Edna slept Robert had foraged the island. He was childishly gratified to discover her appetite, and to see the relish with which she ate the food which he had procured for her.

"Shall we go right away?" she asked, after draining her glass and brushing together the crumbs of the crusty loaf.

"The sun isn't as low as it will be in two hours," he answered.

"The sun will be gone in two hours."

"Well, let it go; who cares!"

They waited a good while under the orange trees, till Madame Antoine came back, panting, waddling, with a thousand apologies to explain her absence. Tonie did not dare to return. He was shy, and would not willingly face any woman except his mother.

It was very pleasant to stay there under the orange trees, while the sun dipped lower and lower, turning the western sky to flaming copper and gold. The shadows lengthened and crept out like stealthy, grotesque monsters across the grass.

Edna and Robert both sat upon the ground—that is, he lay upon the ground beside her, occasionally picking at the hem of her muslin gown.

Madame Antoine seated her fat body, broad and squat, upon a bench beside the door. She had been talking all the afternoon, and had wound herself up to the story-telling pitch.

And what stories she told them! But twice in her life she had left the *Chênière Caminada*, and then for the briefest span. All her years she had squatted and waddled there upon the island, gathering legends of the Baratarians and the sea. The night came on, with the moon to lighten it. Edna could hear the whispering voices of dead men and the click of muffled gold.

When she and Robert stepped into Tonie's boat, with the red lateen sail, misty spirit forms were prowling in the shadows and among the reeds, and upon the water were phantom ships, speeding to cover.

XIV

THE YOUNGEST BOY, Etienne, had been very naughty, Madame Ratignolle said, as she delivered him into the hands of his mother. He had been unwilling to go to bed and had made a scene; whereupon she had taken charge of him and pacified him as well as she could. Raoul had been in bed and asleep for two hours.

The youngster was in his long white nightgown, that kept tripping him up as Madame Ratignolle led him along by the hand. With the other chubby fist he rubbed his eyes, which were heavy with sleep and ill humor. Edna took him in her arms, and seating herself in the rocker, began to coddle and caress him, calling him all manner of tender names, soothing him to sleep.

It was not more than nine o'clock. No one had yet gone to bed but the children.

Léonce had been very uneasy at first, Madame Ratignolle said, and had wanted to start at once for the *Chênière*. But Monsieur Farival had assured him that his wife was only overcome with sleep and fatigue, that Tonie would bring her safely back later in the day; and he had thus been dissuaded from crossing the bay. He had gone over to Klein's, looking up some cotton broker whom he wished to see in regard to securities, exchanges, stocks, bonds, or something of the sort, Madame Ratignolle did not remember what. He said he would not remain away late. She herself was suffering from heat and oppression, she said. She carried a bottle of salts and a large fan. She would not consent to remain with Edna, for Monsieur Ratignolle was alone, and he detested above all things to be left alone.

When Etienne had fallen asleep Edna bore him into the back room, and Robert went and lifted the mosquito bar that she might lay the child comfortably in his bed. The quadroon had vanished. When they emerged from the cottage Robert bade Edna good-night.

"Do you know we have been together the whole livelong day, Robert—since early this morning?" she said at parting.

"All but the hundred years when you were sleeping. Good-night."

He pressed her hand and went away in the direction of the beach. He did not join any of the others, but walked alone toward the Gulf.

Edna stayed outside, awaiting her husband's return. She had no desire to sleep or to retire; nor did she feel like going over to sit with the Ratignolles, or to join Madame Lebrun and a group whose animated voices reached her as they sat in conversation before the house. She let her mind wander back over her stay at Grand Isle; and she tried to discover wherein this summer had been different from any and every other summer of her life. She could only realize that she herself—her present self—was in some way different from the other self. That she was seeing with different eyes and making the acquaintance of new conditions in herself that colored and changed her environment, she did not yet suspect.

She wondered why Robert had gone away and left her. It did not occur to her to think he might have grown tired of being with her the livelong day. She was not tired, and she felt that he was not. She regretted that he had gone. It was so much more natural to have him stay, when he was not absolutely required to leave her.

As Edna waited for her husband she sang low a little song that Robert had sung as they crossed the bay. It began with "Ah! *Si tu savais*," and every verse ended with "*si tu savais.*"[1]

Robert's voice was not pretentious. It was musical and true. The voice, the notes, the whole refrain haunted her memory.

XV

WHEN EDNA ENTERED the dining-room one evening a little late, as was her habit, an unusually animated conversation seemed to be going on.

[1] ["Oh! If you knew . . ." This is a French version of the song "Couldst Thou But Know," by the Irish composer Michael William Balfe (1808–1870).]

Several persons were talking at once, and Victor's voice was predominating, even over that of his mother. Edna had returned late from her bath, had dressed in some haste, and her face was flushed. Her head, set off by her dainty white gown, suggested a rich, rare blossom. She took her seat at table between old Monsieur Farival and Madame Ratignolle.

As she seated herself and was about to begin to eat her soup, which had been served when she entered the room, several persons informed her simultaneously that Robert was going to Mexico. She laid her spoon down and looked about her bewildered. He had been with her, reading to her all the morning, and had never even mentioned such a place as Mexico. She had not seen him during the afternoon; she had heard some one say he was at the house, upstairs with his mother. This she had thought nothing of, though she was surprised when he did not join her later in the afternoon, when she went down to the beach.

She looked across at him, where he sat beside Madame Lebrun, who presided. Edna's face was a blank picture of bewilderment, which she never thought of disguising. He lifted his eyebrows with the pretext of a smile as he returned her glance. He looked embarrassed and uneasy.

"When is he going?" she asked of everybody in general, as if Robert were not there to answer for himself.

"To-night!" "This very evening!" "Did you ever!" "What possesses him!" were some of the replies she gathered, uttered simultaneously in French and English.

"Impossible!" she exclaimed. "How can a person start off from Grand Isle to Mexico at a moment's notice, as if he were going over to Klein's or to the wharf or down to the beach?"

"I said all along I was going to Mexico; I've been saying so for years!" cried Robert, in an excited and irritable tone, with the air of a man defending himself against a swarm of stinging insects.

Madame Lebrun knocked on the table with her knife handle.

"Please let Robert explain why he is going, and why he is going to-night," she called out. "Really, this table is getting to be more and more like Bedlam every day, with everybody talking at once. Sometimes—I hope God will forgive me—but positively, sometimes I wish Victor would lose the power of speech."

Victor laughed sardonically as he thanked his mother for her holy wish, of which he failed to see the benefit to anybody, except that it might afford her a more ample opportunity and license to talk herself.

Monsieur Farival thought that Victor should have been taken out in mid-ocean in his earliest youth and drowned. Victor thought there would be more logic in thus disposing of old people with an established claim for making themselves universally obnoxious. Madame Lebrun grew a trifle hysterical; Robert called his brother some sharp, hard names.

"There's nothing much to explain, mother," he said; though he explained, nevertheless—looking chiefly at Edna—that he could only meet the gentleman whom he intended to join at Vera Cruz by taking such and such a steamer, which left New Orleans on such a day; that Beaudelet was going out with his lugger-load of vegetables that night, which gave him an opportunity of reaching the city and making his vessel in time.

"But when did you make up your mind to all this?" demanded Monsieur Farival.

"This afternoon," returned Robert, with a shade of annoyance.

"At what time this afternoon?" persisted the old gentleman, with nagging determination, as if he were cross-questioning a criminal in a court of justice.

"At four o'clock this afternoon, Monsieur Farival," Robert replied, in a high voice and with a lofty air, which reminded Edna of some gentleman on the stage.

She had forced herself to eat most of her soup, and now she was picking the flaky bits of a *court bouillon*[1] with her fork.

The lovers were profiting by the general conversation on Mexico to speak in whispers of matters which they rightly considered were interesting to no one but themselves. The lady in black had once received a pair of prayer-beads of curious workmanship from Mexico, with very special indulgence attached to them, but she had never been able to ascertain whether the indulgence extended outside the Mexican border. Father Fochel of the Cathedral had attempted to explain it; but he had not done so to her satisfaction. And she begged that Robert would interest himself, and discover, if possible, whether she was entitled to the indulgence accompanying the remarkably curious Mexican prayer-beads.

Madame Ratignolle hoped that Robert would exercise extreme caution in dealing with the Mexicans, who, she considered, were a treacherous people, unscrupulous and revengeful. She trusted she did them no injustice in thus condemning them as a race. She had known personally but one Mexican, who made and sold excellent tamales, and whom she would have trusted implicitly, so soft-spoken was he. One day he was arrested for stabbing his wife. She never knew whether he had been hanged or not.

Victor had grown hilarious, and was attempting to tell an anecdote

[1] [A type of fish stew.]

about a Mexican girl who served chocolate one winter in a restaurant in Dauphine Street. No one would listen to him but old Monsieur Farival, who went into convulsions over the droll story.

Edna wondered if they had all gone mad, to be talking and clamoring at that rate. She herself could think of nothing to say about Mexico or the Mexicans.

"At what time do you leave?" she asked Robert.

"At ten," he told her. "Beaudelet wants to wait for the moon."

"Are you all ready to go?"

"Quite ready, I shall only take a handbag, and shall pack my trunk in the city."

He turned to answer some question put to him by his mother, and Edna, having finished her black coffee, left the table.

She went directly to her room. The little cottage was close and stuffy after leaving the outer air. But she did not mind; there appeared to be a hundred different things demanding her attention indoors. She began to set the toilet-stand to rights, grumbling at the negligence of the quadroon, who was in the adjoining room putting the children to bed. She gathered together stray garments that were hanging on the backs of chairs, and put each where it belonged in closet or bureau drawer. She changed her gown for a more comfortable and commodious wrapper. She rearranged her hair, combing and brushing it with unusual energy. Then she went in and assisted the quadroon in getting the boys to bed.

They were very playful and inclined to talk—to do anything but lie quiet and go to sleep. Edna sent the quadroon away to her supper and told her she need not return. Then she sat and told the children a story. Instead of soothing it excited them, and added to their wakefulness. She left them in heated argument, speculating about the conclusion of the tale which their mother promised to finish the following night.

The little black girl came in to say that Madame Lebrun would like to have Mrs. Pontellier go and sit with them over at the house till Mr. Robert went away. Edna returned answer that she had already undressed, that she did not feel quite well, but perhaps she would go over to the house later. She started to dress again, and got as far advanced as to remove her *peignoir*. But changing her mind once more she resumed the *peignoir*, and went outside and sat down before her door. She was overheated and irritable, and fanned herself energetically for a while. Madame Ratignolle came down to discover what was the matter.

"All that noise and confusion at the table must have upset me," replied Edna, "and moreover, I hate shocks and surprises. The idea of Robert starting off in such a ridiculously sudden and dramatic way! As if it were a matter of life and death! Never saying a word about it all morning when he was with me."

"Yes," agreed Madame Ratignolle. "I think it was showing us all—you especially—very little consideration. It wouldn't have surprised me in any of the others; those Lebruns are all given to heroics. But I must say I should never have expected such a thing from Robert. Are you not coming down? Come on, dear; it doesn't look friendly."

"No," said Edna, a little sullenly. "I can't go to the trouble of dressing again; I don't feel like it."

"You needn't dress; you look all right; fasten a belt around your waist. Just look at me!"

"No," persisted Edna; "but you go on. Madame Lebrun might be offended if we both stayed away."

Madame Ratignolle kissed Edna good-night, and went away, being in truth rather desirous of joining in the general and animated conversation which was still in progress concerning Mexico and the Mexicans.

Somewhat later Robert came up, carrying his hand-bag.

"Aren't you feeling well?" he asked.

"Oh, well enough. Are you going right away?"

He lit a match and looked at his watch. "In twenty minutes," he said. The sudden and brief flare of the match emphasized the darkness for a while. He sat down upon a stool which the children had left out on the porch.

"Get a chair," said Edna.

"This will do," he replied. He put on his soft hat and nervously took it off again, and wiping his face with his handkerchief, complained of the heat.

"Take the fan," said Edna, offering it to him.

"Oh, no! Thank you. It does no good; you have to stop fanning some time, and feel all the more uncomfortable afterward."

"That's one of the ridiculous things which men always say. I have never known one to speak otherwise of fanning. How long will you be gone?"

"Forever, perhaps. I don't know. It depends upon a good many things."

"Well, in case it shouldn't be forever, how long will it be?"

"I don't know."

"This seems to me perfectly preposterous and uncalled for. I don't like it. I don't understand your motive for silence and mystery, never saying a word to me about it this morning." He remained silent, not offering to defend himself. He only said, after a moment:

"Don't part from me in an ill-humor. I never knew you to be out of patience with me before."

"I don't want to part in any ill-humor," she said. "But can't you understand? I've grown used to seeing you, to having you with me all the time, and your action seems unfriendly, even unkind. You don't even offer an excuse for it. Why, I was planning to be together, thinking of how pleasant it would be to see you in the city next winter."

"So was I," he blurted. "Perhaps that's the—" He stood up suddenly and held out his hand. "Good-by, my dear Mrs. Pontellier; good-by. You won't—I hope you won't completely forget me." She clung to his hand, striving to detain him.

"Write to me when you get there, won't you, Robert?" she entreated.

"I will, thank you. Good-by."

How unlike Robert! The merest acquaintance would have said something more emphatic than "I will, thank you; good-by," to such a request.

He had evidently already taken leave of the people over at the house, for he descended the steps and went to join Beaudelet, who was out there with an oar across his shoulder waiting for Robert. They walked away in the darkness. She could only hear Beaudelet's voice; Robert had apparently not even spoken a word of greeting to his companion.

Edna bit her handkerchief convulsively, striving to hold back and to hide, even from herself as she would have hidden from another, the emotion which was troubling—tearing—her. Her eyes were brimming with tears.

For the first time she recognized anew the symptoms of infatuation which she had felt incipiently as a child, as a girl in her earliest teens, and later as a young woman. The recognition did not lessen the reality, the poignancy of the revelation by any suggestion or promise of instability. The past was nothing to her; offered no lesson which she was willing to heed. The future was a mystery which she never attempted to penetrate. The present alone was significant; was hers, to torture her as it was doing then with the biting conviction that she had lost that which she had held, that she had been denied that which her impassioned, newly awakened being demanded.

XVI

"Do you miss your friend greatly?" asked Mademoiselle Reisz one morning as she came creeping up behind Edna, who had just left her cottage on her way to the beach. She spent much of her time in the water since she had acquired finally the art of swimming. As their stay at Grand

Isle drew near its close, she felt that she could not give too much time to a diversion which afforded her the only real pleasurable moments that she knew. When Mademoiselle Reisz came and touched her upon the shoulder and spoke to her, the woman seemed to echo the thought which was ever in Edna's mind; or, better, the feeling which constantly possessed her.

Robert's going had some way taken the brightness, the color, the meaning out of everything. The conditions of her life were in no way changed, but her whole existence was dulled, like a faded garment which seems to be no longer worth wearing. She sought him everywhere—in others whom she induced to talk about him. She went up in the mornings to Madame Lebrun's room, braving the clatter of the old sewing-machine. She sat there and chatted at intervals as Robert had done. She gazed around the room at the pictures and photographs hanging upon the wall, and discovered in some corner an old family album, which she examined with the keenest interest, appealing to Madame Lebrun for enlightenment concerning the many figures and faces which she discovered between its pages.

There was a picture of Madame Lebrun with Robert as a baby, seated in her lap, a round-faced infant with a fist in his mouth. The eyes alone in the baby suggested the man. And that was he also in kilts, at the age of five, wearing long curls and holding a whip in his hand. It made Edna laugh, and she laughed, too, at the portrait in his first long trousers; while another interested her, taken when he left for college, looking thin, long-faced, with eyes full of fire, ambition and great intentions. But there was no recent picture, none which suggested the Robert who had gone away five days ago, leaving a void and wilderness behind him.

"Oh, Robert stopped having his pictures taken when he had to pay for them himself! He found wiser use for his money, he says," explained Madame Lebrun. She had a letter from him, written before he left New Orleans. Edna wished to see the letter, and Madame Lebrun told her to look for it either on the table or the dresser, or perhaps it was on the mantelpiece.

The letter was on the bookshelf. It possessed the greatest interest and attraction for Edna; the envelope, its size and shape, the post-mark, the handwriting. She examined every detail of the outside before opening it. There were only a few lines, setting forth that he would leave the city that afternoon, that he had packed his trunk in good shape, that he was well, and sent her his love and begged to be affectionately remembered to all. There was no special message to Edna except a postscript saying that if Mrs. Pontellier desired to finish the book which he had been reading to her, his mother would find it in his room, among other books there on the table. Edna experienced a pang of jealousy because he had written to his mother rather than to her.

Every one seemed to take for granted that she missed him. Even her husband, when he came down the Saturday following Robert's departure, expressed regret that he had gone.

"How do you get on without him, Edna?" he asked.

"It's very dull without him," she admitted. Mr. Pontellier had seen Robert in the city, and Edna asked him a dozen questions or more. Where had they met? On Carondelet Street, in the morning. They had gone "in" and had a drink and a cigar together. What had they talked about? Chiefly about his prospects in Mexico, which Mr. Pontellier thought were promising. How did he look? How did he seem—grave, or gay, or how? Quite cheerful, and wholly taken up with the idea of his trip, which Mr. Pontellier found altogether natural in a young fellow about to seek fortune and adventure in a strange, queer country.

Edna tapped her foot impatiently, and wondered why the children persisted in playing in the sun when they might be under the trees. She went down and led them out of the sun, scolding the quadroon for not being more attentive.

It did not strike her as in the least grotesque that she should be making of Robert the object of conversation and leading her husband to speak of him. The sentiment which she entertained for Robert in no way resembled that which she felt for her husband, or had ever felt, or ever expected to feel. She had all her life long been accustomed to harbor thoughts and emotions which never voiced themselves. They had never taken the form of struggles. They belonged to her and were her own, and she entertained the conviction that she had a right to them and that they concerned no one but herself. Edna had once told Madame Ratignolle that she would never sacrifice herself for her children, or for any one. Then had followed a rather heated argument; the two women did not appear to understand each other or to be talking the same language. Edna tried to appease her friend, to explain.

"I would give up the unessential; I would give my money, I would give my life for my children; but I wouldn't give myself. I can't make it more clear; it's only something which I am beginning to comprehend, which is revealing itself to me."

"I don't know what you would call the essential, or what you mean by the unessential," said Madame Ratignolle, cheerfully; "but a woman who would give her life for her children could do no more than that—your Bible tells you so. I'm sure I couldn't do more than that."

"Oh, yes you could!" laughed Edna.

She was not surprised at Mademoiselle Reisz's question the morning that lady, following her to the beach, tapped her on the shoulder and asked if she did not greatly miss her young friend.

"Oh, good morning, Mademoiselle; is it you? Why, of course I miss Robert. Are you going down to bathe?"

"Why should I go down to bathe at the very end of the season when I haven't been in the surf all summer," replied the woman, disagreeably.

"I beg your pardon," offered Edna, in some embarrassment, for she should have remembered that Mademoiselle Reisz's avoidance of the water had furnished a theme for much pleasantry. Some among them thought it was on account of her false hair, or the dread of getting the violets wet, while others attributed it to the natural aversion for water sometimes believed to accompany the artistic temperament. Mademoiselle offered Edna some chocolates in a paper bag, which she took from her pocket, by way of showing that she bore no ill feeling. She habitually ate chocolates for their sustaining quality; they contained much nutriment in small compass, she said. They saved her from starvation, as Madame Lebrun's table was utterly impossible; and no one save so impertinent a woman as Madame Lebrun could think of offering such food to people and requiring them to pay for it.

"She must feel very lonely without her son," said Edna, desiring to change the subject. "Her favorite son, too. It must have been quite hard to let him go."

Mademoiselle laughed maliciously.

"Her favorite son! Oh, dear! Who could have been imposing such a tale upon you? Aline Lebrun lives for Victor, and for Victor alone. She has spoiled him into the worthless creature he is. She worships him and the ground he walks on. Robert is very well in a way, to give up all the money he can earn to the family, and keep the barest pittance for himself. Favorite son, indeed! I miss the poor fellow myself, my dear. I liked to see him and to hear him about the place—the only Lebrun who is worth a pinch of salt. He comes to see me often in the city. I like to play to him. That Victor! hanging would be too good for him. It's a wonder Robert hasn't beaten him to death long ago."

"I thought he had great patience with his brother," offered Edna, glad to be talking about Robert, no matter what was said.

"Oh! he thrashed him well enough a year or two ago," said Mademoiselle. "It was about a Spanish girl, whom Victor considered that he had some sort of claim upon. He met Robert one day talking to the girl, or walking with her, or bathing with her, or carrying her basket—I don't remember what;—and he became so insulting and abusive that Robert gave him a thrashing on the spot that has kept him comparatively in order for a good while. It's about time he was getting another."

"Was her name Mariequita?" asked Edna.

"Mariequita—yes, that was it; Mariequita. I had forgotten. Oh, she's a sly one, and a bad one, that Mariequita!"

Edna looked down at Mademoiselle Reisz and wondered how she could have listened to her venom so long. For some reason she felt depressed, almost unhappy. She had not intended to go into the water; but she donned her bathing suit, and left Mademoiselle alone, seated under the shade of the children's tent. The water was growing cooler as the season advanced. Edna plunged and swam about with an abandon that thrilled and invigorated her. She remained a long time in the water, half hoping that Mademoiselle Reisz would not wait for her.

But Mademoiselle waited. She was very amiable during the walk back, and raved much over Edna's appearance in her bathing suit. She talked about music. She hoped that Edna would go to see her in the city, and wrote her address with the stub of a pencil on a piece of card which she found in her pocket.

"When do you leave?" asked Edna.

"Next Monday; and you?"

"The following week," answered Edna, adding, "It has been a pleasant summer, hasn't it, Mademoiselle?"

"Well," agreed Mademoiselle Reisz, with a shrug, "rather pleasant, if it hadn't been for the mosquitoes and the Farival twins."

XVII

THE PONTELLIERS POSSESSED a very charming home on Esplanade Street in New Orleans. It was a large, double cottage, with a broad front veranda, whose round, fluted columns supported the sloping roof. The house was painted a dazzling white; the outside shutters, or jalousies, were green. In the yard, which was kept scrupulously neat, were flowers and plants of every description which flourishes in South Louisiana. Within doors the appointments were perfect after the conventional type. The softest carpets and rugs covered the floors; rich and tasteful draperies hung at doors and windows. There were paintings, selected with judgment and discrimination, upon the walls. The cut glass, the silver, the heavy damask which daily appeared upon the table were the envy of many women whose husbands were less generous than Mr. Pontellier.

Mr. Pontellier was very fond of walking about his house examining its various appointments and details, to see that nothing was amiss. He greatly valued his possessions, chiefly because they were his, and derived genuine pleasure from contemplating a painting, a statuette, a rare lace curtain—no matter what—after he had bought it and placed it among his household gods.

On Tuesday afternoons—Tuesday being Mrs. Pontellier's reception day—there was a constant stream of callers—women who came in carriages or in the street cars, or walked when the air was soft and distance permitted. A light-colored mulatto boy, in dress coat and bearing a diminutive silver tray for the reception of cards, admitted them. A maid, in white fluted cap, offered the callers liqueur, coffee, or chocolate, as they might desire. Mrs. Pontellier, attired in a handsome reception gown, remained in the drawing-room the entire afternoon receiving her visitors. Men sometimes called in the evening with their wives.

This had been the programme which Mrs. Pontellier had religiously followed since her marriage, six years before. Certain evenings during the week she and her husband attended the opera or sometimes the play.

Mr. Pontellier left his home in the mornings between nine and ten o'clock, and rarely returned before half-past six or seven in the evening—dinner being served at half-past seven.

He and his wife seated themselves at table one Tuesday evening, a few weeks after their return from Grand Isle. They were alone together. The boys were being put to bed; the patter of their bare, escaping feet could be heard occasionally, as well as the pursuing voice of the quadroon, lifted in mild protest and entreaty. Mrs. Pontellier did not wear her usual Tuesday reception gown; she was in ordinary house dress. Mr. Pontellier, who was observant about such things, noticed it, as he served the soup and handed it to the boy in waiting.

"Tired out, Edna? Whom did you have? Many callers?" he asked. He tasted his soup and began to season it with pepper, salt, vinegar, mustard—everything within reach.

"There were a good many," replied Edna, who was eating her soup with evident satisfaction. "I found their cards when I got home; I was out."

"Out!" exclaimed her husband, with something like genuine consternation in his voice as he laid down the vinegar cruet and looked at her through his glasses. "Why, what could have taken you out on Tuesday? What did you have to do?"

"Nothing. I simply felt like going out, and I went out."

"Well, I hope you left some suitable excuse," said her husband, somewhat appeased, as he added a dash of cayenne pepper to the soup.

"No, I left no excuse. I told Joe to say I was out, that was all."

"Why, my dear, I should think you'd understand by this time that people don't do such things; we've got to observe *les convenances*[1] if we ever expect to get on and keep up with the procession. If you felt that you had to leave home this afternoon, you should have left some suitable explanation for your absence.

"This soup is really impossible; it's strange that woman hasn't learned yet to make a decent soup. Any free-lunch stand in town serves a better one. Was Mrs. Belthrop here?"

"Bring the tray with the cards, Joe. I don't remember who was here."

The boy retired and returned after a moment, bringing the tiny silver tray, which was covered with ladies' visiting cards. He handed it to Mrs. Pontellier.

"Give it to Mr. Pontellier," she said.

Joe offered the tray to Mr. Pontellier, and removed the soup.

Mr. Pontellier scanned the names of his wife's callers, reading some of them aloud, with comments as he read.

" 'The Misses Delasidas.' I worked a big deal in futures for their father this morning; nice girls; it's time they were getting married. 'Mrs. Belthrop.' I tell you what it is, Edna; you can't afford to snub Mrs. Belthrop. Why, Belthrop could buy and sell us ten times over. His business is worth a good, round sum to me. You'd better write her a note. 'Mrs. James Highcamp.' Hugh! the less you have to do with Mrs. Highcamp, the better. 'Madame Laforcé.' Came all the way from Carrolton, too, poor old soul. 'Miss Wiggs,' 'Mrs. Eleanor Boltons.' " He pushed the cards aside.

"Mercy!" exclaimed Edna, who had been fuming. "Why are you taking the thing so seriously and making such a fuss over it?"

"I'm not making any fuss over it. But it's just such seeming trifles that we've got to take seriously; such things count."

The fish was scorched. Mr. Pontellier would not touch it. Edna said she did not mind a little scorched taste. The roast was in some way not to his fancy, and he did not like the manner in which the vegetables were served.

"It seems to me," he said, "we spend money enough in this house to procure at least one meal a day which a man could eat and retain his self-respect."

[1] ["The conventions."]

"You used to think the cook was a treasure," returned Edna, indifferently.

"Perhaps she was when she first came; but cooks are only human. They need looking after, like any other class of persons that you employ. Suppose I didn't look after the clerks in my office, just let them run things their own way; they'd soon make a nice mess of me and my business."

"Where are you going?" asked Edna, seeing that her husband arose from table without having eaten a morsel except a taste of the highly-seasoned soup.

"I'm going to get my dinner at the club. Good night." He went into the hall, took his hat and stick from the stand, and left the house.

She was somewhat familiar with such scenes. They had often made her very unhappy. On a few previous occasions she had been completely deprived of any desire to finish her dinner. Sometimes she had gone into the kitchen to administer a tardy rebuke to the cook. Once she went to her room and studied the cookbook during an entire evening, finally writing out a menu for the week, which left her harassed with a feeling that, after all, she had accomplished no good that was worth the name.

But that evening Edna finished her dinner alone, with forced deliberation. Her face was flushed and her eyes flamed with some inward fire that lighted them. After finishing her dinner she went to her room, having instructed the boy to tell any other callers that she was indisposed.

It was a large, beautiful room, rich and picturesque in the soft, dim light which the maid had turned low. She went and stood at an open window and looked out upon the deep tangle of the garden below. All the mystery and witchery of the night seemed to have gathered there amid the perfumes and the dusky and tortuous outlines of flowers and foliage. She was seeking herself and finding herself in just such sweet, half-darkness which met her moods. But the voices were not soothing that came to her from the darkness and the sky above and the stars. They jeered and sounded mournful notes without promise, devoid even of hope. She turned back into the room and began to walk to and fro down its whole length, without stopping, without resting. She carried in her hands a thin handkerchief, which she tore into ribbons, rolled into a ball, and flung from her. Once she stopped, and taking off her wedding ring, flung it upon the carpet. When she saw it lying there, she stamped her heel upon it, striving to crush it. But her small boot heel did not make an indenture, not a mark upon the little glittering circlet.

In a sweeping passion she seized a glass vase from the table and flung it upon the tiles of the hearth. She wanted to destroy something. The crash and clatter were what she wanted to hear.

A maid, alarmed at the din of breaking glass, entered the room to discover what was the matter.

"A vase fell upon the hearth," said Edna. "Never mind; leave it till morning."

"Oh! you might get some of the glass in your feet, ma'am," insisted the young woman, picking up bits of the broken vase that were scattered upon the carpet. "And here's your ring, ma'am, under the chair."

Edna held out her hand, and taking the ring, slipped it upon her finger.

XVIII

THE FOLLOWING MORNING Mr. Pontellier, upon leaving for his office, asked Edna if she would not meet him in town in order to look at some new fixtures for the library.

"I hardly think we need new fixtures, Léonce. Don't let us get anything new; you are too extravagant. I don't believe you ever think of saving or putting by."

"The way to become rich is to make money, my dear Edna, not to save it," he said. He regretted that she did not feel inclined to go with him and select new fixtures. He kissed her good-by, and told her she was not looking well and must take care of herself. She was unusually pale and very quiet.

She stood on the front veranda as he quitted the house, and absently picked a few sprays of jessamine that grew upon a trellis near by. She inhaled the odor of the blossoms and thrust them into the bosom of her white morning gown. The boys were dragging along the banquette a small "express wagon," which they had filled with blocks and sticks. The quadroon was following them with little quick steps, having assumed a fictitious animation and alacrity for the occasion. A fruit vender was crying his wares in the street.

Edna looked straight before her with a self-absorbed expression upon her face. She felt no interest in anything about her. The street, the children, the fruit vender, the flowers growing there under her eyes, were all part and parcel of an alien world which had suddenly become antagonistic.

She went back into the house. She had thought of speaking to the cook concerning her blunders of the previous night; but Mr. Pontellier had saved her that disagreeable mission, for which she was so poorly fitted.

Mr. Pontellier's arguments were usually convincing with those whom he employed. He left home feeling quite sure that he and Edna would sit down that evening, and possibly a few subsequent evenings, to a dinner deserving of the name.

Edna spent an hour or two in looking over some of her old sketches. She could see their shortcomings and defects, which were glaring in her eyes. She tried to work a little, but found she was not in the humor. Finally she gathered together a few of the sketches—those which she considered the least discreditable; and she carried them with her when, a little later, she dressed and left the house. She looked handsome and distinguished in her street gown. The tan of the seashore had left her face, and her forehead was smooth, white, and polished beneath her heavy, yellow-brown hair. There were a few freckles on her face, and a small, dark mole near the under lip and one on the temple, half-hidden in her hair.

As Edna walked along the street she was thinking of Robert. She was still under the spell of her infatuation. She had tried to forget him, realizing the inutility of remembering. But the thought of him was like an obsession, ever pressing itself upon her. It was not that she dwelt upon details of their acquaintance, or recalled in any special or peculiar way his personality; it was his being, his existence, which dominated her thought, fading sometimes as if it would melt into the mist of the forgotten, reviving again with an intensity which filled her with an incomprehensible longing.

Edna was on her way to Madame Ratignolle's. Their intimacy, begun at Grand Isle, had not declined, and they had seen each other with some frequency since their return to the city. The Ratignolles lived at no great distance from Edna's home, on the corner of a side street, where Monsieur Ratignolle owned and conducted a drug store which enjoyed a steady and prosperous trade. His father had been in the business before him, and Monsieur Ratignolle stood well in the community and bore an enviable reputation for integrity and clear-headedness. His family lived in commodious apartments over the store, having an entrance on the side within the *porte cochère*. There was something which Edna thought very French, very foreign, about their whole manner of living. In the large and pleasant salon which extended across the width of the house, the Ratignolles entertained their friends once a fortnight with a *soirée musicale,*[1] sometimes diversified by card-playing. There was a friend who played upon the 'cello. One brought his flute and another his violin,

[1] [An evening of musical entertainment.]

while there were some who sang and a number who performed upon the piano with various degrees of taste and agility. The Ratignolles' *soirées musicales* were widely known, and it was considered a privilege to be invited to them.

Edna found her friend engaged in assorting the clothes which had returned that morning from the laundry. She at once abandoned her occupation upon seeing Edna, who had been ushered without ceremony into her presence.

" 'Cité can do it as well as I; it is really her business," she explained to Edna, who apologized for interrupting her. And she summoned a young black woman, whom she instructed, in French, to be very careful in checking off the list which she handed her. She told her to notice particularly if a fine linen handkerchief of Monsieur Ratignolle's, which was missing last week, had been returned; and to be sure to set to one side such pieces as required mending and darning.

Then placing an arm around Edna's waist, she led her to the front of the house, to the salon, where it was cool and sweet with the odor of great roses that stood upon the hearth in jars.

Madame Ratignolle looked more beautiful than ever there at home, in a negligé which left her arms almost wholly bare and exposed the rich, melting curves of her white throat.

"Perhaps I shall be able to paint your picture some day," said Edna with a smile when they were seated. She produced the roll of sketches and started to unfold them. "I believe I ought to work again. I feel as if I wanted to be doing something. What do you think of them? Do you think it worth while to take it up again and study some more? I might study for a while with Laidpore."

She knew that Madame Ratignolle's opinion in such a matter would be next to valueless, that she herself had not alone decided, but determined; but she sought the words of praise and encouragement that would help her to put heart into her venture.

"Your talent is immense, dear!"

"Nonsense!" protested Edna, well pleased.

"Immense, I tell you," persisted Madame Ratignolle, surveying the sketches one by one, at close range, then holding them at arm's length, narrowing her eyes, and dropping her head on one side. "Surely, this Bavarian peasant is worthy of framing; and this basket of apples! never have I seen anything more lifelike. One might almost be tempted to reach out a hand and take one."

Edna could not control a feeling which bordered upon complacency at her friend's praise, even realizing, as she did, its true worth. She retained a few of the sketches, and gave all the rest to Madame Ratignolle, who appreciated the gift far beyond its value and proudly exhibited the pictures to her husband when he came up from the store a little later for his midday dinner.

Mr. Ratignolle was one of those men who are called the salt of the earth. His cheerfulness was unbounded, and it was matched by his goodness of heart, his broad charity, and common sense. He and his wife spoke English with an accent which was only discernible through its un-English emphasis and a certain carefulness and deliberation. Edna's husband spoke English with no accent whatever. The Ratignolles understood each other perfectly. If ever the fusion of two human beings into one has been accomplished on this sphere it was surely in their union.

As Edna seated herself at table with them she thought, "Better a dinner of herbs," though it did not take her long to discover that was no dinner of herbs, but a delicious repast, simple, choice, and in every way satisfying.

Monsieur Ratignolle was delighted to see her, though he found her looking not so well as at Grand Isle, and he advised a tonic. He talked a good deal on various topics, a little politics, some city news and neighborhood gossip. He spoke with an animation and earnestness that gave an exaggerated importance to every syllable he uttered. His wife was keenly interested in everything he said, laying down her fork the better to listen, chiming in, taking the words out of his mouth.

Edna felt depressed rather than soothed after leaving them. The little glimpse of domestic harmony which had been offered her, gave her no regret, no longing. It was not a condition of life which fitted her, and she could see in it but an appalling and hopeless ennui. She was moved by a kind of commiseration for Madame Ratignolle,—a pity for that colorless existence which never uplifted its possessor beyond the region of blind contentment, in which no moment of anguish ever visited her soul, in which she would never have the taste of life's delirium. Edna vaguely wondered what she meant by "life's delirium." It had crossed her thought like some unsought, extraneous impression.

XIX

EDNA COULD NOT help but think that it was very foolish, very childish, to have stamped upon her wedding ring and smashed the crystal vase upon the tiles. She was visited by no more outbursts, moving her to such futile expedients. She began to do as she liked and to feel as she liked. She completely abandoned her Tuesdays at home, and did not return the visits of those who had called upon her. She made no ineffectual efforts to conduct her household *en bonne ménagère,*[1] going and coming as it suited her fancy, and, so far as she was able, lending herself to any passing caprice.

Mr. Pontellier had been a rather courteous husband so long as he met a certain tacit submissiveness in his wife. But her new and unexpected line of conduct completely bewildered him. It shocked him. Then her absolute disregard for her duties as a wife angered him. When Mr. Pontellier became rude, Edna grew insolent. She had resolved never to take another step backward.

"It seems to me the utmost folly for a woman at the head of a household, and the mother of children, to spend in an atelier days which would be better employed contriving for the comfort of her family."

"I feel like painting," answered Edna. "Perhaps I shan't always feel like it."

"Then in God's name paint! but don't let the family go to the devil. There's Madame Ratignolle; because she keeps up her music, she doesn't let everything else go to chaos. And she's more of a musician than you are a painter."

"She isn't a musician, and I'm not a painter. It isn't on account of painting that I let things go."

"On account of what, then?"

"Oh! I don't know. Let me alone; you bother me."

It sometimes entered Mr. Pontellier's mind to wonder if his wife were not growing a little unbalanced mentally. He could see plainly that she was not herself. That is, he could not see that she was becoming herself and daily casting aside that fictitious self which we assume like a garment with which to appear before the world.

Her husband let her alone as she requested, and went away to his office. Edna went up to her atelier—a bright room in the top of the house. She was working with great energy and interest, without accomplishing anything, however, which satisfied her even in the smallest degree. For a time she had the whole household enrolled in the service of art. The boys posed for her. They thought it amusing at first, but the occupation soon lost its attractiveness when they discovered that it was not a game arranged especially for their entertainment. The quadroon sat for hours before Edna's palette, patient as a savage, while the house-maid took charge of the children, and the drawing-room went undusted. But the

[1] [Like a good housewife.]

house-maid, too, served her term as model when Edna perceived that the young woman's back and shoulders were molded on classic lines, and that her hair, loosened from its confining cap, became an inspiration. While Edna worked she sometimes sang low the little air, "*Ah! si tu savais!*"

It moved her with recollections. She could hear again the ripple of the water, the flapping sail. She could see the glint of the moon upon the bay, and could feel the soft, gusty beating of the hot south wind. A subtle current of desire passed through her body, weakening her hold upon the brushes and making her eyes burn.

There were days when she was very happy without knowing why. She was happy to be alive and breathing, when her whole being seemed to be one with the sunlight, the color, the odors, the luxuriant warmth of some perfect Southern day. She liked then to wander alone into strange and unfamiliar places. She discovered many a sunny, sleepy corner, fashioned to dream in. And she found it good to dream and to be alone and unmolested.

There were days when she was unhappy, she did not know why,—when it did not seem worth while to be glad or sorry, to be alive or dead; when life appeared to her like a grotesque pandemonium and humanity like worms struggling blindly toward inevitable annihilation. She could not work on such a day, nor weave fancies to stir her pulses and warm her blood.

XX

IT WAS DURING such a mood that Edna hunted up Mademoiselle Reisz. She had not forgotten the rather disagreeable impression left upon her by their last interview; but she nevertheless felt a desire to see her—above all, to listen while she played upon the piano. Quite early in the afternoon she started upon her quest for the pianist. Unfortunately she had mislaid or lost Mademoiselle Reisz's card, and looking up her address in the city directory, she found that the woman lived on Bienville Street, some distance away. The directory which fell into her hands was a year or more old, however, and upon reaching the number indicated, Edna discovered that the house was occupied by a respectable family of mulattoes who had *chambres garnies*[1] to let. They had been living there for six months, and knew absolutely nothing of a Mademoiselle Reisz. In fact,

[1] [Furnished rooms.]

they knew nothing of any of their neighbors; their lodgers were all people of the highest distinction, they assured Edna. She did not linger to discuss class distinctions with Madame Pouponne, but hastened to a neighboring grocery store, feeling sure that Mademoiselle would have left her address with the proprietor.

He knew Mademoiselle Reisz a good deal better than he wanted to know her, he informed his questioner. In truth, he did not want to know her at all, or anything concerning her—the most disagreeable and unpopular woman who ever lived in Bienville Street. He thanked heaven she had left the neighborhood, and was equally thankful that he did not know where she had gone.

Edna's desire to see Mademoiselle Reisz had increased tenfold since these unlooked-for obstacles had arisen to thwart it. She was wondering who could give her the information she sought, when it suddenly occurred to her that Madame Lebrun would be the one most likely to do so. She knew it was useless to ask Madame Ratignolle, who was on the most distant terms with the musician, and preferred to know nothing concerning her. She had once been almost as emphatic in expressing herself upon the subject as the corner grocer.

Edna knew that Madame Lebrun had returned to the city, for it was the middle of November. And she also knew where the Lebruns lived, on Chartres Street.

Their home from the outside looked like a prison, with iron bars before the door and lower windows. The iron bars were a relic of the old *régime*, and no one had ever thought of dislodging them. At the side was a high fence enclosing the garden. A gate or door opening upon the street was locked. Edna rang the bell at this side garden gate, and stood upon the banquette, waiting to be admitted.

It was Victor who opened the gate for her. A black woman, wiping her hands upon her apron, was close at his heels. Before she saw them Edna could hear them in altercation, the woman—plainly an anomaly—claiming the right to be allowed to perform her duties, one of which was to answer the bell.

Victor was surprised and delighted to see Mrs. Pontellier, and he made no attempt to conceal either his astonishment or his delight. He was a dark-browed, good-looking youngster of nineteen, greatly resembling his mother, but with ten times her impetuosity. He instructed the black woman to go at once and inform Madame Lebrun that Mrs. Pontellier desired to see her. The woman grumbled a refusal to do part of her duty when she had not been permitted to do it all, and started back to her interrupted task of weeding the garden. Whereupon Victor administered a rebuke in the form of a volley of abuse, which, owing to its rapidity and incoherence, was all but incomprehensible to Edna. Whatever it was, the rebuke was convincing, for the woman dropped her hoe and went mumbling into the house.

Edna did not wish to enter. It was very pleasant there on the side porch, where there were chairs, a wicker lounge, and a small table. She seated herself, for she was tired from her long tramp; and she began to rock gently and smooth out the folds of her silk parasol. Victor drew up his chair beside her. He at once explained that the black woman's offensive conduct was all due to imperfect training, as he was not there to take her in hand. He had only come up from the island the morning before, and expected to return the next day. He stayed all winter at the island; he lived there, and kept the place in order and got things ready for the summer visitors.

But a man needed occasional relaxation, he informed Mrs. Pontellier, and every now and again he drummed up a pretext to bring him to the city. My! but he had had a time of it the evening before! He wouldn't want his mother to know, and he began to talk in a whisper. He was scintillant with recollections. Of course, he couldn't think of telling Mrs. Pontellier all about it, she being a woman and not comprehending such things. But it all began with a girl peeping and smiling at him through the shutters as he passed by. Oh! but she was a beauty! Certainly he smiled back, and went up and talked to her. Mrs. Pontellier did not know him if she supposed he was one to let an opportunity like that escape him. Despite herself, the youngster amused her. She must have betrayed in her look some degree of interest or entertainment. The boy grew more daring, and Mrs. Pontellier might have found herself, in a little while, listening to a highly colored story but for the timely appearance of Madame Lebrun.

That lady was still clad in white, according to her custom of the summer. Her eyes beamed an effusive welcome. Would not Mrs. Pontellier go inside? Would she partake of some refreshment? Why had she not been there before? How was that dear Mr. Pontellier and how were those sweet children? Had Mrs. Pontellier ever known such a warm November?

Victor went and reclined on the wicker lounge behind his mother's chair, where he commanded a view of Edna's face. He had taken her parasol from her hands while he spoke to her, and he now lifted it and twirled it above him as he lay on his back. When Madame Lebrun complained that it was *so* dull coming back to the city; that she saw *so* few people now; that even Victor, when he came up from the island for a day or two, had so much to occupy him and engage his time; then it was that the youth went into contortions on the lounge and winked mischievously at Edna. She somehow felt like a confederate in crime, and tried to look severe and disapproving.

There had been but two letters from Robert, with little in them, they told her. Victor said it was really not worth while to go inside for the letters, when his mother entreated him to go in search of them. He remembered the contents, which in truth he rattled off very glibly when put to the test.

One letter was written from Vera Cruz and the other from the City of Mexico. He had met Montel, who was doing everything toward his advancement. So far, the financial situation was no improvement over the one he had left in New Orleans, but of course the prospects were vastly better. He wrote of the City of Mexico, the buildings, the people and their habits, the conditions of life which he found there. He sent his love to the family. He inclosed a check to his mother, and hoped she would affectionately remember him to all his friends. That was about the substance of the two letters. Edna felt that if there had been a message for her, she would have received it. The despondent frame of mind in which she had left home began again to overtake her, and she remembered that she wished to find Mademoiselle Reisz.

Madame Lebrun knew where Mademoiselle Reisz lived. She gave Edna the address, regretting that she would not consent to stay and spend the remainder of the afternoon, and pay a visit to Mademoiselle Reisz some other day. The afternoon was already well advanced.

Victor escorted her out upon the banquette, lifted her parasol, and held it over her while he walked to the car with her. He entreated her to bear in mind that the disclosures of the afternoon were strictly confidential. She laughed and bantered him a little, remembering too late that she should have been dignified and reserved.

"How handsome Mrs. Pontellier looked!" said Madame Lebrun to her son.

"Ravishing!" he admitted. "The city atmosphere has improved her. Some way she doesn't seem like the same woman."

XXI

Some people contended that the reason Mademoiselle Reisz always chose apartments up under the roof was to discourage the approach of beggars, peddlars and callers. There were plenty of windows in her little front room. They were for the most part dingy, but as they were nearly always open it did not make so much difference. They often admitted into the room a good deal of smoke and soot; but at the same time all the light and air that there was came through them. From her windows could be seen the crescent of the river, the masts of ships and the big chimneys of the Mississippi steamers. A magnificent piano crowded the apartment. In the next room she slept, and in the third and last she harbored a gasoline stove on which she cooked her meals when disinclined to descend to the neighboring restaurant. It was there also that she ate, keeping her belongings in a rare old buffet, dingy and battered from a hundred years of use.

When Edna knocked at Mademoiselle Reisz's front room door and entered, she discovered that person standing beside the window, engaged in mending or patching an old prunella gaiter. The little musician laughed all over when she saw Edna. Her laugh consisted of a contortion of the face and all the muscles of the body. She seemed strikingly homely, standing there in the afternoon light. She still wore the shabby lace and the artificial bunch of violets on the side of her head.

"So you remembered me at last," said Mademoiselle. "I had said to myself, 'Ah, bah! she will never come.' "

"Did you want me to come?" asked Edna with a smile.

"I had not thought much about it," answered Mademoiselle. The two had seated themselves on a little bumpy sofa which stood against the wall. "I am glad, however, that you came. I have the water boiling back there, and was just about to make some coffee. You will drink a cup with me. And how is *la belle dame?* Always handsome! always healthy! always contented!" She took Edna's hand between her strong wiry fingers, holding it loosely without warmth, and executing a sort of double theme upon the back and palm.

"Yes," she went on; "I sometimes thought: 'She will never come. She promised as those women in society always do, without meaning it. She will not come.' For I really don't believe you like me, Mrs. Pontellier."

"I don't know whether I like you or not," replied Edna, gazing down at the little woman with a quizzical look.

The candor of Mrs. Pontellier's admission greatly pleased Mademoiselle Reisz. She expressed her gratification by repairing forthwith to the region of the gasoline stove and rewarding her guest with the promised cup of coffee. The coffee and the biscuit accompanying it proved very acceptable to Edna, who had declined refreshment at Madame Lebrun's and was now beginning to feel hungry. Mademoiselle set the tray which she brought in upon a small table near at hand, and seated herself once again on the lumpy sofa.

"I have had a letter from your friend," she remarked, as she poured a little cream into Edna's cup and handed it to her.

"My friend?"

"Yes, your friend Robert. He wrote to me from the City of Mexico."

"Wrote to *you?*" repeated Edna in amazement, stirring her coffee absently.

"Yes, to me. Why not? Don't stir all the warmth out of your coffee; drink it. Though the letter might as well have been sent to you; it was nothing but Mrs. Pontellier from beginning to end."

"Let me see it," requested the young woman, entreatingly.

"No; a letter concerns no one but the person who writes it and the one to whom it is written."

"Haven't you just said it concerned me from beginning to end?"

"It was written about you, not to you. 'Have you seen Mrs. Pontellier? How is she looking?' he asks. 'As Mrs. Pontellier says,' or 'as Mrs. Pontellier once said.' 'If Mrs. Pontellier should call upon you, play for her that Impromptu of Chopin's, my favorite. I heard it here a day or two ago, but not as you play it. I should like to know how it affects her,' and so on, as if he supposed we were constantly in each other's society."

"Let me see the letter."

"Oh, no."

"Have you answered it?"

"No."

"Let me see the letter."

"No, and again, no."

"Then play the Impromptu for me."

"It is growing late; what time do you have to be home?"

"Time doesn't concern me. Your question seems a little rude. Play the Impromptu."

"But you have told me nothing of yourself. What are you doing?"

"Painting!" laughed Edna. "I am becoming an artist. Think of it!"

"Ah! an artist! You have pretensions, Madame."

"Why pretensions? Do you think I could not become an artist?"

"I do not know you well enough to say. I do not know your talent or your temperament. To be an artist includes much; one must possess many gifts—absolute gifts—which have not been acquired by one's own effort. And, moreover, to succeed, the artist must possess the courageous soul."

"What do you mean by the courageous soul?"

"Courageous, *ma foi!* The brave soul. The soul that dares and defies."

"Show me the letter and play for me the Impromptu. You see that I have persistence. Does that quality count for anything in art?"

"It counts with a foolish old woman whom you have captivated," replied Mademoiselle, with her wriggling laugh.

The letter was right there at hand in the drawer of the little table upon which Edna had just placed her coffee cup. Mademoiselle opened the drawer and drew forth the letter, the topmost one. She placed it in Edna's hands, and without further comment arose and went to the piano.

Mademoiselle played a soft interlude. It was an improvisation. She sat low at the instrument, and the lines of her body settled into ungraceful curves and angles that gave it an appearance of deformity. Gradually and imperceptibly the interlude melted into the soft opening minor chords of the Chopin Impromptu.

Edna did not know when the Impromptu began or ended. She sat in the sofa corner reading Robert's letter by the fading light. Mademoiselle had glided from the Chopin into the quivering love-notes of Isolde's song, and back again to the Impromptu with its soulful and poignant longing.

The shadows deepened in the little room. The music grew strange and fantastic—turbulent, insistent, plaintive and soft with entreaty. The shadows grew deeper. The music filled the room. It floated out upon the night, over the housetops, the crescent of the river, losing itself in the silence of the upper air.

Edna was sobbing, just as she had wept one midnight at Grand Isle when strange, new voices awoke in her. She arose in some agitation to take her departure. "May I come again, Mademoiselle?" she asked at the threshold.

"Come whenever you feel like it. Be careful; the stairs and landings are dark; don't stumble."

Mademoiselle reëntered and lit a candle. Robert's letter was on the floor. She stooped and picked it up. It was crumpled and damp with tears. Mademoiselle smoothed the letter out, restored it to the envelope, and replaced it in the table drawer.

XXII

One morning on his way into town Mr. Pontellier stopped at the house of his old friend and family physician, Doctor Mandelet. The Doctor was a semi-retired physician, resting, as the saying is, upon his laurels. He bore a reputation for wisdom rather than skill—leaving the active practice of medicine to his assistants and younger contemporaries—and was much sought for in matters of consultation. A few families, united to him by bonds of friendship, he still attended when they required the services of a physician. The Pontelliers were among these.

Mr. Pontellier found the Doctor reading at the open window of his study. His house stood rather far back from the street, in the center of a delightful garden, so that it was quiet and peaceful at the old gentleman's study window. He was a great reader. He stared up disapprovingly over his eye-glasses as Mr. Pontellier entered, wondering who had the temerity to disturb him at that hour of the morning.

"Ah, Pontellier! Not sick, I hope. Come and have a seat. What news do you bring this morning?" He was quite portly, with a profusion of gray hair, and small blue eyes which age had robbed of much of their brightness but none of their penetration.

"Oh! I'm never sick, Doctor. You know that I come of tough fiber—of that old Creole race of Pontelliers that dry up and finally blow away. I came to consult—no, not precisely to consult—to talk to you about Edna. I don't know what ails her."

"Madame Pontellier not well?" marveled the Doctor. "Why, I saw her—I think it was a week ago—walking along Canal Street, the picture of health, it seemed to me."

"Yes, yes; she seems quite well," said Mr. Pontellier, leaning forward and whirling his stick between his two hands; "but she doesn't act well. She's odd, she's not like herself. I can't make her out, and I thought perhaps you'd help me."

"How does she act?" inquired the doctor.

"Well, it isn't easy to explain," said Mr. Pontellier, throwing himself back in his chair. "She lets the housekeeping go to the dickens."

"Well, well; women are not all alike, my dear Pontellier. We've got to consider—"

"I know that; I told you I couldn't explain. Her whole attitude—toward me and everybody and everything—has changed. You know I have a quick temper, but I don't want to quarrel or be rude to a woman, especially my wife; yet I'm driven to it, and feel like ten thousand devils after I've made a fool of myself. She's making it devilishly uncomfortable for me," he went on nervously. "She's got some sort of notion in her head concerning the eternal rights of women; and—you understand—we meet in the morning at the breakfast table."

The old gentleman lifted his shaggy eyebrows, protruded his thick nether lip, and tapped the arms of his chair with his cushioned finger-tips.

"What have you been doing to her, Pontellier?"

"Doing! *Parbleu!*"

"Has she," asked the Doctor, with a smile, "has she been associating of late with a circle of pseudo-intellectual women—super-spiritual superior beings? My wife has been telling me about them."

"That's the trouble," broke in Mr. Pontellier, "she hasn't been associating with any one. She has abandoned her Tuesdays at home, has thrown over all her acquaintances, and goes tramping about by herself, moping in the street-cars, getting in after dark. I tell you she's peculiar. I don't like it; I feel a little worried over it."

This was a new aspect for the Doctor. "Nothing hereditary?" he asked, seriously. "Nothing peculiar about her family antecedents, is there?"

"Oh, no, indeed! She comes of sound old Presbyterian Kentucky stock. The old gentleman, her father, I have heard, used to atone for his week-day sins with his Sunday devotions. I know for a fact, that his race horses literally ran away with the prettiest bit of Kentucky farming land I ever laid eyes upon. Margaret—you know Margaret—she has all the Presbyterianism undiluted. And the youngest is something of a vixen. By the way, she gets married in a couple of weeks from now."

"Send your wife up to the wedding," exclaimed the Doctor, foreseeing a happy solution. "Let her stay among her own people for a while; it will do her good."

"That's what I want her to do. She won't go to the marriage. She says a wedding is one of the most lamentable spectacles on earth. Nice thing for a woman to say to her husband!" exclaimed Mr. Pontellier, fuming anew at the recollection.

"Pontellier," said the Doctor, after a moment's reflection, "let your wife alone for a while. Don't bother her, and don't let her bother you. Woman, my dear friend, is a very peculiar and delicate organism—a sensitive and highly organized woman, such as I know Mrs. Pontellier to be, is especially peculiar. It would require an inspired psychologist to deal successfully with them. And when ordinary fellows like you and me attempt to cope with their idiosyncrasies the result is bungling. Most women are moody and whimsical. This is some passing whim of your wife, due to some cause or causes which you and I needn't try to fathom. But it will pass happily over, especially if you let her alone. Send her around to see me."

"Oh! I couldn't do that; there'd be no reason for it," objected Mr. Pontellier.

"Then I'll go around and see her," said the Doctor. "I'll drop in to dinner some evening *en bon ami*."[1]

[1] ["As a friend."]

"Do! by all means," urged Mr. Pontellier. "What evening will you come? Say Thursday. Will you come Thursday?" he asked, rising to take his leave.

"Very well; Thursday. My wife may possibly have some engagement for me Thursday. In case she has, I shall let you know. Otherwise, you may expect me."

Mr. Pontellier turned before leaving to say:

"I am going to New York on business very soon. I have a big scheme on hand, and want to be on the field proper to pull the ropes and handle the ribbons. We'll let you in on the inside if you say so, Doctor," he laughed.

"No, I thank you, my dear sir," returned the Doctor. "I leave such ventures to you younger men with the fever of life still in your blood."

"What I wanted to say," continued Mr. Pontellier, with his hand on the knob; "I may have to be absent a good while. Would you advise me to take Edna along?"

"By all means, if she wishes to go. If not, leave her here. Don't contradict her. The mood will pass, I assure you. It may take a month, two, three months—possibly longer, but it will pass; have patience."

"Well, good-by, *à jeudi*,"[1] said Mr. Pontellier, as he let himself out.

The Doctor would have liked during the course of conversation to ask, "Is there any man in the case?" but he knew his Creole too well to make such a blunder as that.

He did not resume his book immediately, but sat for a while meditatively looking out into the garden.

XXIII

EDNA'S FATHER WAS in the city, and had been with them several days. She was not very warmly or deeply attached to him, but they had certain tastes in common, and when together they were companionable. His coming was in the nature of a welcome disturbance; it seemed to furnish a new direction for her emotions.

He had come to purchase a wedding gift for his daughter, Janet, and an outfit for himself in which he might make a creditable appearance at her marriage. Mr. Pontellier had selected the bridal gift, as every one immediately connected with him always deferred to his taste in such matters. And his suggestions on the question of dress—which too often assumes the nature of a problem—were of inestimable value to his father-in-law.

[1] ["Until Thursday."]

But for the past few days the old gentleman had been upon Edna's hands, and in his society she was becoming acquainted with a new set of sensations. He had been a colonel in the Confederate army, and still maintained, with the title, the military bearing which had always accompanied it. His hair and mustache were white and silky, emphasizing the rugged bronze of his face. He was tall and thin, and wore his coats padded, which gave a fictitious breadth and depth to his shoulders and chest. Edna and her father looked very distinguished together, and excited a good deal of notice during their perambulations. Upon his arrival she began by introducing him to her atelier and making a sketch of him. He took the whole matter very seriously. If her talent had been tenfold greater than it was, it would not have surprised him, convinced as he was that he had bequeathed to all of his daughters the germs of a masterful capability, which only depended upon their own efforts to be directed toward successful achievement.

Before her pencil he sat rigid and unflinching, as he had faced the cannon's mouth in days gone by. He resented the intrusion of the children, who gaped with wondering eyes at him, sitting so stiff up there in their mother's bright atelier. When they drew near he motioned them away with an expressive action of the foot, loath to disturb the fixed lines of his countenance, his arms, or his rigid shoulders.

Edna, anxious to entertain him, invited Mademoiselle Reisz to meet him, having promised him a treat in her piano playing; but Mademoiselle declined the invitation. So together they attended a *soirée musicale* at the Ratignolles'. Monsieur and Madame Ratignolle made much of the Colonel, installing him as the guest of honor and engaging him at once to dine with them the following Sunday, or any day which he might select. Madame coquetted with him in the most captivating and naïve manner, with eyes, gestures, and a profusion of compliments, till the Colonel's old head felt thirty years younger on his padded shoulders. Edna marveled, not comprehending. She herself was almost devoid of coquetry.

There were one or two men whom she observed at the *soirée musicale*; but she would never have felt moved to any kittenish display to attract their notice—to any feline or feminine wiles to express herself toward them. Their personality attracted her in an agreeable way. Her fancy selected them, and she was glad when a lull in the music gave them an opportunity to meet her and talk with her. Often on the street the glance of strange eyes had lingered in her memory, and sometimes had disturbed her.

Mr. Pontellier did not attend these *soirées musicales*. He considered them *bourgeois*, and found more diversion at the club. To Madame

Ratignolle he said the music dispensed at her *soirées* was too "heavy," too far beyond his untrained comprehension. His excuse flattered her. But she disapproved of Mr. Pontellier's club, and she was frank enough to tell Edna so.

"It's a pity Mr. Pontellier doesn't stay home more in the evenings. I think you would be more—well, if you don't mind my saying it—more united, if he did."

"Oh! dear no!" said Edna, with a blank look in her eyes. "What should I do if he stayed home? We wouldn't have anything to say to each other."

She had not much of anything to say to her father, for that matter; but he did not antagonize her. She discovered that he interested her, though she realized that he might not interest her long; and for the first time in her life she felt as if she were thoroughly acquainted with him. He kept her busy serving him and ministering to his wants. It amused her to do so. She would not permit a servant or one of the children to do anything for him which she might do herself. Her husband noticed, and thought it was the expression of a deep filial attachment which he had never suspected.

The Colonel drank numerous "toddies" during the course of the day, which left him, however, imperturbed. He was an expert at concocting strong drinks. He had even invented some, to which he had given fantastic names, and for whose manufacture he required diverse ingredients that it devolved upon Edna to procure for him.

When Doctor Mandelet dined with the Pontelliers on Thursday he could discern in Mrs. Pontellier no trace of that morbid condition which her husband had reported to him. She was excited and in a manner radiant. She and her father had been to the race course, and their thoughts when they seated themselves at table were still occupied with the events of the afternoon, and their talk was still of the track. The Doctor had not kept pace with turf affairs. He had certain recollections of racing in what he called "the good old times" when the Lecompte stables flourished, and he drew upon this fund of memories so that he might not be left out and seem wholly devoid of the modern spirit. But he failed to impose upon the Colonel, and was even far from impressing him with this trumped-up knowledge of bygone days. Edna had staked her father on his last venture, with the most gratifying results to both of them. Besides, they had met some very charming people, according to the Colonel's impressions. Mrs. Mortimer Merriman and Mrs. James Highcamp, who were there with Alcée Arobin, had joined them and had enlivened the hours in a fashion that warmed him to think of.

Mr. Pontellier himself had no particular leaning toward horse-racing, and was even rather inclined to discourage it as a pastime, especially when he considered the fate of that blue-grass farm in Kentucky. He endeavored, in a general way, to express a particular disapproval, and only succeeded in arousing the ire and opposition of his father-in-law. A pretty dispute followed, in which Edna warmly espoused her father's cause and the Doctor remained neutral.

He observed his hostess attentively from under his shaggy brows, and noted a subtle change which had transformed her from the listless woman he had known into a being who, for the moment, seemed palpitant with the forces of life. Her speech was warm and energetic. There was no repression in her glance or gesture. She reminded him of some beautiful, sleek animal waking up in the sun.

The dinner was excellent. The claret was warm and the champagne was cold, and under their beneficent influence the threatened unpleasantness melted and vanished with the fumes of the wine.

Mr. Pontellier warmed up and grew reminiscent. He told some amusing plantation experiences, recollections of old Iberville and his youth, when he hunted 'possum in company with some friendly darky; thrashed the pecan trees, shot the grosbec, and roamed the woods and fields in mischievous idleness.

The Colonel, with little sense of humor and of the fitness of things, related a somber episode of those dark and bitter days, in which he had acted a conspicuous part and always formed a central figure. Nor was the Doctor happier in his selection, when he told the old, ever new and curious story of the waning of a woman's love, seeking strange, new channels, only to return to its legitimate source after days of fierce unrest. It was one of the many little human documents which had been unfolded to him during his long career as a physician. The story did not seem especially to impress Edna. She had one of her own to tell, of a woman who paddled away with her lover one night in a pirogue and never came back. They were lost amid the Baratarian Islands, and no one ever heard of them or found trace of them from that day to this. It was a pure invention. She said that Madame Antoine had related it to her. That, also, was an invention. Perhaps it was a dream she had had. But every glowing word seemed real to those who listened. They could feel the hot breath of the Southern night; they could hear the long sweep of the pirogue through the glistening moonlit water, the beating of birds' wings, rising startled from among the reeds in the salt-water pools; they could see the faces of the lovers, pale, close together, rapt in oblivious forgetfulness, drifting into the unknown.

The champagne was cold, and its subtle fumes played fantastic tricks with Edna's memory that night.

Outside, away from the glow of the fire and the soft lamplight, the night was chill and murky. The Doctor doubled his old-fashioned cloak across his breast as he strode home through the darkness. He knew his fellow-creatures better than most men; knew that inner life which so seldom unfolds itself to unanointed eyes. He was sorry he had accepted Pontellier's invitation. He was growing old, and beginning to need rest and an imperturbed spirit. He did not want the secrets of other lives thrust upon him.

"I hope it isn't Arobin," he muttered to himself as he walked. "I hope to heaven it isn't Alcée Arobin."

XXIV

EDNA AND HER father had a warm, and almost violent dispute upon the subject of her refusal to attend her sister's wedding. Mr. Pontellier declined to interfere, to interpose either his influence or his authority. He was following Doctor Mandelet's advice, and letting her do as she liked. The Colonel reproached his daughter for her lack of filial kindness and respect, her want of sisterly affection and womanly consideration. His arguments were labored and unconvincing. He doubted if Janet would accept any excuse—forgetting that Edna had offered none. He doubted if Janet would ever speak to her again, and he was sure Margaret would not.

Edna was glad to be rid of her father when he finally took himself off with his wedding garments and his bridal gifts, with his padded shoulders, his Bible reading, his "toddies" and ponderous oaths.

Mr. Pontellier followed him closely. He meant to stop at the wedding on his way to New York and endeavor by every means which money and love could devise to atone somewhat for Edna's incomprehensible action.

"You are too lenient, too lenient by far, Léonce," asserted the Colonel. "Authority, coercion are what is needed. Put your foot down good and hard; the only way to manage a wife. Take my word for it."

The Colonel was perhaps unaware that he had coerced his own wife into her grave. Mr. Pontellier had a vague suspicion of it which he thought it needless to mention at that late day.

Edna was not so consciously gratified at her husband's leaving home as she had been over the departure of her father. As the day approached when he was to leave her for a comparatively long stay, she grew melting and affectionate, remembering his many acts of consideration and his repeated expressions of an ardent attachment. She was solicitous about his health and his welfare. She bustled around, looking after his clothing, thinking about heavy underwear, quite as Madame Ratignolle would have done under similar circumstances. She cried when he went away, calling him her dear, good friend, and she was quite certain she would grow lonely before very long and go to join him in New York.

But after all, a radiant peace settled upon her when she at last found herself alone. Even the children were gone. Old Madame Pontellier had come herself and carried them off to Iberville with their quadroon. The old madame did not venture to say she was afraid they would be neglected during Léonce's absence; she hardly ventured to think so. She was hungry for them—even a little fierce in her attachment. She did not want them to be wholly "children of the pavement," she always said when begging to have them for a space. She wished them to know the country, with its streams, its fields, its woods, its freedom, so delicious to the young. She wished them to taste something of the life their father had lived and known and loved when he, too, was a little child.

When Edna was at last alone, she breathed a big, genuine sigh of relief. A feeling that was unfamiliar but very delicious came over her. She walked all through the house, from one room to another, as if inspecting it for the first time. She tried the various chairs and lounges, as if she had never sat and reclined upon them before. And she perambulated around the outside of the house, investigating, looking to see if windows and shutters were secure and in order. The flowers were like new acquaintances; she approached them in a familiar spirit, and made herself at home among them. The garden walks were damp, and Edna called to the maid to bring out her rubber sandals. And there she stayed, and stooped, digging around the plants, trimming, picking dead, dry leaves. The children's little dog came out, interfering, getting in her way. She scolded him, laughed at him, played with him. The garden smelled so good and looked so pretty in the afternoon sunlight. Edna plucked all the bright flowers she could find, and went into the house with them, she and the little dog.

Even the kitchen assumed a sudden interesting character which she had never before perceived. She went in to give directions to the cook, to say that the butcher would have to bring much less meat, that they would require only half their usual quantity of bread, of milk and groceries. She told the cook that she herself would be greatly occupied during Mr. Pontellier's absence, and she begged her to take all thought and responsibility of the larder upon her own shoulders.

That night Edna dined alone. The candelabra, with a few candles in the center of the table, gave all the light she needed. Outside the circle of light in which she sat, the large dining-room looked solemn and shadowy. The cook, placed upon her mettle, served a delicious repast—a luscious tenderloin broiled à point. The wine tasted good; the marron glacé seemed to be just what she wanted. It was so pleasant, too, to dine in a comfortable peignoir.

She thought a little sentimentally about Léonce and the children, and wondered what they were doing. As she gave a dainty scrap or two to the doggie, she talked intimately to him about Etienne and Raoul. He was beside himself with astonishment and delight over these companionable advances, and showed his appreciation by his little quick, snappy barks and a lively agitation.

Then Edna sat in the library after dinner and read Emerson until she grew sleepy. She realized that she had neglected her reading, and determined to start anew upon a course of improving studies, now that her time was completely her own to do with as she liked.

After a refreshing bath, Edna went to bed. And as she snuggled comfortably beneath the eiderdown a sense of restfulness invaded her, such as she had not known before.

XXV

When the weather was dark and cloudy Edna could not work. She needed the sun to mellow and temper her mood to the sticking point. She had reached a stage when she seemed to be no longer feeling her way, working, when in the humor, with sureness and ease. And being devoid of ambition, and striving not toward accomplishment, she drew satisfaction from the work in itself.

On rainy or melancholy days Edna went out and sought the society of the friends she had made at Grand Isle. Or else she stayed indoors and nursed a mood with which she was becoming too familiar for her own comfort and peace of mind. It was not despair; but it seemed to her as if life were passing by, leaving its promise broken and unfulfilled. Yet there were other days when she listened, was led on and deceived by fresh promises which her youth held out to her.

She went again to the races, and again. Alcée Arobin and Mrs. Highcamp called for her one bright afternoon in Arobin's drag. Mrs. Highcamp was a worldly but unaffected, intelligent, slim, tall blonde woman in the forties, with an indifferent manner and blue eyes that stared. She had a daughter who served her as a pretext for cultivating the society of young men of fashion. Alcée Arobin was one of them. He was a familiar figure at the race course, the opera, the fashionable clubs. There was a perpetual smile in his eyes, which seldom failed to awaken a corresponding cheerfulness in any one who looked into them and listened to his good-humored voice. His manner was quiet, and at times a little insolent. He possessed a good figure, a pleasing face, not overburdened with depth of thought or feeling; and his dress was that of the conventional man of fashion.

He admired Edna extravagantly, after meeting her at the races with her father. He had met her before on other occasions, but she had seemed to him unapproachable until that day. It was at his instigation that Mrs. Highcamp called to ask her to go with them to the Jockey Club to witness the turf event of the season.

There were possibly a few track men out there who knew the race horse as well as Edna, but there was certainly none who knew it better. She sat between her two companions as one having authority to speak. She laughed at Arobin's pretensions, and deplored Mrs. Highcamp's ignorance. The race horse was a friend and intimate associate of her childhood. The atmosphere of the stables and the breath of the blue grass paddock revived in her memory and lingered in her nostrils. She did not perceive that she was talking like her father as the sleek geldings ambled in review before them. She played for very high stakes, and fortune favored her. The fever of the game flamed in her cheeks and eyes, and it got into her blood and into her brain like an intoxicant. People turned their heads to look at her, and more than one lent an attentive ear to her utterances, hoping thereby to secure the elusive but ever-desired "tip." Arobin caught the contagion of excitement which drew him to Edna like a magnet. Mrs. Highcamp remained, as usual, unmoved, with her indifferent stare and uplifted eyebrows.

Edna stayed and dined with Mrs. Highcamp upon being urged to do so. Arobin also remained and sent away his drag.

The dinner was quiet and uninteresting, save for the cheerful efforts of Arobin to enliven things. Mrs. Highcamp deplored the absence of her daughter from the races, and tried to convey to her what she had missed by going to the "Dante reading" instead of joining them. The girl held a geranium leaf up to her nose and said nothing, but looked knowing and noncommittal. Mr. Highcamp was a plain, bald-headed man, who only talked under compulsion. He was unresponsive. Mrs. Highcamp was full of delicate courtesy and consideration toward her husband. She addressed most of her conversation to him at table. They sat in the library after dinner and read the evening papers together under the drop-light; while the younger people went into the drawing-room near by and talked.

Miss Highcamp played some selections from Grieg upon the piano. She seemed to have apprehended all of the composer's coldness and none of his poetry. While Edna listened she could not help wondering if she had lost her taste for music.

When the time came for her to go home, Mr. Highcamp grunted a lame offer to escort her, looking down at his slippered feet with tactless concern. It was Arobin who took her home. The car ride was long, and it was late when they reached Esplanade Street. Arobin asked permission to enter for a second to light his cigarette—his match safe was empty. He filled his match safe, but did not light his cigarette until he left her, after she had expressed her willingness to go to the races with him again.

Edna was neither tired nor sleepy. She was hungry again, for the Highcamp dinner, though of excellent quality, had lacked abundance. She rummaged in the larder and brought forth a slice of "Gruyère" and some crackers. She opened a bottle of beer which she found in the icebox. Edna felt extremely restless and excited. She vacantly hummed a fantastic tune as she poked at the wood embers on the hearth and munched a cracker.

She wanted something to happen—something, anything; she did not know what. She regretted that she had not made Arobin stay a half hour to talk over the horses with her. She counted the money she had won. But there was nothing else to do, so she went to bed, and tossed there for hours in a sort of monotonous agitation.

In the middle of the night she remembered that she had forgotten to write her regular letter to her husband; and she decided to do so next day and tell him about her afternoon at the Jockey Club. She lay wide awake composing a letter which was nothing like the one which she wrote next day. When the maid awoke her in the morning Edna was dreaming of Mr. Highcamp playing the piano at the entrance of a music store on Canal Street, while his wife was saying to Alcée Arobin, as they boarded an Esplanade Street car:

"What a pity that so much talent has been neglected! but I must go."

When, a few days later, Alcée Arobin again called for Edna in his drag, Mrs. Highcamp was not with him. He said they would pick her up. But as that lady had not been apprised of his intention of picking her up, she was not at home. The daughter was just leaving the house to attend the meeting of a branch Folk Lore Society, and regretted that she could not accompany them. Arobin appeared nonplused, and asked Edna if there were any one else she cared to ask.

She did not deem it worth while to go in search of any of the fashionable acquaintances from whom she had withdrawn herself. She thought of Madame Ratignolle, but knew that her fair friend did not leave the house, except to take a languid walk around the block with her husband after nightfall. Mademoiselle Reisz would have laughed at such a request from Edna. Madame Lebrun might have enjoyed the outing, but for some reason Edna did not want her. So they went alone, she and Arobin.

The afternoon was intensely interesting to her. The excitement came back upon her like a remittent fever. Her talk grew familiar and confidential. It was no labor to become intimate with Arobin. His manner invited easy confidence. The preliminary stage of becoming acquainted was one which he always endeavored to ignore when a pretty and engaging woman was concerned.

He stayed and dined with Edna. He stayed and sat beside the wood fire. They laughed and talked; and before it was time to go he was telling her how different life might have been if he had known her years before. With ingenuous frankness he spoke of what a wicked, ill-disciplined boy he had been, and impulsively drew up his cuff to exhibit upon his wrist the scar from a saber cut which he had received in a duel outside of Paris when he was nineteen. She touched his hand as she scanned the red cicatrice on the inside of his white wrist. A quick impulse that was somewhat spasmodic impelled her fingers to close in a sort of clutch upon his hand. He felt the pressure of her pointed nails in the flesh of his palm.

She arose hastily and walked toward the mantel.

"The sight of a wound or scar always agitates and sickens me," she said. "I shouldn't have looked at it."

"I beg your pardon," he entreated, following her; "it never occurred to me that it might be repulsive."

He stood close to her, and the effrontery in his eyes repelled the old, vanishing self in her, yet drew all her awakening sensuousness. He saw enough in her face to impel him to take her hand and hold it while he said his lingering good night.

"Will you go to the races again?" he asked.

"No," she said. "I've had enough of the races. I don't want to lose all the money I've won, and I've got to work when the weather is bright, instead of—"

"Yes; work; to be sure. You promised to show me your work. What morning may I come up to your atelier? To-morrow?"

"No!"

"Day after?"

"No, no."

"Oh, please don't refuse me! I know something of such things. I might help you with a stray suggestion or two."

"No. Good night. Why don't you go after you have said good night? I don't like you," she went on in a high, excited pitch, attempting to draw away her hand. She felt that her words lacked dignity and sincerity, and she knew that he felt it.

"I'm sorry you don't like me. I'm sorry I offended you. How have I offended you? What have I done? Can't you forgive me?" And he bent and pressed his lips upon her hand as if he wished never more to withdraw them.

"Mr. Arobin," she complained, "I'm greatly upset by the excitement of the afternoon; I'm not myself. My manner must have misled you in some way. I wish you to go, please." She spoke in a monotonous, dull tone. He took his hat from the table, and stood with eyes turned from her, looking into the dying fire. For a moment or two he kept an impressive silence.

"Your manner has not misled me, Mrs. Pontellier," he said finally. "My own emotions have done that. I couldn't help it. When I'm near you, how could I help it? Don't think anything of it, don't bother, please. You see, I go when you command me. If you wish me to stay away, I shall do so. If you let me come back, I—oh! you will let me come back?"

He cast one appealing glance at her, to which she made no response. Alcée Arobin's manner was so genuine that it often deceived even himself.

Edna did not care or think whether it were genuine or not. When she was alone she looked mechanically at the back of her hand which he had kissed so warmly. Then she leaned her head down on the mantelpiece. She felt somewhat like a woman who in a moment of passion is betrayed into an act of infidelity, and realizes the significance of the act without being wholly awakened from its glamour. The thought was passing vaguely through her mind, "What would he think?"

She did not mean her husband; she was thinking of Robert Lebrun. Her husband seemed to her now like a person whom she had married without love as an excuse.

She lit a candle and went up to her room. Alcée Arobin was absolutely nothing to her. Yet his presence, his manners, the warmth of his glances, and above all the touch of his lips upon her hand had acted like a narcotic upon her.

She slept a languorous sleep, interwoven with vanishing dreams.

XXVI

ALCÉE AROBIN WROTE Edna an elaborate note of apology, palpitant with sincerity. It embarrassed her; for in a cooler, quieter moment it appeared to her absurd that she should have taken his action so seriously, so dramatically. She felt sure that the significance of the whole occurrence had lain in her own self-consciousness. If she ignored his note it would give undue importance to a trivial affair. If she replied to it in a serious spirit it would still leave in his mind the impression that she had in a susceptible moment yielded to his influence. After all, it was no great matter to have one's hand kissed. She was provoked at his having written the apology. She answered in as light and bantering a spirit as she fancied it deserved, and said she would be glad to have him look in upon her at work whenever he felt the inclination and his business gave him the opportunity.

He responded at once by presenting himself at her home with all his disarming naïveté. And then there was scarcely a day which followed that she did not see him or was not reminded of him. He was prolific in pretexts. His attitude became one of good-humored subservience and tacit adoration. He was ready at all times to submit to her moods, which were as often kind as they were cold. She grew accustomed to him. They became intimate and friendly by imperceptible degrees, and then by leaps. He sometimes talked in a way that astonished her at first and brought the crimson into her face; in a way that pleased her at last, appealing to the animalism that stirred impatiently within her.

There was nothing which so quieted the turmoil of Edna's senses as a visit to Mademoiselle Reisz. It was then, in the presence of that personality which was offensive to her, that the woman, by her divine art, seemed to reach Edna's spirit and set it free.

It was misty, with heavy, lowering atmosphere, one afternoon, when Edna climbed the stairs to the pianist's apartments under the roof. Her clothes were dripping with moisture. She felt chilled and pinched as she entered the room. Mademoiselle was poking at a rusty stove that smoked a little and warmed the room indifferently. She was endeavoring to heat a pot of chocolate on the stove. The room looked cheerless and dingy to Edna as she entered. A bust of Beethoven, covered with a hood of dust, scowled at her from the mantelpiece.

"Ah! here comes the sunlight!" exclaimed Mademoiselle, rising from her knees before the stove. "Now it will be warm and bright enough; I can let the fire alone."

She closed the stove door with a bang, and approaching, assisted in removing Edna's dripping mackintosh.

"You are cold; you look miserable. The chocolate will soon be hot. But would you rather have a taste of brandy? I have scarcely touched the bottle which you brought me for my cold." A piece of red flannel was wrapped around Mademoiselle's throat; a stiff neck compelled her to hold her head on one side.

"I will take some brandy," said Edna, shivering as she removed her gloves and overshoes. She drank the liquor from the glass as a man would have done. Then flinging herself upon the uncomfortable sofa she said, "Mademoiselle, I am going to move away from my house on Esplanade Street."

"Ah!" ejaculated the musician, neither surprised nor especially interested. Nothing ever seemed to astonish her very much. She was endeavoring to adjust the bunch of violets which had become loose from its fastening in her hair. Edna drew her down upon the sofa, and taking a pin from her own hair, secured the shabby artificial flowers in their accustomed place.

"Aren't you astonished?"

"Passably. Where are you going? to New York? to Iberville? to your father in Mississippi? where?"

"Just two steps away," laughed Edna, "in a little four-room house around the corner. It looks so cozy, so inviting and restful, whenever I pass by; and it's for rent. I'm tired looking after that big house. It never seemed like mine, anyway—like home. It's too much trouble. I have to keep too many servants. I am tired bothering with them."

"That is not your true reason, *ma belle*. There is no use in telling me lies. I don't know your reason, but you have not told me the truth." Edna did not protest or endeavor to justify herself.

"The house, the money that provides for it, are not mine. Isn't that enough reason?"

"They are your husband's," returned Mademoiselle, with a shrug and a malicious elevation of the eyebrows.

"Oh! I see there is no deceiving you. Then let me tell you: It is a caprice. I have a little money of my own from my mother's estate, which my father sends me by driblets. I won a large sum this winter on the races, and I am beginning to sell my sketches. Laidpore is more and more pleased with my work; he says it grows in force and individuality. I cannot judge of that myself, but I feel that I have gained in ease and confidence.

However, as I said, I have sold a good many through Laidpore. I can live in the tiny house for little or nothing, with one servant. Old Celestine, who works occasionally for me, says she will come stay with me and do my work. I know I shall like it, like the feeling of freedom and independence."

"What does your husband say?"

"I have not told him yet. I only thought of it this morning. He will think I am demented, no doubt. Perhaps you think so."

Mademoiselle shook her head slowly. "Your reason is not yet clear to me," she said.

Neither was it quite clear to Edna herself; but it unfolded itself as she sat for a while in silence. Instinct had prompted her to put away her husband's bounty in casting off her allegiance. She did not know how it would be when he returned. There would have to be an understanding, an explanation. Conditions would some way adjust themselves, she felt; but whatever came, she had resolved never again to belong to another than herself.

"I shall give a grand dinner before I leave the old house!" Edna exclaimed. "You will have to come to it, Mademoiselle. I will give you everything that you like to eat and to drink. We shall sing and laugh and be merry for once." And she uttered a sigh that came from the very depths of her being.

If Mademoiselle happened to have received a letter from Robert during the interval of Edna's visits, she would give her the letter unsolicited. And she would seat herself at the piano and play as her humor prompted her while the young woman read the letter.

The little stove was roaring; it was red-hot, and the chocolate in the tin sizzled and sputtered. Edna went forward and opened the stove door, and Mademoiselle rising, took a letter from under the bust of Beethoven and handed it to Edna.

"Another! so soon!" she exclaimed, her eyes filled with delight. "Tell me, Mademoiselle, does he know that I see his letters?"

"Never in the world! He would be angry and would never write to me again if he thought so. Does he write to you? Never a line. Does he send you a message? Never a word. It is because he loves you, poor fool, and is trying to forget you, since you are not free to listen to him or to belong to him."

"Why do you show me his letters, then?"

"Haven't you begged for them? Can I refuse you anything? Oh! you cannot deceive me," and Mademoiselle approached her beloved instrument and began to play. Edna did not at once read the letter. She sat holding it in her hand, while the music penetrated her whole being like an effulgence, warming and brightening the dark places of her soul. It prepared her for joy and exultation.

"Oh!" she exclaimed, letting the letter fall to the floor. "Why did you not tell me?" She went and grasped Mademoiselle's hands up from the keys. "Oh! unkind! malicious! Why did you not tell me?"

"That he was coming back? No great news, *ma foi*. I wonder he did not come long ago."

"But when, when?" cried Edna, impatiently. "He does not say when."

"He says 'very soon.' You know as much about it as I do; it is all in the letter."

"But why? Why is he coming? Oh, if I thought—" and she snatched the letter from the floor and turned the pages this way and that way, looking for the reason, which was left untold.

"If I were young and in love with a man," said Mademoiselle, turning on the stool and pressing her wiry hands between her knees as she looked down at Edna, who sat on the floor holding the letter, "it seems to me he would have to be some *grand esprit*; a man with lofty aims and ability to reach them; one who stood high enough to attract the notice of his fellow-men. It seems to me if I were young and in love I should never deem a man of ordinary caliber worthy of my devotion."

"Now it is you who are telling lies and seeking to deceive me, Mademoiselle; or else you have never been in love, and know nothing about it. Why," went on Edna, clasping her knees and looking up into Mademoiselle's twisted face, "do you suppose a woman knows why she loves? Does she select? Does she say to herself: 'Go to! Here is a distinguished statesman with presidential possibilities; I shall proceed to fall in love with him.' Or, 'I shall set my heart upon this musician, whose fame is on every tongue?' Or, 'This financier, who controls the world's money markets?' "

"You are purposely misunderstanding me, *ma reine*.[1] Are you in love with Robert?"

"Yes," said Edna. It was the first time she had admitted it, and a glow overspread her face, blotching it with red spots.

"Why?" asked her companion. "Why do you love him when you ought not to?"

Edna, with a motion or two, dragged herself on her knees before Mademoiselle Reisz, who took the glowing face between her two hands.

"Why? Because his hair is brown and grows away from his temples;

[1] ["My love." (Literally, "My queen.")]

because he opens and shuts his eyes, and his nose is a little out of drawing; because he has two lips and a square chin, and a little finger which he can't straighten from having played baseball too energetically in his youth. Because—"

"Because you do, in short," laughed Mademoiselle. "What will you do when he comes back?" she asked.

"Do? Nothing, except feel glad and happy to be alive."

She was already glad and happy to be alive at the mere thought of his return. The murky, lowering sky, which had depressed her a few hours before, seemed bracing and invigorating as she splashed through the streets on her way home.

She stopped at a confectioner's and ordered a huge box of bonbons for the children in Iberville. She slipped a card in the box, on which she scribbled a tender message and sent an abundance of kisses.

Before dinner in the evening Edna wrote a charming letter to her husband, telling him of her intention to move for a while into the little house around the block, and to give a farewell dinner before leaving, regretting that he was not there to share it, to help her out with the menu and assist her in entertaining the guests. Her letter was brilliant and brimming with cheerfulness.

XXVII

"WHAT IS THE matter with you?" asked Arobin that evening. "I never found you in such a happy mood." Edna was tired by that time, and was reclining on the lounge before the fire.

"Don't you know the weather prophet has told us we shall see the sun pretty soon?"

"Well, that ought to be reason enough," he acquiesced. "You wouldn't give me another if I sat here all night imploring you." He sat close to her on a low tabouret, and as he spoke his fingers lightly touched the hair that fell a little over her forehead. She liked the touch of his fingers through her hair, and closed her eyes sensitively.

"One of these days," she said, "I'm going to pull myself together for a while and think—try to determine what character of a woman I am; for, candidly, I don't know. By all the codes which I am acquainted with, I am a devilishly wicked specimen of the sex. But some way I can't convince myself that I am. I must think about it."

"Don't. What's the use? Why should you bother thinking about it when I can tell you what manner of woman you are." His fingers strayed occasionally down to her warm, smooth cheeks and firm chin, which was growing a little full and double.

"Oh, yes! You will tell me that I am adorable; everything that is captivating. Spare yourself the effort."

"No; I shan't tell you anything of the sort, though I shouldn't be lying if I did."

"Do you know Mademoiselle Reisz?" she asked irrelevantly.

"The pianist? I know her by sight. I've heard her play."

"She says queer things sometimes in a bantering way that you don't notice at the time and you find yourself thinking about afterward."

"For instance?"

"Well, for instance, when I left her to-day, she put her arms around me and felt my shoulder blades, to see if my wings were strong, she said. 'The bird that would soar above the level plain of tradition and prejudice must have strong wings. It is a sad spectacle to see the weaklings bruised, exhausted, fluttering back to earth.' "

"Whither would you soar?"

"I'm not thinking of any extraordinary flights. I only half comprehend her."

"I've heard she's partially demented," said Arobin.

"She seems to me wonderfully sane," Edna replied.

"I'm told she's extremely disagreeable and unpleasant. Why have you introduced her at a moment when I desired to talk of you?"

"Oh! talk of me if you like," cried Edna, clasping her hands beneath her head; "but let me think of something else while you do."

"I'm jealous of your thoughts to-night. They're making you a little kinder than usual; but some way I feel as if they were wandering, as if they were not here with me." She only looked at him and smiled. His eyes were very near. He leaned upon the lounge with an arm extended across her, while the other hand still rested upon her hair. They continued silently to look into each other's eyes. When he leaned forward and kissed her, she clasped his head, holding his lips to hers.

It was the first kiss of her life to which her nature had really responded. It was a flaming torch that kindled desire.

XXVIII

EDNA CRIED A little that night after Arobin left her. It was only one phase of the multitudinous emotions which had assailed her. There was with her an overwhelming feeling of irresponsibility. There was the shock of the unexpected and the unaccustomed. There was her husband's reproach looking at her from the external things around her which he had provided for her external existence. There was Robert's reproach making itself felt by a quicker, fiercer, more overpowering love, which had awakened within her toward him. Above all, there was understanding. She felt as if a mist had been lifted from her eyes, enabling her to look upon and comprehend the significance of life, that monster made up of beauty and brutality. But among the conflicting sensations which assailed her, there was neither shame nor remorse. There was a dull pang of regret because it was not the kiss of love which had inflamed her, because it was not love which had held this cup of life to her lips.

XXIX

WITHOUT EVEN WAITING for an answer from her husband regarding his opinion or wishes in the matter, Edna hastened her preparations for quitting her home on Esplanade Street and moving into the little house around the block. A feverish anxiety attended her every action in that direction. There was no moment of deliberation, no interval of repose between the thought and its fulfillment. Early upon the morning following those hours passed in Arobin's society, Edna set about securing her new abode and hurrying her arrangements for occupying it. Within the precincts of her home she felt like one who has entered and lingered within the portals of some forbidden temple in which a thousand muffled voices bade her begone.

Whatever was her own in the house, everything which she had acquired aside from her husband's bounty, she caused to be transported to the other house, supplying simple and meager deficiencies from her own resources.

Arobin found her with rolled sleeves, working in company with the house-maid when he looked in during the afternoon. She was splendid and robust, and had never appeared handsomer than in the old blue gown, with a red silk handkerchief knotted at random around her head to protect her hair from the dust. She was mounted upon a high step-ladder, unhooking a picture from the wall when he entered. He had found the front door open, and had followed his ring by walking in unceremoniously.

"Come down!" he said. "Do you want to kill yourself?" She greeted him with affected carelessness, and appeared absorbed in her occupation.

If he had expected to find her languishing, reproachful, or indulging in sentimental tears, he must have been greatly surprised.

He was no doubt prepared for any emergency, ready for any one of the foregoing attitudes, just as he bent himself easily and naturally to the situation which confronted him.

"Please come down," he insisted, holding the ladder and looking up at her.

"No," she answered; "Ellen is afraid to mount the ladder. Joe is working over at the 'pigeon house'—that's the name Ellen gives it, because it's so small and looks like a pigeon house—and some one has to do this."

Arobin pulled off his coat, and expressed himself ready and willing to tempt fate in her place. Ellen brought him one of her dust-caps, and went into contortions of mirth, which she found it impossible to control, when she saw him put it on before the mirror as grotesquely as he could. Edna herself could not refrain from smiling when she fastened it at his request. So it was he who in turn mounted the ladder, unhooking pictures and curtains, and dislodging ornaments as Edna directed. When he had finished he took off his dust-cap and went out to wash his hands.

Edna was sitting on the tabouret, idly brushing the tips of a feather duster along the carpet when he came in again.

"Is there anything more you will let me do?" he asked.

"That is all," she answered. "Ellen can manage the rest." She kept the young woman occupied in the drawing-room, unwilling to be left alone with Arobin.

"What about the dinner?" he asked; "the grand event, the *coup d'état?*"

"It will be day after to-morrow. Why do you call it the '*coup d'état?*' Oh! it will be very fine; all my best of everything—crystal, silver and gold, Sèvres, flowers, music, and champagne to swim in. I'll let Léonce pay the bills. I wonder what he'll say when he sees the bills."

"And you ask me why I call it a *coup d'état?*" Arobin had put on his coat, and he stood before her and asked if his cravat was plumb. She told him it was, looking no higher than the tip of his collar.

"When do you go to the 'pigeon house?'—with all due acknowledgment to Ellen."

"Day after to-morrow, after the dinner. I shall sleep there."

"Ellen, will you very kindly get me a glass of water?" asked Arobin. "The dust in the curtains, if you will pardon me for hinting such a thing, has parched my throat to a crisp."

"While Ellen gets the water," said Edna, rising, "I will say good-by and let you go. I must get rid of this grime, and I have a million things to do and think of."

"When shall I see you?" asked Arobin, seeking to detain her, the maid having left the room.

"At the dinner, of course. You are invited."

"Not before?—not to-night or to-morrow morning or to-morrow noon or night? or the day after morning or noon? Can't you see yourself, without my telling you, what an eternity it is?"

He had followed her into the hall and to the foot of the stairway, looking up at her as she mounted with her face half turned to him.

"Not an instant sooner," she said. But she laughed and looked at him with eyes that at once gave him courage to wait and made it torture to wait.

XXX

THOUGH EDNA HAD spoken of the dinner as a very grand affair, it was in truth a very small affair and very select, in so much as the guests invited were few and were selected with discrimination. She had counted upon an even dozen seating themselves at her round mahogany board, forgetting for the moment that Madame Ratignolle was to the last degree *souffrante*[1] and unpresentable, and not foreseeing that Madame Lebrun would send a thousand regrets at the last moment. So there were only ten, after all, which made a cozy, comfortable number.

There were Mr. and Mrs. Merriman, a pretty, vivacious little woman in the thirties; her husband, a jovial fellow, something of a shallow-pate, who laughed a good deal at other people's witticisms, and had thereby made himself extremely popular. Mrs. Highcamp had accompanied them. Of course, there was Alcée Arobin; and Mademoiselle Reisz had consented to come. Edna had sent her a fresh bunch of violets with black lace trimmings for her hair. Monsieur Ratignolle brought himself and his wife's excuses. Victor Lebrun, who happened to be in the city, bent upon relaxation, had accepted with alacrity. There was a Miss Mayblunt, no longer in her teens, who looked at the world through lorgnettes and with the keenest interest. It was thought and said that she was intellectual; it was suspected of her that she wrote under a *nom de guerre*. She had come with a gentleman by the name of Gouvernail, connected with one of the

[1] [Ill.]

daily papers, of whom nothing special could be said, except that he was observant and seemed quiet and inoffensive. Edna herself made the tenth, and at half-past eight they seated themselves at table, Arobin and Monsieur Ratignolle on either side of their hostess.

Mrs. Highcamp sat between Arobin and Victor Lebrun. Then came Mrs. Merriman, Mr. Gouvernail, Miss Mayblunt, Mr. Merriman, and Mademoiselle Reisz next to Monsieur Ratignolle.

There was something extremely gorgeous about the appearance of the table, an effect of splendor conveyed by a cover of pale yellow satin under strips of lace-work. There were wax candles in massive brass candelabra, burning softly under yellow silk shades; full, fragrant roses, yellow and red, abounded. There were silver and gold, as she had said there would be, and crystal which glittered like the gems which the women wore.

The ordinary stiff dining chairs had been discarded for the occasion and replaced by the most commodious and luxurious which could be collected throughout the house. Mademoiselle Reisz, being exceedingly diminutive, was elevated upon cushions, as small children are sometimes hoisted at table upon bulky volumes.

"Something new, Edna?" exclaimed Miss Mayblunt, with lorgnette directed toward a magnificent cluster of diamonds that sparkled, that almost sputtered, in Edna's hair, just over the center of her forehead.

"Quite new; 'brand' new, in fact; a present from my husband. It arrived this morning from New York. I may as well admit that this is my birthday, and that I am twenty-nine. In good time I expect you to drink my health. Meanwhile, I shall ask you to begin with this cocktail, composed—would you say 'composed?' " with an appeal to Miss Mayblunt—"composed by my father in honor of Sister Janet's wedding."

Before each guest stood a tiny glass that looked and sparkled like a garnet gem.

"Then, all things considered," spoke Arobin, "it might not be amiss to start out by drinking the Colonel's health in the cocktail which he composed, on the birthday of the most charming of women—the daughter whom he invented."

Mr. Merriman's laugh at this sally was such a genuine outburst and so contagious that it started the dinner with an agreeable swing that never slackened.

Miss Mayblunt begged to be allowed to keep her cocktail untouched before her, just to look at. The color was marvelous! She could compare it to nothing she had ever seen, and the garnet lights which it emitted were unspeakably rare. She pronounced the Colonel an artist, and stuck to it.

Monsieur Ratignolle was prepared to take things seriously: the *mets*, the *entre-mets*,[1] the service, the decorations, even the people. He looked up from his pompono and inquired of Arobin if he were related to the gentleman of that name who formed one of the firm of Laitner and Arobin, lawyers. The young man admitted that Laitner was a warm personal friend, who permitted Arobin's name to decorate the firm's letterheads and to appear upon a shingle that graced Perdido Street.

"There are so many inquisitive people and institutions abounding," said Arobin, "that one is really forced as a matter of convenience these days to assume the virtue of an occupation if he has it not."

Monsieur Ratignolle stared a little, and turned to ask Mademoiselle Reisz if she considered the symphony concerts up to the standard which had been set the previous winter. Mademoiselle Reisz answered Monsieur Ratignolle in French, which Edna thought a little rude, under the circumstances, but characteristic. Mademoiselle had only disagreeable things to say of the symphony concerts, and insulting remarks to make of all the musicians of New Orleans, singly and collectively. All her interest seemed to be centered upon the delicacies placed before her.

Mr. Merriman said that Mr. Arobin's remark about inquisitive people reminded him of a man from Waco the other day at the St. Charles Hotel—but as Mr. Merriman's stories were always lame and lacking point, his wife seldom permitted him to complete them. She interrupted him to ask if he remembered the name of the author whose book she had bought the week before to send to a friend in Geneva. She was talking "books" with Mr. Gouvernail and trying to draw from him his opinion upon current literary topics. Her husband told the story of the Waco man privately to Miss Mayblunt, who pretended to be greatly amused and to think it extremely clever.

Mrs. Highcamp hung with languid but unaffected interest upon the warm and impetuous volubility of her left-hand neighbor, Victor Lebrun. Her attention was never for a moment withdrawn from him after seating herself at table; and when he turned to Mrs. Merriman, who was prettier and more vivacious than Mrs. Highcamp, she waited with easy indifference for an opportunity to reclaim his attention. There was the occasional sound of music, of mandolins, sufficiently removed to be an agreeable accompaniment rather than an interruption to the conversation. Outside the soft, monotonous splash of a fountain could be heard; the sound penetrated into the room with the heavy odor of jessamine that came through the open windows.

[1] [The main courses, the side dishes.]

The golden shimmer of Edna's satin gown spread in rich folds on either side of her. There was a soft fall of lace encircling her shoulders. It was the color of her skin, without the glow, the myriad living tints that one may sometimes discover in vibrant flesh. There was something in her attitude, in her whole appearance when she leaned her head against the high-backed chair and spread her arms, which suggested the regal woman, the one who rules, who looks on, who stands alone.

But as she sat there amid her guests, she felt the old ennui overtaking her; the hopelessness which so often assailed her, which came upon her like an obsession, like something extraneous, independent of volition. It was something which announced itself; a chill breath that seemed to issue from some vast cavern wherein discords wailed. There came over her the acute longing which always summoned into her spiritual vision the presence of the beloved one, overpowering her at once with a sense of the unattainable.

The moments glided on, while a feeling of good fellowship passed around the circle like a mystic cord, holding and binding these people together with jest and laughter. Monsieur Ratignolle was the first to break the pleasant charm. At ten o'clock he excused himself. Madame Ratignolle was waiting for him at home. She was *bien souffrante*, and she was filled with vague dread, which only her husband's presence could allay.

Mademoiselle Reisz arose with Monsieur Ratignolle, who offered to escort her to the car. She had eaten well; she had tasted the good, rich wines, and they must have turned her head, for she bowed pleasantly to all as she withdrew from table. She kissed Edna upon the shoulder, and whispered: "*Bonne nuit, ma reine; soyez sage.*"[1] She had been a little bewildered upon rising, or rather, descending from her cushions, and Monsieur Ratignolle gallantly took her arm and led her away.

Mrs. Highcamp was weaving a garland of roses, yellow and red. When she had finished the garland, she laid it lightly upon Victor's black curls. He was reclining far back in the luxurious chair, holding a glass of champagne to the light.

As if a magician's wand had touched him, the garland of roses transformed him into a vision of Oriental beauty. His cheeks were the color of crushed grapes, and his dusky eyes glowed with a languishing fire.

"*Sapristi!*" exclaimed Arobin.

But Mrs. Highcamp had one more touch to add to the picture. She took from the back of her chair a white silken scarf, with which she had covered her shoulders in the early part of the evening. She draped it

[1] ["Good night, my love; be good."]

across the boy in graceful folds, and in a way to conceal his black, conventional evening dress. He did not seem to mind what she did to him, only smiled, showing a faint gleam of white teeth, while he continued to gaze with narrowing eyes at the light through his glass of champagne.

"Oh! to be able to paint in color rather than in words!" exclaimed Miss Mayblunt, losing herself in a rhapsodic dream as she looked at him.

> " 'There was a graven image of Desire
> Painted with red blood on a ground of gold.' "[1]

murmured Gouvernail, under his breath.

The effect of the wine upon Victor was, to change his accustomed volubility into silence. He seemed to have abandoned himself to a reverie, and to be seeing pleasing visions in the amber bead.

"Sing," entreated Mrs. Highcamp. "Won't you sing to us?"

"Let him alone," said Arobin.

"He's posing," offered Mr. Merriman; "let him have it out."

"I believe he's paralyzed," laughed Mrs. Merriman. And leaning over the youth's chair, she took the glass from his hand and held it to his lips. He sipped the wine slowly, and when he had drained the glass she laid it upon the table and wiped his lips with her little filmy handkerchief.

"Yes, I'll sing for you," he said, turning in his chair toward Mrs. Highcamp. He clasped his hands behind his head, and looking up at the ceiling began to hum a little, trying his voice like a musician tuning an instrument. Then, looking at Edna, he began to sing:

> "Ah! si tu savais!"

"Stop!" she cried, "don't sing that. I don't want you to sing it," and she laid her glass so impetuously and blindly upon the table as to shatter it against a caraffe. The wine spilled over Arobin's legs and some of it trickled down upon Mrs. Highcamp's black gauze gown. Victor had lost all idea of courtesy, or else he thought his hostess was not in earnest, for he laughed and went on:

> "Ah! si tu savais
> Ce que tes yeux me disent"—[2]

[1] [The first two lines from the sonnet "A Cameo" by Algernon Charles Swinburne.]
[2] ["Oh! if you knew/ What your eyes say to me"]

"Oh! you mustn't! you mustn't," exclaimed Edna, and pushing back her chair she got up, and going behind him placed her hand over his mouth. He kissed the soft palm that pressed upon his lips.

"No, no, I won't, Mrs. Pontellier. I didn't know you meant it," looking up at her with caressing eyes. The touch of his lips was like a pleasing sting to her hand. She lifted the garland of roses from his head and flung it across the room.

"Come, Victor; you've posed long enough. Give Mrs. Highcamp her scarf."

Mrs. Highcamp undraped the scarf from about him with her own hands. Miss Mayblunt and Mr. Gouvernail suddenly conceived the notion that it was time to say good night. And Mr. and Mrs. Merriman wondered how it could be so late.

Before parting from Victor, Mrs. Highcamp invited him to call upon her daughter, who she knew would be charmed to meet him and talk French and sing French songs with him. Victor expressed his desire and intention to call upon Miss Highcamp at the first opportunity which presented itself. He asked if Arobin were going his way. Arobin was not.

The mandolin players had long since stolen away. A profound stillness had fallen upon the broad, beautiful street. The voices of Edna's disbanding guests jarred like a discordant note upon the quiet harmony of the night.

XXXI

"WELL?" QUESTIONED AROBIN, who had remained with Edna after the others had departed.

"Well," she reiterated, and stood up, stretching her arms, and feeling the need to relax her muscles after having been so long seated.

"What next?" he asked.

"The servants are all gone. They left when the musicians did. I have dismissed them. The house has to be closed and locked, and I shall trot around to the pigeon house, and shall send Celestine over in the morning to straighten things up."

He looked around, and began to turn out some of the lights.

"What about upstairs?" he inquired.

"I think it is all right; but there may be a window or two unlatched. We had better look; you might take a candle and see. And bring me my wrap and hat on the foot of the bed in the middle room."

He went up with the light, and Edna began closing doors and windows. She hated to shut in the smoke and the fumes of the wine. Arobin found her cape and hat, which he brought down and helped her to put on.

When everything was secured and the lights put out, they left through the front door, Arobin locking it and taking the key, which he carried for Edna. He helped her down the steps.

"Will you have a spray of jessamine?" he asked, breaking off a few blossoms as he passed.

"No; I don't want anything."

She seemed disheartened, and had nothing to say. She took his arm, which he offered her, holding up the weight of her satin train with the other hand. She looked down, noticing the black line of his leg moving in and out so close to her against the yellow shimmer of her gown. There was the whistle of a railway train somewhere in the distance, and the midnight bells were ringing. They met no one in their short walk.

The "pigeon-house" stood behind a locked gate, and a shallow *parterre* that had been somewhat neglected. There was a small front porch, upon which a long window and the front door opened. The door opened directly into the parlor; there was no side entry. Back in the yard was a room for servants, in which old Celestine had been ensconced.

Edna had left a lamp burning low upon the table. She had succeeded in making the room look habitable and homelike. There were some books on the table and a lounge near at hand. On the floor was a fresh matting, covered with a rug or two; and on the walls hung a few tasteful pictures. But the room was filled with flowers. These were a surprise to her. Arobin had sent them, and had had Celestine distribute them during Edna's absence. Her bed-room was adjoining, and across a small passage were the dining-room and kitchen.

Edna seated herself with every appearance of discomfort.

"Are you tired?" he asked.

"Yes, and chilled, and miserable. I feel as if I had been wound up to a certain pitch—too tight—and something inside of me had snapped." She rested her head against the table upon her bare arm.

"You want to rest," he said, "and to be quiet. I'll go; I'll leave you and let you rest."

"Yes," she replied.

He stood up beside her and smoothed her hair with his soft, magnetic hand. His touch conveyed to her a certain physical comfort. She could have fallen quietly asleep there if he had continued to pass his hand over her hair. He brushed the hair upward from the nape of her neck.

"I hope you will feel better and happier in the morning," he said. "You have tried to do too much in the past few days. The dinner was the last straw; you might have dispensed with it."

"Yes," she admitted; "it was stupid."

"No, it was delightful; but it has worn you out." His hand had strayed to her beautiful shoulders, and he could feel the response of her flesh to his touch. He seated himself beside her and kissed her lightly upon the shoulder.

"I thought you were going away," she said, in an uneven voice.

"I am, after I have said good night."

"Good night," she murmured.

He did not answer, except to continue to caress her. He did not say good night until she had become supple to his gentle, seductive entreaties.

XXXII

When Mr. Pontellier learned of his wife's intention to abandon her home and take up her residence elsewhere, he immediately wrote her a letter of unqualified disapproval and remonstrance. She had given reasons which he was unwilling to acknowledge as adequate. He hoped she had not acted upon her rash impulse; and he begged her to consider first, foremost, and above all else, what people would say. He was not dreaming of scandal when he uttered this warning; that was a thing which would never have entered into his mind to consider in connection with his wife's name or his own. He was simply thinking of his financial integrity. It might get noised about that the Pontelliers had met with reverses, and were forced to conduct their *ménage* on a humbler scale than heretofore. It might do incalculable mischief to his business prospects.

But remembering Edna's whimsical turn of mind of late, and foreseeing that she had immediately acted upon her impetuous determination, he grasped the situation with his usual promptness and handled it with his well-known business tact and cleverness.

The same mail which brought to Edna his letter of disapproval carried instructions—the most minute instructions—to a well-known architect concerning the remodeling of his home, changes which he had long contemplated, and which he desired carried forward during his temporary absence.

Expert and reliable packers and movers were engaged to convey the furniture, carpets, pictures—everything movable, in short—to places of security. And in an incredibly short time the Pontellier house was turned over to the artisans. There was to be an addition—a small snuggery; there was to be frescoing, and hardwood flooring was to be put into such rooms as had not yet been subjected to this improvement.

Furthermore, in one of the daily papers appeared a brief notice to the effect that Mr. and Mrs. Pontellier were contemplating a summer sojourn abroad, and that their handsome residence on Esplanade Street was undergoing sumptuous alterations, and would not be ready for occupancy until their return. Mr. Pontellier had saved appearances!

Edna admired the skill of his maneuver, and avoided any occasion to balk his intentions. When the situation as set forth by Mr. Pontellier was accepted and taken for granted, she was apparently satisfied that it should be so.

The pigeon-house pleased her. It at once assumed the intimate character of a home, while she herself invested it with a charm which it reflected like a warm glow. There was with her a feeling of having descended in the social scale, with a corresponding sense of having risen in the spiritual. Every step which she took toward relieving herself from obligations added to her strength and expansion as an individual. She began to look with her own eyes; to see and to apprehend the deeper undercurrents of life. No longer was she content to "feed upon opinion" when her own soul had invited her.

After a little while, a few days, in fact, Edna went up and spent a week with her children in Iberville. They were delicious February days, with all the summer's promise hovering in the air.

How glad she was to see the children! She wept for very pleasure when she felt their little arms clasping her; their hard, ruddy cheeks pressed against her own glowing cheeks. She looked into their faces with hungry eyes that could not be satisfied with looking. And what stories they had to tell their mother! About the pigs, the cows, the mules! About riding to the mill behind Gluglu; fishing back in the lake with their Uncle Jasper; picking pecans with Lidie's little black brood, and hauling chips in their express wagon. It was a thousand times more fun to haul real chips for old lame Susie's real fire than to drag painted blocks along the banquette on Esplanade Street!

She went with them herself to see the pigs and the cows, to look at the darkies laying the cane, to thrash the pecan trees, and catch fish in the back lake. She lived with them a whole week long, giving them all of herself, and gathering and filling herself with their young existence. They listened, breathless, when she told them the house in Esplanade Street was crowded with workmen, hammering, nailing, sawing, and filling the place with clatter. They wanted to know where their bed was; what had been done with their rocking-horse; and where did Joe sleep, and where had Ellen gone, and the cook? But, above all, they were fired with a desire to see the little house around the block. Was there any place to play? Were there any boys next door? Raoul, with pessimistic foreboding, was convinced that there were only girls next door. Where would they sleep, and where would papa sleep? She told them the fairies would fix it all right.

The old Madame was charmed with Edna's visit, and showered all manner of delicate attentions upon her. She was delighted to know that the Esplanade Street house was in a dismantled condition. It gave her the promise and pretext to keep the children indefinitely.

It was with a wrench and a pang that Edna left her children. She carried away with her the sound of their voices and the touch of their cheeks. All along the journey homeward their presence lingered with her like the memory of a delicious song. But by the time she had regained the city the song no longer echoed in her soul. She was again alone.

XXXIII

It happened sometimes when Edna went to see Mademoiselle Reisz that the little musician was absent, giving a lesson or making some small necessary household purchase. The key was always left in a secret hiding-place in the entry, which Edna knew. If Mademoiselle happened to be away, Edna would usually enter and wait for her return.

When she knocked at Mademoiselle Reisz's door one afternoon there was no response; so unlocking the door, as usual, she entered and found the apartment deserted, as she had expected. Her day had been quite filled up, and it was for a rest, for a refuge, and to talk about Robert, that she sought out her friend.

She had worked at her canvas—a young Italian character study—all the morning, completing the work without the model; but there had been many interruptions, some incident to her modest housekeeping, and others of a social nature.

Madame Ratignolle had dragged herself over, avoiding the too public thoroughfares, she said. She complained that Edna had neglected her much of late. Besides, she was consumed with curiosity to see the little house and the manner in which it was conducted. She wanted to hear all about the dinner party; Monsieur Ratignolle had left *so* early. What had happened after he left? The champagne and grapes which Edna sent over were *too* delicious. She had so little appetite; they had refreshed and toned her stomach. Where on earth was she going to put Mr. Pontellier in that little house, and the boys? And then she made Edna promise to go to her when her hour of trial overtook her.

"At any time—any time of the day or night, dear," Edna assured her.

Before leaving Madame Ratignolle said:

"In some way you seem to me like a child, Edna. You seem to act without a certain amount of reflection which is necessary in this life. That is the reason I want to say you mustn't mind if I advise you to be a little careful while you are living here alone. Why don't you have some one come and stay with you? Wouldn't Mademoiselle Reisz come?"

"No; she wouldn't wish to come, and I shouldn't want her always with me."

"Well, the reason—you know how evil-minded the world is—some one was talking of Alcée Arobin visiting you. Of course, it wouldn't matter if Mr. Arobin had not such a dreadful reputation. Monsieur Ratignolle was telling me that his attentions alone are considered enough to ruin a woman's name."

"Does he boast of his successes?" asked Edna, indifferently, squinting at her picture.

"No, I think not. I believe he is a decent fellow as far as that goes. But his character is so well known among the men. I shan't be able to come back and see you; it was very, very imprudent to-day."

"Mind the step!" cried Edna.

"Don't neglect me," entreated Madame Ratignolle; "and don't mind what I said about Arobin, or having some one to stay with you."

"Of course not," Edna laughed. "You may say anything you like to me." They kissed each other good-by. Madame Ratignolle had not far to go, and Edna stood on the porch a while watching her walk down the street.

Then in the afternoon Mrs. Merriman and Mrs. Highcamp had made their "party call." Edna felt that they might have dispensed with the formality. They had also come to invite her to play *vingt-et-un*[1] one evening at Mrs. Merriman's. She was asked to go early, to dinner, and Mr.

[1] [Twenty-one (a card game).]

Merriman or Mr. Arobin would take her home. Edna accepted in a half-hearted way. She sometimes felt very tired of Mrs. Highcamp and Mrs. Merriman.

Late in the afternoon she sought refuge with Mademoiselle Reisz, and stayed there alone, waiting for her, feeling a kind of repose invade her with the very atmosphere of the shabby, unpretentious little room.

Edna sat at the window, which looked out over the house-tops and across the river. The window frame was filled with pots of flowers, and she sat and picked the dry leaves from a rose geranium. The day was warm, and the breeze which blew from the river was very pleasant. She removed her hat and laid it on the piano. She went on picking the leaves and digging around the plants with her hat pin. Once she thought she heard Mademoiselle Reisz approaching. But it was a young black girl, who came in, bringing a small bundle of laundry, which she deposited in the adjoining room, and went away.

Edna seated herself at the piano, and softly picked out with one hand the bars of a piece of music which lay open before her. A half-hour went by. There was the occasional sound of people going and coming in the lower hall. She was growing interested in her occupation of picking out the aria, when there was a second rap at the door. She vaguely wondered what these people did when they found Mademoiselle's door locked.

"Come in," she called, turning her face toward the door. And this time it was Robert Lebrun who presented himself. She attempted to rise; she could not have done so without betraying the agitation which mastered her at sight of him, so she fell back upon the stool, only exclaiming, "Why, Robert!"

He came and clasped her hand, seemingly without knowing what he was saying or doing.

"Mrs. Pontellier! How do you happen—oh! how well you look! Is Mademoiselle Reisz not here? I never expected to see you."

"When did you come back?" asked Edna in an unsteady voice, wiping her face with her handkerchief. She seemed ill at ease on the piano stool, and he begged her to take the chair by the window. She did so, mechanically, while he seated himself on the stool.

"I returned day before yesterday," he answered, while he leaned his arm on the keys, bringing forth a crash of discordant sound.

"Day before yesterday!" she repeated, aloud; and went on thinking to herself, "day before yesterday," in a sort of an uncomprehending way. She had pictured him seeking her at the very first hour, and he had lived under the same sky since day before yesterday; while only by accident had he stumbled upon her. Mademoiselle must have lied when she said, "Poor fool, he loves you."

"Day before yesterday," she repeated, breaking off a spray of Mademoiselle's geranium; "then if you had not met me here to-day you wouldn't—when—that is, didn't you mean to come and see me?"

"Of course, I should have gone to see you. There have been so many things—" he turned the leaves of Mademoiselle's music nervously. "I started in at once yesterday with the old firm. After all there is as much chance for me here as there was there—that is, I might find it profitable some day. The Mexicans were not very congenial."

So he had come back because the Mexicans were not congenial; because business was as profitable here as there; because of any reason, and not because he cared to be near her. She remembered the day she sat on the floor, turning the pages of his letter, seeking the reason which was left untold.

She had not noticed how he looked—only feeling his presence; but she turned deliberately and observed him. After all, he had been absent but a few months, and was not changed. His hair—the color of hers—waved back from his temples in the same way as before. His skin was not more burned than it had been at Grand Isle. She found in his eyes, when he looked at her for one silent moment, the same tender caress, with an added warmth and entreaty which had not been there before—the same glance which had penetrated to the sleeping places of her soul and awakened them.

A hundred times Edna had pictured Robert's return, and imagined their first meeting. It was usually at her home, whither he had sought her out at once. She always fancied him expressing or betraying in some way his love for her. And here, the reality was that they sat ten feet apart, she at the window, crushing geranium leaves in her hand and smelling them, he twirling around on the piano stool, saying:

"I was very much surprised to hear of Mr. Pontellier's absence; it's a wonder Mademoiselle Reisz did not tell me; and your moving—mother told me yesterday. I should think you would have gone to New York with him, or to Iberville with the children, rather than be bothered here with housekeeping. And you are going abroad, too, I hear. We shan't have you at Grand Isle next summer; it won't seem—do you see much of Mademoiselle Reisz? She often spoke of you in the few letters she wrote."

"Do you remember that you promised to write to me when you went away?" A flush overspread his whole face.

"I couldn't believe that my letters would be of any interest to you."

"That is an excuse; it isn't the truth." Edna reached for her hat on the piano. She adjusted it, sticking the hat pin through the heavy coil of hair with some deliberation.

"Are you not going to wait for Mademoiselle Reisz?" asked Robert.

"No; I have found when she is absent this long, she is liable not to come back till late." She drew on her gloves, and Robert picked up his hat.

"Won't you wait for her?" asked Edna.

"Not if you think she will not be back till late," adding, as if suddenly aware of some discourtesy in his speech, "and I should miss the pleasure of walking home with you." Edna locked the door and put the key back in its hiding-place.

They went together, picking their way across muddy streets and sidewalks encumbered with the cheap display of small tradesmen. Part of the distance they rode in the car, and after disembarking, passed the Pontellier mansion, which looked broken and half torn asunder. Robert had never known the house, and looked at it with interest.

"I never knew you in your home," he remarked.

"I am glad you did not."

"Why?" She did not answer. They went on around the corner, and it seemed as if her dreams were coming true after all, when he followed her into the little house.

"You must stay and dine with me, Robert. You see I am all alone, and it is so long since I have seen you. There is so much I want to ask you."

She took off her hat and gloves. He stood irresolute, making some excuse about his mother who expected him; he even muttered something about an engagement. She struck a match and lit the lamp on the table; it was growing dusk. When he saw her face in the lamp-light, looking pained, with all the soft lines gone out of it, he threw his hat aside and seated himself.

"Oh! you know I want to stay if you will let me!" he exclaimed. All the softness came back. She laughed, and went and put her hand on his shoulder.

"This is the first moment you have seemed like the old Robert. I'll go tell Celestine." She hurried away to tell Celestine to set an extra place. She even sent her off in search of some added delicacy which she had not thought of for herself. And she recommended great care in dripping the coffee and having the omelet done to a proper turn.

When she reëntered, Robert was turning over magazines, sketches, and things that lay upon the table in great disorder. He picked up a photograph, and exclaimed:

"Alcée Arobin! What on earth is his picture doing here?"

"I tried to make a sketch of his head one day," answered Edna, "and he thought the photograph might help me. It was at the other house. I thought it had been left there. I must have packed it up with my drawing materials."

"I should think you would give it back to him if you have finished with it."

"Oh! I have a great many such photographs. I never think of returning them. They don't amount to anything." Robert kept on looking at the picture.

"It seems to me—do you think his head worth drawing? Is he a friend of Mr. Pontellier's? You never said you knew him."

"He isn't a friend of Mr. Pontellier's; he's a friend of mine. I always knew him—that is, it is only of late that I know him pretty well. But I'd rather talk about you, and know what you have been seeing and doing and feeling out there in Mexico." Robert threw aside the picture.

"I've been seeing the waves and the white beach of Grand Isle; the quiet, grassy street of the *Chênière*; the old fort at Grande Terre. I've been working like a machine, and feeling like a lost soul. There was nothing interesting."

She leaned her head upon her hand to shade her eyes from the light.

"And what have you been seeing and doing and feeling all these days?" he asked.

"I've been seeing the waves and the white beach of Grand Isle; the quiet, grassy street of the *Chênière Caminada*; the old sunny fort at Grande Terre. I've been working with a little more comprehension than a machine, and still feeling like a lost soul. There was nothing interesting."

"Mrs. Pontellier, you are cruel," he said, with feeling, closing his eyes and resting his head back in his chair. They remained in silence till old Celestine announced dinner.

XXXIV

THE DINING-ROOM WAS very small. Edna's round mahogany would have almost filled it. As it was there was but a step or two from the little table to the kitchen, to the mantel, the small buffet, and the side door that opened out on the narrow brick-paved yard.

A certain degree of ceremony settled upon them with the announcement of dinner. There was no return to personalities. Robert related incidents of his sojourn in Mexico, and Edna talked of events likely to interest him, which had occurred during his absence. The dinner was of ordinary quality, except for the few delicacies which she had sent out to purchase. Old Celestine, with a bandana *tignon* twisted about her head, hobbled in and out, taking a personal interest in everything; and she lingered occasionally to talk patois with Robert, whom she had known as a boy.

He went out to a neighboring cigar stand to purchase cigarette papers, and when he came back he found that Celestine had served the black coffee in the parlor.

"Perhaps I shouldn't have come back," he said. "When you are tired of me, tell me to go."

"You never tire me. You must have forgotten the hours and hours at Grand Isle in which we grew accustomed to each other and used to being together."

"I have forgotten nothing at Grand Isle," he said, not looking at her, but rolling a cigarette. His tobacco pouch, which he laid upon the table, was a fantastic embroidered silk affair, evidently the handiwork of a woman.

"You used to carry your tobacco in a rubber pouch," said Edna, picking up the pouch and examining the needlework.

"Yes; it was lost."

"Where did you buy this one? In Mexico?"

"It was given to me by a Vera Cruz girl; they are very generous," he replied, striking a match and lighting his cigarette.

"They are very handsome, I suppose, those Mexican women; very picturesque, with their black eyes and their lace scarfs."

"Some are; others are hideous. Just as you find women everywhere."

"What was she like—the one who gave you the pouch? You must have known her very well."

"She was very ordinary. She wasn't of the slightest importance. I knew her well enough."

"Did you visit at her house? Was it interesting? I should like to know and hear about the people you met, and the impressions they made on you."

"There are some people who leave impressions not so lasting as the imprint of an oar upon the water."

"Was she such a one?"

"It would be ungenerous for me to admit that she was of that order and kind." He thrust the pouch back in his pocket, as if to put away the subject with the trifle which had brought it up.

Arobin dropped in with a message from Mrs. Merriman, to say that the card party was postponed on account of the illness of one of her children.

"How do you do, Arobin?" said Robert, rising from the obscurity.

"Oh! Lebrun. To be sure! I heard yesterday you were back. How did they treat you down in Mexique?"

"Fairly well."

"But not well enough to keep you there. Stunning girls, though, in Mexico. I thought I should never get away from Vera Cruz when I was down there a couple of years ago."

"Did they embroider slippers and tobacco pouches and hat-bands and things for you?" asked Edna.

"Oh! my! no! I didn't get so deep in their regard. I fear they made more impression on me than I made on them."

"You were less fortunate than Robert, then."

"I am always less fortunate than Robert. Has he been imparting tender confidences?"

"I've been imposing myself long enough," said Robert, rising, and shaking hands with Edna. "Please convey my regards to Mr. Pontellier when you write."

He shook hands with Arobin and went away.

"Fine fellow, that Lebrun," said Arobin when Robert had gone. "I never heard you speak of him."

"I knew him last summer at Grand Isle," she replied. "Here is that photograph of yours. Don't you want it?"

"What do I want with it? Throw it away." She threw it back on the table.

"I'm not going to Mrs. Merriman's," she said. "If you see her, tell her so. But perhaps I had better write. I think I shall write now, and say that I am sorry her child is sick, and tell her not to count on me."

"It would be a good scheme," acquiesced Arobin. "I don't blame you; stupid lot!"

Edna opened the blotter, and having procured paper and pen, began to write the note. Arobin lit a cigar and read the evening paper, which he had in his pocket.

"What is the date?" she asked. He told her.

"Will you mail this for me when you go out?"

"Certainly." He read to her little bits out of the newspaper, while she straightened things on the table.

"What do you want to do?" he asked, throwing aside the paper. "Do you want to go out for a walk or a drive or anything? It would be a fine night to drive."

"No; I don't want to do anything but just be quiet. You go away and amuse yourself. Don't stay."

"I'll go away if I must; but I shan't amuse myself. You know that I only live when I am near you."

He stood up to bid her good night.

"Is that one of the things you always say to women?"

"I have said it before, but I don't think I ever came so near meaning it," he answered with a smile. There were no warm lights in her eyes; only a dreamy, absent look.

"Good night. I adore you. Sleep well," he said, and he kissed her hand and went away.

She stayed alone in a kind of reverie—a sort of stupor. Step by step she lived over every instant of the time she had been with Robert after he had entered Mademoiselle Reisz's door. She recalled his words, his looks. How few and meager they had been for her hungry heart! A vision—a transcendently seductive vision of a Mexican girl arose before her. She writhed with a jealous pang. She wondered when he would come back. He had not said he would come back. She had been with him, had heard his voice and touched his hand. But some way he had seemed nearer to her off there in Mexico.

XXXV

THE MORNING WAS full of sunlight and hope. Edna could see before her no denial—only the promise of excessive joy. She lay in bed awake, with bright eyes full of speculation. "He loves you, poor fool." If she could but get that conviction firmly fixed in her mind, what mattered about the rest? She felt she had been childish and unwise the night before in giving herself over to despondency. She recapitulated the motives which no doubt explained Robert's reserve. They were not insurmountable; they would not hold if he really loved her; they could not hold against her own passion, which he must come to realize in time. She pictured him going to his business that morning. She even saw how he was dressed; how he walked down one street, and turned the corner of another; saw him bending over his desk, talking to people who entered the office, going to his lunch, and perhaps watching for her on the street. He would come to her in the afternoon or evening, sit and roll his cigarette, talk a little, and go away as he had done the night before. But how delicious it would be to have him there with her! She would have no regrets, nor seek to penetrate his reserve if he still chose to wear it.

Edna ate her breakfast only half dressed. The maid brought her a delicious printed scrawl from Raoul, expressing his love, asking her to send him some bonbons, and telling her they had found that morning ten tiny white pigs all lying in a row beside Lidie's big white pig.

A letter also came from her husband, saying he hoped to be back early in March, and then they would get ready for that journey abroad which he had promised her so long, which he felt now fully able to afford; he felt able to travel as people should, without any thought of small economies—thanks to his recent speculations in Wall Street.

Much to her surprise she received a note from Arobin, written at midnight from the club. It was to say good morning to her, to hope that she had slept well, to assure her of his devotion, which he trusted she in some faintest manner returned.

All these letters were pleasing to her. She answered the children in a cheerful frame of mind, promising them bonbons, and congratulating them upon their happy find of the little pigs.

She answered her husband with friendly evasiveness,—not with any fixed design to mislead him, only because all sense of reality had gone out of her life; she had abandoned herself to Fate, and awaited the consequences with indifference.

To Arobin's note she made no reply. She put it under Celestine's stove-lid.

Edna worked several hours with much spirit. She saw no one but a picture dealer, who asked her if it were true that she was going abroad to study in Paris.

She said possibly she might, and he negotiated with her for some Parisian studies to reach him in time for the holiday trade in December.

Robert did not come that day. She was keenly disappointed. He did not come the following day, nor the next. Each morning she awoke with hope, and each night she was a prey to despondency. She was tempted to seek him out. But far from yielding to the impulse, she avoided any occasion which might throw her in his way. She did not go to Mademoiselle Reisz's nor pass by Madame Lebrun's, as she might have done if he had still been in Mexico.

When Arobin, one night, urged her to drive with him, she went—out to the lake, on the Shell Road. His horses were full of mettle, and even a little unmanageable. She liked the rapid gait at which they spun along, and the quick, sharp sound of the horses' hoofs on the hard road.

They did not stop anywhere to eat or to drink. Arobin was not needlessly imprudent. But they ate and they drank when they regained Edna's little dining-room—which was comparatively early in the evening.

It was late when he left her. It was getting to be more than a passing whim with Arobin to see her and be with her. He had detected the latent sensuality, which unfolded under his delicate sense of her nature's requirements like a torpid, torrid, sensitive blossom.

There was no despondency when she fell asleep that night; nor was there hope when she awoke in the morning.

XXXVI

THERE WAS A garden out in the suburbs; a small, leafy corner, with a few green tables under the orange trees. An old cat slept all day on the stone step in the sun, and an old *mulatresse* slept her idle hours away in her chair at the open window, till some one happened to knock on one of the green tables. She had milk and cream cheese to sell, and bread and butter. There was no one who could make such excellent coffee or fry a chicken so golden brown as she.

The place was too modest to attract the attention of people of fashion, and so quiet as to have escaped the notice of those in search of pleasure and dissipation. Edna had discovered it accidentally one day when the high-board gate stood ajar. She caught sight of a little green table, blotched with the checkered sunlight that filtered through the quivering leaves overhead. Within she had found the slumbering *mulatresse*, the drowsy cat, and a glass of milk which reminded her of the milk she had tasted in Iberville.

She often stopped there during her perambulations; sometimes taking a book with her, and sitting an hour or two under the trees when she found the place deserted. Once or twice she took a quiet dinner there alone, having instructed Celestine beforehand to prepare no dinner at home. It was the last place in the city where she would have expected to meet any one she knew.

Still she was not astonished when, as she was partaking of a modest dinner late in the afternoon, looking into an open book, stroking the cat, which had made friends with her—she was not greatly astonished to see Robert come in at the tall garden gate.

"I am destined to see you only by accident," she said, shoving the cat off the chair beside her. He was surprised, ill at ease, almost embarrassed at meeting her thus so unexpectedly.

"Do you come here often?" he asked.

"I almost live here," she said.

"I used to drop in very often for a cup of Catiche's good coffee. This is the first time since I came back."

"She'll bring you a plate, and you will share my dinner. There's always enough for two—even three." Edna had intended to be indifferent and as reserved as he when she met him; she had reached the determination by a laborious train of reasoning, incident to one of her despondent moods. But her resolve melted when she saw him before her, seated there beside her in the little garden, as if a designing Providence had led him into her path.

"Why have you kept away from me, Robert?" she asked, closing the book that lay open upon the table.

"Why are you so personal, Mrs. Pontellier? Why do you force me to idiotic subterfuges?" he exclaimed with sudden warmth. "I suppose there's no use telling you I've been very busy, or that I've been sick, or that I've been to see you and not found you at home. Please let me off with any one of these excuses."

"You are the embodiment of selfishness," she said. "You save yourself something—I don't know what—but there is some selfish motive, and in sparing yourself you never consider for a moment what I think, or how I feel your neglect and indifference. I suppose this is what you would call unwomanly; but I have got into a habit of expressing myself. It doesn't matter to me, and you may think me unwomanly if you like."

"No; I only think you cruel, as I said the other day. Maybe not intentionally cruel; but you seem to be forcing me into disclosures which can result in nothing; as if you would have me bare a wound for the pleasure of looking at it, without the intention or power of healing it."

"I'm spoiling your dinner, Robert; never mind what I say. You haven't eaten a morsel."

"I only came in for a cup of coffee." His sensitive face was all disfigured with excitement.

"Isn't this a delightful place?" she remarked. "I am so glad it has never actually been discovered. It is so quiet, so sweet, here. Do you notice there is scarcely a sound to be heard? It's so out of the way; and a good walk from the car. However, I don't mind walking. I always feel so sorry for women who don't like to walk; they miss so much—so many rare little glimpses of life; and we women learn so little of life on the whole.

"Catiche's coffee is always hot. I don't know how she manages it, here in the open air. Celestine's coffee gets cold bringing it from the kitchen to the dining-room. Three lumps! How can you drink it so sweet? Take some of the cress with your chop; it's so biting and crisp. Then there's the advantage of being able to smoke with your coffee out here. Now, in the city—aren't you going to smoke?"

"After a while," he said, laying a cigar on the table.

"Who gave it to you?" she laughed.

"I bought it. I suppose I'm getting reckless; I bought a whole box." She was determined not to be personal again and make him uncomfortable.

The cat made friends with him, and climbed into his lap when he smoked his cigar. He stroked her silky fur, and talked a little about her. He looked at Edna's book, which he had read; and he told her the end, to save her the trouble of wading through it, he said.

Again he accompanied her back to her home; and it was after dusk when they reached the little "pigeon-house." She did not ask him to remain, which he was grateful for, as it permitted him to stay without the discomfort of blundering through an excuse which he had no intention of considering. He helped her to light the lamp; then she went into her room to take off her hat and to bathe her face and hands.

When she came back Robert was not examining the pictures and magazines as before; he sat off in the shadow, leaning his head back on the chair as if in a reverie. Edna lingered a moment beside the table, arranging the books there. Then she went across the room to where he sat. She bent over the arm of his chair and called his name.

"Robert," she said, "are you asleep?"

"No," he answered, looking up at her.

She leaned over and kissed him—a soft, cool, delicate kiss, whose voluptuous sting penetrated his whole being—then she moved away from him. He followed, and took her in his arms, just holding her close to him. She put her hand up to his face and pressed his cheek against her own. The action was full of love and tenderness. He sought her lips again. Then he drew her down upon the sofa beside him and held her hand in both of his.

"Now you know," he said, "now you know what I have been fighting against since last summer at Grand Isle; what drove me away and drove me back again."

"Why have you been fighting against it?" she asked. Her face glowed with soft lights.

"Why? Because you were not free; you were Léonce Pontellier's wife. I couldn't help loving you if you were ten times his wife; but so long as I went away from you and kept away I could help telling you so." She put her free hand up to his shoulder, and then against his cheek, rubbing it softly. He kissed her again. His face was warm and flushed.

"There in Mexico I was thinking of you all the time, and longing for you."

"But not writing to me," she interrupted.

"Something put into my head that you cared for me; and I lost my senses. I forgot everything but a wild dream of your some way becoming my wife."

"Your wife!"

"Religion, loyalty, everything would give way if only you cared."

"Then you must have forgotten that I was Léonce Pontellier's wife."

"Oh! I was demented, dreaming of wild, impossible things, recalling men who had set their wives free, we have heard of such things."

"Yes, we have heard of such things."

"I came back full of vague, mad intentions. And when I got here—"

"When you got here you never came near me!" She was still caressing his cheek.

"I realized what a cur I was to dream of such a thing, even if you had been willing."

She took his face between her hands and looked into it as if she would never withdraw her eyes more. She kissed him on the forehead, the eyes, the cheeks, and the lips.

"You have been a very, very foolish boy, wasting your time dreaming of impossible things when you speak of Mr. Pontellier setting me free! I am no longer one of Mr. Pontellier's possessions to dispose of or not. I give myself where I choose. If he were to say, 'Here, Robert, take her and be happy; she is yours,' I should laugh at you both."

His face grew a little white. "What do you mean?" he asked.

There was a knock at the door. Old Celestine came in to say that Madame Ratignolle's servant had come around the back way with a message that Madame had been taken sick and begged Mrs. Pontellier to go to her immediately.

"Yes, yes," said Edna, rising; "I promised. Tell her yes—to wait for me. I'll go back with her."

"Let me walk over with you," offered Robert.

"No," she said; "I will go with the servant." She went into her room to put on her hat, and when she came in again she sat once more upon the sofa beside him. He had not stirred. She put her arms about his neck.

"Good-by, my sweet Robert. Tell me good-by." He kissed her with a degree of passion which had not before entered into his caress, and strained her to him.

"I love you," she whispered, "only you; no one but you. It was you who awoke me last summer out of a life-long, stupid dream. Oh! you have made me so unhappy with your indifference. Oh! I have suffered, suffered! Now you are here we shall love each other, my Robert. We shall be everything to each other. Nothing else in the world is of any consequence. I must go to my friend; but you will wait for me? No matter how late; you will wait for me, Robert?"

"Don't go; don't go! Oh! Edna, stay with me," he pleaded. "Why should you go? Stay with me, stay with me."

"I shall come back as soon as I can; I shall find you here." She buried her face in his neck, and said good-by again. Her seductive voice, together with his great love for her, had enthralled his senses, had deprived him of every impulse but the longing to hold her and keep her.

XXXVII

EDNA LOOKED IN at the drug store. Monsieur Ratignolle was putting up a mixture himself, very carefully, dropping a red liquid into a tiny glass. He was grateful to Edna for having come; her presence would be a comfort to his wife. Madame Ratignolle's sister, who had always been with her at such trying times, had not been able to come up from the plantation, and Adèle had been inconsolable until Mrs. Pontellier so kindly promised to come to her. The nurse had been with them at night for the past week, as she lived a great distance away. And Dr. Mandelet had been coming and going all the afternoon. They were then looking for him any moment.

Edna hastened upstairs by a private stairway that led from the rear of the store to the apartments above. The children were all sleeping in a back room. Madame Ratignolle was in the salon, whither she had strayed in her suffering impatience. She sat on the sofa, clad in an ample white *peignoir*, holding a handkerchief tight in her hand with a nervous clutch. Her face was drawn and pinched, her sweet blue eyes haggard and unnatural. All her beautiful hair had been drawn back and plaited. It lay in a long braid on the sofa pillow, coiled like a golden serpent. The nurse, a comfortable looking *Griffe*[1] woman in white apron and cap, was urging her to return to her bedroom.

"There is no use, there is no use," she said at once to Edna. "We must

[1] [The offspring of a mulatto and either a black or an American Indian.]

get rid of Mandelet; he is getting too old and careless. He said he would be here at half-past seven; now it must be eight. See what time it is, Joséphine."

The woman was possessed of a cheerful nature, and refused to take any situation too seriously, especially a situation with which she was so familiar. She urged Madame to have courage and patience. But Madame only set her teeth hard into her under lip, and Edna saw the sweat gather in beads on her white forehead. After a moment or two she uttered a profound sigh and wiped her face with the handkerchief rolled in a ball. She appeared exhausted. The nurse gave her a fresh handkerchief, sprinkled with cologne water.

"This is too much!" she cried. "Mandelet ought to be killed! Where is Alphonse? Is it possible I am to be abandoned like this—neglected by every one?"

"Neglected, indeed!" exclaimed the nurse. Wasn't she there? And here was Mrs. Pontellier leaving, no doubt, a pleasant evening at home to devote to her? And wasn't Monsieur Ratignolle coming that very instant through the hall? And Joséphine was quite sure she had heard Doctor Mandelet's coupé. Yes, there it was, down at the door.

Adèle consented to go back to her room. She sat on the edge of a little low couch next to her bed.

Doctor Mandelet paid no attention to Madame Ratignolle's upbraidings. He was accustomed to them at such times, and was too well convinced of her loyalty to doubt it.

He was glad to see Edna, and wanted her to go with him into the salon and entertain him. But Madame Ratignolle would not consent that Edna should leave her for an instant. Between agonizing moments, she chatted a little, and said it took her mind off her sufferings.

Edna began to feel uneasy. She was seized with a vague dread. Her own like experiences seemed far away, unreal, and only half remembered. She recalled faintly an ecstasy of pain, the heavy odor of chloroform, a stupor which had deadened sensation, and an awakening to find a little new life to which she had given being, added to the great unnumbered multitude of souls that come and go.

She began to wish she had not come; her presence was not necessary. She might have invented a pretext for staying away; she might even invent a pretext now for going. But Edna did not go. With an inward agony, with a flaming, outspoken revolt against the ways of Nature, she witnessed the scene of torture.

She was still stunned and speechless with emotion when later she leaned over her friend to kiss her and softly say good-by. Adèle, pressing her cheek, whispered in an exhausted voice: "Think of the children, Edna. Oh think of the children! Remember them!"

XXXVIII

EDNA STILL FELT dazed when she got outside in the open air. The Doctor's coupé had returned for him and stood before the *porte cochère*. She did not wish to enter the coupé, and told Doctor Mandelet she would walk; she was not afraid, and would go alone. He directed his carriage to meet him at Mrs. Pontellier's, and he started to walk home with her.

Up—away up, over the narrow street between the tall houses, the stars were blazing. The air was mild and caressing, but cool with the breath of spring and the night. They walked slowly, the Doctor with a heavy, measured tread and his hands behind him; Edna, in an absent-minded way, as she had walked one night at Grand Isle, as if her thoughts had gone ahead of her and she was striving to overtake them.

"You shouldn't have been there, Mrs. Pontellier," he said. "That was no place for you. Adèle is full of whims at such times. There were a dozen women she might have had with her, unimpressionable women. I felt that it was cruel, cruel. You shouldn't have gone."

"Oh, well!" she answered, indifferently. "I don't know that it matters after all. One has to think of the children some time or other; the sooner the better."

"When is Léonce coming back?"

"Quite soon. Some time in March."

"And you are going abroad?"

"Perhaps—no, I am not going. I'm not going to be forced into doing things. I don't want to go abroad. I want to be let alone. Nobody has any right—except children, perhaps—and even then, it seems to me—or it did seem—" She felt that her speech was voicing the incoherency of her thoughts, and stopped abruptly.

"The trouble is," sighed the Doctor, grasping her meaning intuitively, "that youth is given up to illusions. It seems to be a provision of Nature; a decoy to secure mothers for the race. And Nature takes no account of moral consequences, of arbitrary conditions which we create, and which we feel obliged to maintain at any cost."

"Yes," she said. "The years that are gone seem like dreams—if one might go on sleeping and dreaming—but to wake up and find—oh! well!

perhaps it is better to wake up after all, even to suffer, rather than to remain a dupe to illusions all one's life."

"It seems to me, my dear child," said the Doctor at parting, holding her hand, "you seem to me to be in trouble. I am not going to ask for your confidence. I will only say that if ever you feel moved to give it to me, perhaps I might help you. I know I would understand, and I tell you there are not many who would—not many, my dear."

"Some way I don't feel moved to speak of things that trouble me. Don't think I am ungrateful or that I don't appreciate your sympathy. There are periods of despondency and suffering which take possession of me. But I don't want anything but my own way. That is wanting a good deal, of course, when you have to trample upon the lives, the hearts, the prejudices of others—but no matter—still, I shouldn't want to trample upon the little lives. Oh! I don't know what I'm saying, Doctor. Good night. Don't blame me for anything."

"Yes, I will blame you if you don't come and see me soon. We will talk of things you never have dreamt of talking about before. It will do us both good. I don't want you to blame yourself, whatever comes. Good night, my child."

She let herself in at the gate, but instead of entering she sat upon the step of the porch. The night was quiet and soothing. All the tearing emotion of the last few hours seemed to fall away from her like a somber, uncomfortable garment, which she had but to loosen to be rid of. She went back to that hour before Adèle had sent for her; and her senses kindled afresh in thinking of Robert's words, the pressure of his arms, and the feeling of his lips upon her own. She could picture at that moment no greater bliss on earth than possession of the beloved one. His expression of love had already given him to her in part. When she thought that he was there at hand, waiting for her, she grew numb with the intoxication of expectancy. It was so late; he would be asleep perhaps. She would awaken him with a kiss. She hoped he would be asleep that she might arouse him with her caresses.

Still, she remembered Adèle's voice whispering, "Think of the children; think of them." She meant to think of them; that determination had driven into her soul like a death wound—but not to-night. To-morrow would be time to think of everything.

Robert was not waiting for her in the little parlor. He was nowhere at hand. The house was empty. But he had scrawled on a piece of paper that lay in the lamplight:

"I love you. Good-by—because I love you."

Edna grew faint when she read the words. She went and sat on the sofa.

Then she stretched herself out there, never uttering a sound. She did not sleep. She did not go to bed. The lamp sputtered and went out. She was still awake in the morning, when Celestine unlocked the kitchen door and came in to light the fire.

XXXIX

VICTOR, WITH HAMMER and nails and scraps of scantling, was patching a corner of one of the galleries. Mariequita sat near by, dangling her legs, watching him work, and handing him nails from the tool-box. The sun was beating down upon them. The girl had covered her head with her apron folded into a square pad. They had been talking for an hour or more. She was never tired of hearing Victor describe the dinner at Mrs. Pontellier's. He exaggerated every detail, making it appear a veritable Lucillean feast. The flowers were in tubs, he said. The champagne was quaffed from huge golden goblets. Venus rising from the foam could have presented no more entrancing a spectacle than Mrs. Pontellier, blazing with beauty and diamonds at the head of the board, while the other women were all of them youthful houris, possessed of incomparable charms.

She got it into her head that Victor was in love with Mrs. Pontellier, and he gave her evasive answers, framed so as to confirm her belief. She grew sullen and cried a little, threatening to go off and leave him to his fine ladies. There were a dozen men crazy about her at the *Chênière*; and since it was the fashion to be in love with married people, why, she could run away any time she liked to New Orleans with Célina's husband.

Célina's husband was a fool, a coward, and a pig, and to prove it to her, Victor intended to hammer his head into a jelly the next time he encountered him. This assurance was very consoling to Mariequita. She dried her eyes, and grew cheerful at the prospect.

They were still talking of the dinner and the allurements of city life when Mrs. Pontellier herself slipped around the corner of the house. The two youngsters stayed dumb with amazement before what they considered to be an apparition. But it was really she in flesh and blood, looking tired and a little travel-stained.

"I walked up from the wharf," she said, "and heard the hammering. I supposed it was you, mending the porch. It's a good thing. I was always tripping over those loose planks last summer. How dreary and deserted everything looks!"

It took Victor some little time to comprehend that she had come in Beaudelet's lugger, that she had come alone, and for no purpose but to rest.

"There's nothing fixed up yet, you see. I'll give you my room; it's the only place."

"Any corner will do," she assured him.

"And if you can stand Philomel's cooking," he went on, "though I might try to get her mother while you are here. Do you think she would come?" turning to Mariequita.

Mariequita thought that perhaps Philomel's mother might come for a few days, and money enough.

Beholding Mrs. Pontellier make her appearance, the girl had at once suspected a lovers' rendezvous. But Victor's astonishment was so genuine, and Mrs. Pontellier's indifference so apparent, that the disturbing notion did not lodge long in her brain. She contemplated with the greatest interest this woman who gave the most sumptuous dinners in America, and who had all the men in New Orleans at her feet.

"What time will you have dinner?" asked Edna. "I'm very hungry; but don't get anything extra."

"I'll have it ready in little or no time," he said, bustling and packing away his tools. "You may go to my room to brush up and rest yourself. Mariequita will show you."

"Thank you," said Edna. "But, do you know, I have a notion to go down to the beach and take a good wash and even a little swim, before dinner?"

"The water is too cold!" they both exclaimed. "Don't think of it."

"Well, I might go down and try—dip my toes in. Why, it seems to me the sun is hot enough to have warmed the very depths of the ocean. Could you get me a couple of towels? I'd better go right away, so as to be back in time. It would be a little too chilly if I waited till this afternoon."

Mariequita ran over to Victor's room, and returned with some towels, which she gave to Edna.

"I hope you have fish for dinner," said Edna, as she started to walk away; "but don't do anything extra if you haven't."

"Run and find Philomel's mother," Victor instructed the girl. "I'll go to the kitchen and see what I can do. By Gimminy! Women have no consideration! She might have sent me word."

Edna walked on down to the beach rather mechanically, not noticing anything special except that the sun was hot. She was not dwelling upon any particular train of thought. She had done all the thinking which was necessary after Robert went away, when she lay awake upon the sofa till morning.

She had said over and over to herself: "To-day it is Arobin; to-morrow it will be some one else. It makes no difference to me, it doesn't matter about Léonce Pontellier—but Raoul and Etienne!" She understood now clearly what she had meant long ago when she said to Adèle Ratignolle that she would give up the unessential, but she would never sacrifice herself for her children.

Despondency had come upon her there in the wakeful night, and had never lifted. There was no one thing in the world that she desired. There was no human being whom she wanted near her except Robert; and she even realized that the day would come when he, too, and the thought of him would melt out of her existence, leaving her alone. The children appeared before her like antagonists who had overcome her; who had overpowered and sought to drag her into the soul's slavery for the rest of her days. But she knew a way to elude them. She was not thinking of these things when she walked down to the beach.

The water of the Gulf stretched out before her, gleaming with the million lights of the sun. The voice of the sea is seductive, never ceasing, whispering, clamoring, murmuring, inviting the soul to wander in abysses of solitude. All along the white beach, up and down, there was no living thing in sight. A bird with a broken wing was beating the air above, reeling, fluttering, circling disabled down, down to the water.

Edna had found her old bathing suit still hanging, faded, upon its accustomed peg.

She put it on, leaving her clothing in the bath-house. But when she was there beside the sea, absolutely alone, she cast the unpleasant, pricking garments from her, and for the first time in her life she stood naked in the open air, at the mercy of the sun, the breeze that beat upon her, and the waves that invited her.

How strange and awful it seemed to stand naked under the sky! how delicious! She felt like some new-born creature, opening its eyes in a familiar world that it had never known.

The foamy wavelets curled up to her white feet, and coiled like serpents about her ankles. She walked out. The water was chill, but she walked on. The water was deep, but she lifted her white body and reached out with a long, sweeping stroke. The touch of the sea is sensuous, enfolding the body in its soft, close embrace.

She went on and on. She remembered the night she swam far out, and recalled the terror that seized her at the fear of being unable to regain the shore. She did not look back now, but went on and on, thinking of the blue-grass meadow that she had traversed when a little child, believing that it had no beginning and no end.

Her arms and legs were growing tired.

She thought of Léonce and the children. They were a part of her life. But they need not have thought that they could possess her, body and soul. How Mademoiselle Reisz would have laughed, perhaps sneered, if she knew! "And you call yourself an artist! What pretensions, Madame! The artist must possess the courageous soul that dares and defies."

Exhaustion was pressing upon and over-powering her.

"Good-by—because, I love you." He did not know; he did not understand. He would never understand. Perhaps Doctor Mandelet would have understood if she had seen him—but it was too late; the shore was far behind her, and her strength was gone.

She looked into the distance, and the old terror flamed up for an instant, then sank again. Edna heard her father's voice and her sister Margaret's. She heard the barking of an old dog that was chained to the sycamore tree. The spurs of the cavalry officer clanged as he walked across the porch. There was the hum of bees, and the musky odor of pinks filled the air.

Study Guide

Text by
Debra Geller Lieberman
(J.D., New York University School of Law)
(M.S. Ed., Hunter College)

Dr. M. Fogiel
Chief Editor

Contents

Section One: *Introduction* 121

The Life and Work of Kate Chopin 121

Historical Background 122

Master List of Characters 123

Summary of the Novel 124

Estimated Reading Time 126

Each Chapter includes List of Characters, Summary, Analysis, Study Questions and Answers, and Suggested Essay Topics.

Section Two: *The Awakening* 127

Chapter I 127

Chapter II 130

Chapter III 132

Chapter IV 135

Chapters V and VI 138
Chapter VII 141
Chapter VIII 144
Chapter IX 147
Chapter X 149
Chapter XI 152
Chapter XII 154
Chapter XIII 156
Chapter XIV 159
Chapter XV 161
Chapter XVI 163
Chapter XVII 166
Chapter XVIII 169
Chapter XIX 172
Chapter XX 174
Chapter XXI 177
Chapter XXII 179
Chapter XXIII 182
Chapter XXIV 185
Chapter XXV 187
Chapter XXVI 190
Chapter XXVII and XXVIII 193
Chapter XXIX 195
Chapter XXX 197
Chapter XXXI 200

Chapter XXXII 202
Chapter XXXIII 205
Chapter XXXIV 207
Chapter XXXV 209
Chapter XXXVI 212
Chapter XXXVII 215
Chapter XXXVIII 217
Chapter XXXIX 220

Section Three: *Bibliography* 224

SECTION ONE

Introduction

The Life and Work of Kate Chopin

Kate Chopin was born Katie O'Flaherty in 1850 in St. Louis to an Irish father and a French mother. Her father died in a train crash in 1855. Kate was taught and greatly influenced by her maternal great-grandmother who was an independent, free thinker. She taught Kate through storytelling, in both English and French. Additionally, Kate attended the prestigious Sacred Heart Academy, which promoted intelligence and independent thinking. Kate began her lifelong love of reading and writing there.

In 1861 the Civil War began, and Kate, after ripping down a Union flag posted in front of her home, became known as St. Louis "Littlest Rebel." During the course of the war, Kate lost her brother, her great-grandmother, and her best friend. She later wrote war stories about loss, grief, terror, and fear. She became preoccupied with death.

Kate graduated in 1868 and "came out" to the debutante scene where she was praised for her beauty and cleverness. She, however, hated the life that took her away from reading, writing, and thinking, and she particularly hated the constricting clothes that society women were forced to wear. Despite her inner rebelliousness, she married Oscar Chopin in 1870, moved to New Orleans, and had six children. She loved her husband and children but felt engulfed by her life. She became well known for taking long solitary walks (which scandalized the townspeople).

Oscar died in 1882, and Kate had an affair with a married man named Albert Sampite who later appeared in many of her major works as a character called "Alcée." She moved back to

St. Louis in 1884, and after her mother died in 1885, Kate took up writing more seriously. Her publishing debut came in 1889 with a poem titled "If It Might Be." Her first novel, titled *At Fault*, was published in 1890, but national recognition did not come until her first national publication in 1894, a collection of short stories titled *Bayou Folk*.

Kate's favorite writer was Guy de Maupassant, and like him, much of Kate's fiction was considered scandalous. Nobody, however, denied her talent. She was a prolific and much published writer; she wrote short stories, poems, essays, and novels. Even the bad reviews for *The Awakening* did not hurt Kate's literary reputation. In 1900 she was included in the first edition of *Who's Who in America*, and she continued to have many admirers. However she was deeply wounded by the negative reviews and by people's lack of understanding. She wrote less often after that. Kate died in 1904 after spending the day at the St. Louis World's Fair.

Kate Chopin was a woman ahead of her time. In the 1960s, with the advent of feminism, Kate Chopin was resurrected, and *The Awakening* is considered to be one of the first feminist books.

Historical Background

Kate Chopin grew up in violent, turbulent times. She came from a slaveholding family in a city that was a major center for slave trade. There was constant fighting in St. Louis over secession. The Civil War began in 1861 when she was 11 years old, and she and everyone she knew lived in constant terror. There were times when she was confined to her home because of the fighting in the street. She learned to be self-sufficient from an early age.

After the Civil War ended, a period of strong activism among St. Louis women began. There were many outspoken suffragists, and other women who were beginning to question the path of marriage and motherhood. Susan B. Anthony was traveling and speaking extensively about equality and women's rights. By the 1890s there were many "New Women" making their way in St. Louis. These were single women who became doctors, lawyers, and journalists.

Additionally, the works of Darwin, Spencer, and Huxley were transforming intellectual thought. People were beginning to question things they had always held as truth, including definitions of morality. Finally, the Industrial Revolution was well under way, and the whole world was changing. *The Awakening* was published in 1899, just at the turn of the century, and there was constant tension between tradition and movement, old and new.

The majority of the reviews for *The Awakening* were unfavorable. Although her writing was praised, the book was described as "unhealthy," "unwholesome," "unpleasant," and "a dangerous specimen of sex fiction." Despite the fact that many women had begun to write novels with daring themes by the time *The Awakening* was published, for example, Charlotte Perkins Gilman, even novels with the most radical themes still tended to promote traditional values and have traditional resolutions. Even some of the most radical women still thought that sexual passion was immoral and unhealthy for women. So it is no surprise that even amidst the incredible changes, for women and the country as a whole, Kate Chopin was censured for the choices made by her protagonist, Edna Pontellier. Edna's passion was described by one reviewer as an "ugly, cruel, loathsome monster."

Kate Chopin, herself, and through Edna Pontellier, questioned the traditional idea of woman as wife and mother, without passion and without her own mind. *The Awakening* depicts the powerful "cage of convention" and the futility both Kate and Edna felt in trying to live a life of freedom.

Master List of Characters

Edna Pontellier—*The protagonist of the novel, she is a 28-year-old married woman with children who yearns for more out of life. The novel is about her journey of discovery.*

Léonce Pontellier—*Edna's husband; He is, by all accounts, a good man, but he treats Edna like a possession rather than an equal.*

Madame Lebrun—*The owner of the resort at Grand Isle where the Pontellier family spends their summers.*

Robert Lebrun—*The 26-year-old son of Madame Lebrun; He and Edna fall in love.*

Adèle Ratignolle—*A friend of Edna's; She is a beautiful woman who is devoted to her husband and children. She is pregnant and gives birth during the book.*

Mademoiselle Reisz—*A loner at Grand Isle, she is a gifted pianist who becomes very close to Edna.*

The Farival Twins—*Two young guests at Grand Isle who play the piano for the entertainment of the other guests.*

Monsieur Farival—*Grandfather of the twins.*

Raoul and Etienne—*The Pontellier's two young children.*

Victor Lebrun—*The younger brother of Robert.*

Mariequita—*A "mischievous," carefree Spanish girl who works at Grand Isle.*

The Lovers—*A young, unmarried couple who are oblivious to all but themselves.*

Celestine—*The Pontellier's servant.*

Baudelet—*An old sailor who takes people by boat to Mass at Chênière Caminada.*

Madame Antoine—*A fat village woman at Chênière Caminada whose house Edna stays in when she feels ill.*

Tonie—*The son of Madame Antoine.*

Dr. Mandelet—*A good doctor who tries to help Edna.*

Alcée Arobin—*A young man-about-town with whom Edna has an affair.*

The Highcamps and the Merrimans—*Society people who are friends of Edna's.*

The Colonel—*Edna's father.*

Miss Mayblunt and Gouvernail—*Guests at Edna's dinner party.*

Summary of the Novel

The Awakening begins in Grand Isle, where the Pontellier family is vacationing for the summer. Léonce Pontellier's newspaper reading has been interrupted by the loud talking of the caged parrot so he returns to his own cottage. Edna Pontellier returns from bathing in the ocean with Robert Lebrun, and her husband criticizes her for bathing so late in the day. She and Robert share laughs over something that happened at the ocean, but Léonce is bored with the conversation. He leaves to go to a men's club at a hotel called Klein's. Robert stays with Edna.

When Mr. Pontellier returns late that night, he reprimands Edna for her neglect of the children. She begins to cry, feeling an "indescribable oppression." The next day we meet Adèle Ratignolle, who is pregnant and a classic "mother-woman." Edna, Adèle, and Robert spend the afternoon together, and Robert is very attentive to Edna; they later go swimming together.

At the ocean with Adèle, Edna remembers the times she was in love and how she "accidentally" married Léonce. Adèle warns Robert to stay away from Edna. Some weeks later, all the summer guests gather together for an evening's entertainment. We are introduced to Edna's love of music. At the end of the evening, everyone goes swimming and Robert walks Edna home. Later Edna defies Léonce and stays out in the hammock after he instructs her to go inside.

The next day Edna and Robert go to Mass together at *Chênière Caminada* and spend the whole day together there. Some time later Robert announces that he is leaving for Mexico that night, and Edna tries to hide her feelings, from herself as much as from anyone else. After he is gone, she misses him very much.

At the beach one day, Edna tells Adèle that although she would give her life for her children, she wouldn't give herself. Adèle doesn't understand.

After the summer, they go home to New Orleans, and Edna starts to forego her usual social engagements, for which she is reprimanded by Léonce. She begins taking long, solitary walks. She has lost interest in her home and family and takes up painting. She visits Mademoiselle Reisz and reads a letter from Robert, which makes her cry.

Léonce is worried about his wife and talks to Dr. Mandelet who advises him to let her have her way and maybe it will pass. After Edna's father comes to stay for a while, Léonce and the children go away, and Edna is happily left alone. She paints, reads, and visits with friends. One of her new friends is Alcée Arobin, who is known for being a womanizer. They often go to the track together, and begin to spend time alone together in the evening.

While her family is still away, Edna decides to move out of her house to a smaller one around the corner. One day she goes to visit Mademoiselle Reisz and learns that Robert is coming home; she admits that she loves him. That night she begins her affair with Alcée Arobin and says of his kiss, "It was the first kiss of her life to which her nature had really responded." Later she is disappointed that the response wasn't brought on by love. The night before she moves, Edna has a dinner party, and Alcée stays the night.

One day Edna goes to visit Mademoiselle Reisz and finds Robert there. She is hurt that he has not called on her since his return. He dines with her at her house that night but does not call or come visit after that. She spends more and more time with Alcée, although she still longs for Robert.

Luckily Edna runs into Robert accidentally, and he goes to her home with her. They finally both declare their love, and kiss, but then Edna has to leave to be with Adèle Ratignolle, who is giving birth. When she returns, Robert is gone.

The novel ends with Edna leaving New Orleans and going back to Grand Isle. Shortly after her arrival there, she swims out as far as she can into the ocean, with no strength left to return.

Estimated Reading Time

The average reader should be able to complete *The Awakening* in four to five hours. The short chapters make it easier to read, and certain chapters can be grouped together to aid the reader in understanding the story.

Chapters I through VI take place in Grand Isle and introduce the major conflicts of the novel and set the tone for Edna's awakening.

Chapters VII through XVI are the remaining chapters that take place in Grand Isle. Here we see Edna's various awakenings set in motion.

Chapters XVII through XXX take place in New Orleans. Here we see significant growth in both Edna's rebellion and her resulting conflicts.

Chapters XXXI to XXXVIII also take place in New Orleans and are about Edna's independence.

Chapter XXXIX should be read alone. The story moves back to Grand Isle, and it is the resolution of the novel.

SECTION TWO

The Awakening

Chapter I (pages 1–3)

New Characters:

Edna Pontellier: *the protagonist of the novel; a 28-year-old married woman with children who yearns for more out of life; the novel is about her journey of discovery*

Léonce Pontellier: *Edna's husband; by all accounts, a good man, but treats Edna like a possession rather than an equal*

Madame Lebrun: *the owner of the resort at Grand Isle where the Pontellier family spends their summers*

Robert Lebrun: *the 26-year-old son of Madame Lebrun; falls in love with Edna*

The Farival Twins: *two young guests at Grand Isle who play the piano for the entertainment of the other guests*

Raoul and Etienne: *the Pontellier's two young children*

Summary

Léonce Pontellier is seated in the main building (known as the "House") of a resort on Grand Isle. He is attempting to read a newspaper but is interrupted by the noise of a green and yellow parrot that speaks French and Spanish. He leaves the House and proceeds to his own cottage, where he again picks up his newspaper. He hears lots of noise from the House, including the Farival twins playing the piano, and Mrs. Lebrun, the owner of the resort. He sees his two children, ages four and five, with their quadroon nurse.

Léonce lights up a cigar and sees his wife Edna walking up to the cottage with Robert Lebrun. He reprimands them for bathing in the heat, and gives back her wedding rings, which she had taken off prior to going to the beach. Edna and Robert begin laughing about some adventure they had at the beach and try to relate it to Léonce, but he is obviously bored. Finally, he gets up and leaves for Klein's Hotel to play billiards. He invites Robert, but Robert says he would rather stay with Edna.

Edna inquires whether Léonce will be home for dinner, but he does not answer because it depends on what he finds at Klein's. Edna understands and says good-bye. Léonce promises to bring home bonbons and peanuts for the children.

Analysis

Chopin begins with an image that is very strong in women's fiction: that of a caged bird, which is "tamed for the amusement of the household." Léonce Pontellier "had the privilege of quitting their society when they ceased to be entertaining." He also exercises this privilege with his wife, whom he leaves when he is bored.

The bird's speech is also symbolic here. It imitates very well, repeating phrases it has heard but also speaks a language that nobody understands. Edna fights against being forced simply to mimic the life every other woman leads, but it is questionable whether anybody will understand her if she stops that mimicking. Still Chopin is preparing us for Edna's journey of self-discovery.

Chopin uses a bit of foreshadowing, although very few people today would pick it up. It is in the Farival twins' duet from *Zampa*. *Zampa* is an opera that records a romantic death at sea.

Chopin makes the relationship between Edna and Léonce quite clear from the beginning. After reprimanding her for bathing in the heat, Léonce looks at Edna "as one looks at a valuable piece of personal property which has suffered some damage." In contrast, Edna and Robert's relationship seems to be based on mutual affection; they have adventures and laugh together.

Study Questions

1. What kind of bird is hung in the cage?
2. Why does Léonce return to his own cottage?
3. What are the Farival twins doing at the main house?
4. Who is Edna bathing with?
5. How does Léonce look at Edna when she returns?
6. What does Léonce give to Edna upon her return?
7. What are Edna and Robert laughing about?
8. Where is Léonce going to spend the evening?
9. Why doesn't Robert go with him?
10. Does Léonce keep his promise to the children?

Answers

1. A green and yellow parrot is hung in the cage.
2. Léonce returns to his own cottage because the bird's talking was making it difficult for him to read his newspaper.
3. They are playing a duet from *Zampa* on the piano.
4. Edna is bathing with Robert Lebrun.
5. Léonce looks at Edna as if she were a valuable piece of personal property that had suffered some damage.
6. He gives Edna back her wedding rings, which she had taken off prior to bathing.
7. They are laughing about an adventure they had in the water.
8. He is going to spend the evening at the Klein's Hotel.
9. Robert prefers to stay with Edna.
10. No. He forgets the bonbons and peanuts.

Suggested Essay Topics

1. Describe the attitude of Léonce toward Edna and how it differs from Robert's.
2. What is the symbolism of the caged parrot?

Chapter II (pages 3–5)

Summary

The chapter begins with a description of Edna Pontellier. She has bright yellowish brown eyes and hair, and her eyebrows are a shade darker. She is handsome rather than beautiful, wears a frank expression, and has an engaging manner. Additionally, there is depth to her eyes and a subtlety to her features.

Robert Lebrun is also described for the reader. He is smoking a cigarette because he cannot afford cigars, although he has one that Léonce Pontellier had given to him. He is clean shaven and similar in complexion to Edna.

Robert and Edna chat together about their adventure in the water, and everything that is going on around them, including the children who are playing croquet and the Farival twins. They also talk about themselves and are both very interested in what the other has to say. Robert talks about his long-held desire to go to Mexico and make his fortune and how he remembers Grand Isle when there was no need for guests.

Edna talks about her childhood and her home in Kentucky. She reads a letter from her sister and Robert asks many questions about the family. Finally it is time to dress for dinner. Edna realizes Léonce won't be coming home, and Robert agrees because there were many club men over at Klein's. Robert then plays with the Pontellier children until dinner is ready.

Analysis

The physical description of Edna Pontellier is a clue to her character and the journey she will undertake. Her eyes look at things as if "lost in some inward maze of contemplation of thought." Her eyes have depth, and there is subtlety to her features. She is clearly not an ordinary woman. There is something deep going on inside her, some inner searching. The fact that she is handsome rather than beautiful gives a masculine edge to her and, in fact, her journey takes her into a world that had previously been exclusively male.

Robert, on the other hand, is described as a callow youth on whose face "rested no shadow of care." It is obvious that he is no match for her. Still Chopin makes it clear that they have an easy-going friendship and that they truly enjoy one another's company. This is in direct contrast to Edna's relationship with her husband. For example, Léonce doesn't come home for dinner, because he would rather be with the men at Klein's.

Chopin also introduces another characteristic that sets Edna apart from her peers. She is clearly American, and any French ancestry has been "lost in dilution." Her husband, as well as all the guests at Grand Isle, are French Creole. They have a different set of norms, values, and customs than those with which she grew up.

Study Questions

1. How does Edna look at objects?
2. How does Edna's appearance differ from other women?
3. What about Robert's appearance makes him seem immature?
4. Why does Robert smoke cigarettes?
5. How do we see the intimacy between Robert and Edna at this point?
6. Why does Robert want to go to Mexico?
7. Why does Madame Lebrun take in guests?
8. How is Edna's background different from the other guests at Grand Isle?
9. What is Edna's sister doing in the East?
10. Why does Robert assume Léonce wouldn't be coming home for dinner?

Answers

1. She looks at them as if she were lost in contemplation or thought.
2. Edna is handsome rather than pretty.
3. He is clean shaven and has no shadow of care.

4. He smokes cigarettes because he can't afford cigars.
5. They both chat incessantly and each is interested in what the other has to say.
6. He wants to make his fortune there.
7. She needs to so she can keep up her easy, comfortable lifestyle.
8. She is truly American, and any French has been lost in dilution. The other guests are all French Creole.
9. She is engaged to be married.
10. He assumes that because there were a good many New Orleans clubmen over at Klein's.

Suggested Essay Topics

1. What does Edna's appearance tell us about her personality?
2. How does Edna and Robert's relationship differ from Edna and Léonce's thus far?

Chapter III (pages 5–7)

Summary

Léonce returns from Klein's at eleven o'clock that evening, in high spirits and very talkative. Edna, who was sleeping when he came in, only half answers him as he talks. Léonce finds her lack of interest very discouraging.

Léonce forgot the bonbons and peanuts for the children, but he goes into their room to check on them. He reports back to Edna that Raoul has a fever and needs looking after. Then he sits down and lights up a cigar. Edna responds that Raoul went to bed perfectly well.

Leone reprimands Edna for her neglect of the children, reminding her that it is a mother's place to look after them. He is busy with his business and cannot do both. Edna gets out of bed to check on the children and then refuses to answer Léonce when he questions her upon her return. Léonce finishes his cigar and goes to sleep.

Edna begins to cry and slips outside to rock in the wicker chair. It is past midnight and very quiet, except for the sounds of an old owl and, of course, the sea, which "broke like a mournful lullaby upon the night." Edna now begins crying very hard, and becomes filled with a sense of oppression and anguish. If not for the mosquitos biting her, she might have sat and cried for half the night.

Léonce is up early the next morning, ready and eager to go back to the city until the following weekend. A few days later a box of delicacies arrives from Léonce, which Edna shares with everyone. The Grand Isle ladies declare that Léonce is the best husband in the world, and Edna "was forced to admit that she knew of none better."

Analysis

We are introduced in this chapter to the assigned gender roles Edna is trying to break free of. When Léonce comes home from Klein's, he tells Edna that Raoul is sick and needs looking after. Then he sits down and lights a cigar. It is clearly not his role to take care of the children. He makes this even more clear when he reprimands Edna for her inattention and says "If it was not a mother's place to look after children, whose on earth was it?" This becomes one of the central conflicts of the novel: Edna's love for her children versus her desire for independence.

Later, when Edna goes outside to cry, the sea as symbol is brought in again. All is quiet except for an owl and "the everlasting voice of the sea. . . like a mournful lullaby." The sea is constant and eternal and speaks to Edna. In this case, it is mirroring her sadness, since a "mournful lullaby" is a song that would be sung by a sad mother.

We see the beginning of Edna's change here because she is surprised by her tears. She says that such experiences, meaning Léonce's reprimand, were not uncommon yet she was reacting differently. She was filled with "an indescribable oppression" and a "vague anguish." This is the first sign of her "awakening," although she does not yet recognize it as such.

When Léonce sends Edna a box of delicacies from the city,

she is "forced" to admit to the admiring ladies that she knows of no better husband. This is one of the forces that dooms Edna's journey. Léonce is just as he should be by society's standards; thus, Edna's desired change must confront not only her husband but society as a whole.

Study Questions

1. Why does Edna have trouble talking to Léonce when he comes home from Klein's?
2. What does Léonce do after he tells Edna that Raoul has a fever?
3. What is Léonce's opinion of raising children?
4. Why is Edna so upset after she checks on Raoul?
5. What does the sea sound like when Edna goes outside?
6. What is different about this particular argument with Léonce that causes Edna to cry?
7. What does Edna feel while she cries?
8. Is Edna upset about the fact that she is crying?
9. What does Léonce send to Edna while he is away?
10. Is Léonce considered a good husband?

Answers

1. Edna had been asleep when Léonce came in; he wakes her up.
2. He sits down to smoke a cigar.
3. He believes that it is solely the mother's responsibility.
4. She feels bad because Léonce was right, and Raoul had a fever.
5. It sounds like a mournful lullaby.
6. Edna doesn't know why she is crying, but something is changing inside her.
7. She feels an indescribable oppression and a vague anguish.

8. No. She is enjoying her solitary cry.
9. Léonce sends a box of delicacies from New Orleans.
10. Yes. All the ladies admire him and even Edna is forced to admit she knows of none better.

Suggested Essay Topics

1. What does Edna's cry and accompanying feelings suggest about her "awakening"?
2. Why is it actually a problem for Edna that Léonce is considered to be such a good husband?

Chapter IV (pages 7–10)

New Character:

Adèle Ratignolle: *a friend of Edna's; a beautiful woman who is devoted to her husband and children; she is pregnant*

Summary

This chapter begins with a description of Edna's mothering. Léonce cannot define exactly Edna's failings in this regard, but as an example, if one of the Pontellier children fell, he would not rush to his mother's arms for comfort. Edna is not a "mother-woman": a breed who idolize their children and worship their husbands and have no selves of their own.

One such mother-woman is Adèle Ratignolle, who is described as "the embodiment of every womanly grace and charm." She is very fond of Edna and is with her, doing her usual sewing, the day the box of delicacies arrives from Léonce. She had brought a pattern for Edna to cut for a winter outfit for the children. Edna is not interested in doing this but so as not to offend Adèle, she cuts the pattern.

Edna offers Adèle some bonbons, which Adèle takes with some misgiving because she is pregnant. Adèle had been married seven years and had a baby every two years. Robert, who is there also, tries to reassure Adèle about the bonbon, but Edna blushes when he mentions the pregnancy.

Everyone at Grand Isle that summer is a Creole; Edna is a Creole only by marriage and does not feel entirely comfortable among them. She is especially taken by their freedom of expression and absence of prudery, which nonetheless went hand in hand with a strict chastity. She is embarrassed by Adèle's description of a particularly difficult childbirth and by the plot of a book that everyone else had read and discussed openly.

Analysis

Here we see the contrast between Edna, who is seeking independence, and Adèle Ratignolle, who is a classic "mother-woman." These mother-women "idolized their children, worshipped their husbands, and esteemed it a holy privilege to efface themselves as individuals and grow wings as ministering angels." Adèle's physical description goes along with this. There is nothing subtle about Adèle. She is beautiful, feminine, and maternal. In fact, her hands are never more beautiful than when she is sewing. Physically, as tempermentally, she is in direct contrast to Edna.

Adèle has had a baby every two years since her wedding and is pregnant again. Chopin points out that although she is not showing yet, everyone knows she is pregnant because Adèle talks about it constantly. Because Adèle as mother-woman has no identity beyond wife and mother, it is crucial to her that her pregnancy is known.

Finally Edna's alienation from Creole society is brought out. She blushes when Robert talks about Adèle's pregnancy and was shocked by a racy book that everyone else had read and discussed openly. This openness is in contrast to Edna's strict, moralistic upbringing.

Study Questions

1. What is given as an example of Edna's lack of mothering?
2. What is a "mother-woman"?
3. Who is considered a classic mother-woman?
4. What are three differences between Adèle and Edna's appearances?

5. When are Adèle's hands considered most beautiful?
6. Why did Edna cut a pattern for winter clothes for her children?
7. How do Edna and Robert know that Adèle is pregnant again?
8. Why does Edna blush when Robert tells Adèle it is safe to eat a bonbon?
9. Why doesn't Edna feel entirely comfortable at Grand Isle?
10. According to Edna, what is the most distinguishing characteristic of the Creoles?

Answers

1. If one of the children falls while at play, he does not rush to his mother's arms for comfort.
2. A mother-woman is a woman who idolizes her children, worships her husband, and considers it a privilege to lose her own identity.
3. Adèle Ratignolle is considered a classic mother-woman.
4. (1) Edna's features are subtle and have depth while there is nothing subtle or hidden about Adèle's beauty; (2) Edna's body is lean and symmetrical while Adèle's is plump and (3) Edna is handsome rather than beautiful while Adèle is like a bygone heroine of romance or the fair lady of our dreams.
5. They are most beautiful when they are busy sewing.
6. She does it so as not to insult Adèle.
7. They know because she talks about her "condition" constantly.
8. Edna is not used to people talking about pregnancy so openly.
9. Everyone there is a Creole except Edna.
10. To Edna the most distinguishing characteristic of the Creoles is their absence of prudery.

Suggested Essay Topics

1. How does Edna's desire for independence conflict with the image of the mother-woman?
2. Compare and contrast Edna and Adèle with respect to physical appearance and temperament.

Chapters V and VI (pages 10–13)

Summary

In Chapter V, Adèle continues to sew, while Edna and Robert sit idle, exchanging occasional words and glances that suggest intimacy. Every summer Robert devotes himself to one woman, and this summer it is Edna. The summer before it was Adèle, and they joked a bit about it as Robert described his passion to Edna. It was understood that his words of love were not to be taken seriously. Edna is glad Robert does not speak that way to her.

Edna has her sketchbook with her and begins to draw Adèle. Robert praises the work, but Edna crumples it up because it does not look like Adèle. While Edna is drawing, Robert rests his head against her arm. Even after she pushes him away, he does it again.

The children come up with their nurse, and Edna wants to talk to them but they are interested only in the bonbons. The sun is setting, and Adèle gathers up her sewing to leave. She complains of faintness, and Edna and Robert rush to help her. Afterwards Edna wonders if Adèle had been faking.

Edna watches Adèle walk away and watches her children run and cling to her. She picks up the little one despite her doctor's orders not to lift anything.

After Adèle leaves, Robert asks Edna if she is going bathing. Edna says no, but Robert insists and they walk away together to the beach.

Chapter VI is only one page, and is a break from the plot. First Edna wonders why she first said no, and then so easily yes, to going to the beach with Robert. She is beginning to sense something in herself, but at this point it only confuses her and causes her anguish.

The narrator tells us that Edna is beginning to recognize her place in the world, and hints that most women never see this. And like all such beginnings, it is chaotic and dangerous.

Finally, the sea is described as seductive and sensuous, with a voice that speaks to the soul.

Analysis

In Chapter V, we see further the intimacy between Robert and Edna and learn that Robert devotes himself each summer to one woman. It is obviously understood at Grand Isle that Robert is not to be taken seriously. However, Edna, as we already know, is not familiar with Creole customs and can't help but take him seriously. She finds it offensive when he rests his head on her arm, yet he clearly thinks nothing of it.

We are introduced to Edna's love of beauty and art. Her love of beauty is shown through Adèle, whom Edna likes to gaze at "as she might look upon a faultless Madonna." Her love of art is shown through her sketching. She "felt in it a satisfaction of a kind which no other employment afforded her." Yet she is very critical of herself as an artist; she crumples up a sketch of Adèle because it doesn't look like her, even though it is a "fair enough piece of work."

We also see that she does in fact love her children, although she does not always feel motherly. When they come to the house looking for candy, "she sought to detain them for a little talk and some pleasantry." It sounds as though she were talking about adults rather than children. In fact, the children have no wish to stay. In contrast, Adèle's children flutter around her skirts, and she picks the youngest one up despite her doctor's orders not to lift anything.

Again the sea comes into play, this time with a new adjective attached to it. The breeze that comes up is "charged with the seductive odor of the sea." Later after Robert invites her for a swim, the sea has a "sonorous murmur," which reached her like a "loving but imperative entreaty." The sea is becoming seductive; its pull on her is getting stronger.

Chapter VI is really an interlude in the narrative. Chopin is letting us know that the awakening is beginning; Edna is beginning to see her place in the world and to want more. Chopin is also telling us that such an awakening can be dangerous, even life-threatening. Finally, Chopin is using foreshadowing, telling us that the touch of the sea is an embrace Edna may not want to leave.

Study Questions

1. What is clear about Edna and Robert's relationship?
2. Why is Robert allowed to spend so much time with married women at Grand Isle?
3. How does Edna feel about Adèle's beauty?
4. Why does Edna sketch?
5. Why does Edna repulse Robert's head from her arm?
6. Why does Edna crumple up the picture of Adèle?
7. How is the sea described here?
8. Why did Edna go bathing with Robert?
9. What is Edna beginning to realize?
10. Why is Edna's realization potentially dangerous?

Answers

1. It is clear that they are very intimate.
2. He is considered safe because nobody ever takes him seriously.
3. She loves to gaze at Adèle and wishes to sketch her.
4. Sketching gives her satisfaction that no other work does.
5. She does not think it is proper for Robert to touch her like that.
6. The picture does not look like Adèle.
7. The sea is seductive, sensuous, embracing—like a lover.
8. She was following an impulse that she didn't understand.

9. Edna is beginning to realize her position in the universe and her relation to the rest of the world.
10. It is a beginning, and all beginnings are chaotic and disturbing. Additionally, women are not usually graced with such realizations so there will clearly be consequences.

Suggested Essay Topics

1. Describe the changes Edna has gone through so far.
2. How does the sea fit in with Edna's awakening?

Chapter VII (pages 13–19)

New Characters:

The Lovers: *a young, unmarried couple who are oblivious to all but themselves*

Summary

Edna, usually a woman of outward reserve, is beginning to loosen up a bit at Grand Isle, mostly under the influence of Adèle's beauty and candor.

One morning the women go together to the beach, and although the children are left behind, Adèle brings her needlework. Both women are described as tall, with Adèle having a feminine and matronly figure, while Edna's is "long, clean and symmetrical." Similarly Adèle is dressed in white ruffles while Edna is wearing white and brown linen.

At the beach, the Pontelliers and Ratignolles share adjoining compartments, and Edna pulls a rug and pillows out so the women can sit down in the shade against the front of the building. There are few people about; they see the lovers, the lady in black, and a few others further away.

Edna is gazing at the sea in such an absorbed way that Adèle asks her what she is thinking. Edna begins to talk of her childhood in Kentucky and a particular day when she walked aimlessly through a green meadow. She says she feels the same way sometimes at Grand Isle. Adèle takes her hand and begins caressing it, which is difficult at first for Edna who is not used to expressions of affection.

Next Edna begins thinking and talking about past affections she had for certain young men; she had been very passionate about them. In contrast her marriage to Léonce was "purely an accident," one that closed forever the world of romance for her, although she had grown fond of him. Her feelings for her children were inconsistent; she felt free of unwanted responsibility when they were not around.

Just after these "confessions," Robert approaches with several children. The women get up; Edna joins the children, and Robert walks Adèle back up to her cottage.

Analysis

Here we see that Edna has always been "different" and that she perceived early the difference between "the outward existence which conforms, the inward life which questions."

Again we see the physical descriptions of Edna and Adèle relating to their personalities. Edna's figure is noble and symmetrical while Adèle's (from Chapter IV) is plump and matronly. Here Edna is wearing a cool muslin dress with a streak of brown running through it. Adèle is dressed in pure white, in a fluffy dress with ruffles. Edna's physical being is always described in more masculine terms than Adèle's.

Sitting at the beach, Edna, as always, is focused on the sea. She is gazing so intently that Adèle asks what she is thinking about. Edna, who is usually very reserved, is drawn into unusual candor by Adèle's beauty and charm. She tells Adèle a story about her childhood in Kentucky, walking aimlessly through a green meadow, and adds that she feels that way now sometimes—aimless and unguided. Her awakening is still new to her, and it feels strange. She's heading into uncharted waters and therefore has no guidance.

When Adèle takes Edna's hand, Edna is shocked at first, not being used to expressions of affection. This is part of her repression, something she longs to break free of. She tells Adèle of old passions, of her infatuation with romance. She also tells how she gave it up when she married Léonce. For Edna romance and marriage are mutually exclusive.

Edna also tells Adèle something about her feelings for her children. Edna loves her children but feels weighed down with a responsibility that is suited to her nature. She feels relief when they are away.

Sharing with Adèle is like "the first breath of freedom" for Edna. She feels "intoxicated." It is the first letting go of the repression she grew up with.

Study Questions

1. What is Edna's attitude toward sharing confidences?
2. What is it about Adèle that started to bring Edna out of her shell?
3. Why does Adèle insist on bringing her needlework to the beach?
4. What is the difference in the way Edna and Adèle dressed for the beach?
5. What is Edna gazing at when Adèle begins questioning her thoughts?
6. What does Edna's childhood meadow story tell her and us about her present state?
7. Why is Edna confused when Adèle begins stroking her hand?
8. What is different about Edna's relationship with Léonce and the other men she talks about?
9. How does Edna feel when she is away from her children?
10. How does Edna feel after sharing about herself with Adèle?

Answers

1. She is not used to sharing confidences; she had always understood that she had a secret inner life.
2. Edna is drawn out first by Adèle's beauty and then by her complete candor.

3. As a mother-woman, Adèle cannot be without some reminder of that role.
4. Edna wears a cool white and brown muslin dress that has a fairly severe line. Adèle wears a pure white, frilly, ruffled dress. Edna's dress has a more masculine tone, Adèle's a more feminine.
5. She is gazing at the sea.
6. It tells us that she currently feels aimless and unguided, just as she did then.
7. Edna is not used to any displays of affection.
8. She married Léonce for practical reasons, with no feelings of passion or love. The other men she had been infatuated with, feeling tremendous passion.
9. She feels as if she is free of a responsibility that she is not suited for.
10. She feels intoxicated, as if she has just had her first taste of freedom.

Suggested Essay Topics

1. Compare Edna's feelings for Léonce with her feelings for the soldier, the tragedian, and Robert.
2. Why does Edna's sharing feel like freedom?

Chapter VIII (pages 19–22)

New Character:

Victor Lebrun: *the younger brother of Robert*

Summary

As soon as Robert and Adèle begin their walk away from the beach, Adèle asks Robert to leave Edna alone. She is afraid that Edna might take him seriously. In his defense, Robert tells a story about Alcée Arobin and the consul's wife and several other sordid stories. Then he declares that Edna would never take him seriously. He makes Adèle a cup of bouillon and leaves for the main house.

On his way, he passes the lovers, who are oblivious to everything around them. He looks for Edna and the children, but not seeing them, he goes to his mother's house. She is busy at her sewing machine.

Robert and his mother engage in some conversation and then they call out to Victor, who is driving off somewhere. He refuses to answer, however, and Madame Lebrun becomes very annoyed with the willful Victor. Madame Lebrun speculates that all would be well if only her husband had not died so young.

Madame Lebrun then tells Robert that a suitor of hers would be going to Mexico and has invited Robert to join him.

Analysis

Adèle, sensing Edna's romantic inclinations, warns Robert to stay away from her. She reminds him that Edna is not a Creole and might take him seriously. Robert is offended but understands that he would not be able to keep company with the ladies the way he does if anybody took him seriously. He then tells a story about Alcée Arobin having an affair with somebody's wife. He is trying to differentiate himself from Alcée who obviously does not live by the same rules.

When Robert leaves Adèle's cottage, he sees the lovers, who as usual are oblivious to all but themselves. The lovers symbolize premarriage romance—everything that Edna wants and does not have with Léonce.

Finally we learn that Robert has been invited to Mexico. Although we already know that he has been talking about going for years, this invitation lets us know that he might finally be going.

Study Questions

1. What is different about Adèle's eyes when she talks to Robert?
2. What is Adèle's fear when she asks Robert to leave Edna alone?
3. How does Adèle explain that fear to Robert?

4. Why is it important that nobody take Robert seriously?
5. What does Robert tell Adèle about Alcée Arobin?
6. What is Robert's thought about Edna?
7. How do the lovers walk?
8. Why does Madame Lebrun have someone else working the treadle of her sewing machine?
9. How does Madame Lebrun account for things going wrong in her life and the world?
10. What news does Madame Lebrun have for Robert?

Answers

1. They are filled with thoughtfulness and speculation.
2. She is afraid that Edna will take Robert's attentions seriously.
3. She is afraid because Edna is not a Creole.
4. If Robert's attentions to married women were taken seriously, he would be thought a scoundrel and no proper women would associate with him.
5. Robert tells Adèle about Alcée's affair with the consul's wife.
6. He believes she would never take him seriously.
7. The lovers walk as if there were no ground beneath their feet.
8. Creole women don't do anything that might imperil their health.
9. She blames it on the fact that her husband died so early in their marriage.
10. A friend of hers is going to Vera Cruz and Robert has been invited to join him.

Suggested Essay Topics

1. What has Edna said or done that would make Adèle worry that she might take Robert's affections seriously?

2. How does not being a Creole affect Edna? Why is it difficult for outsiders in any society to adjust and fit in?

Chapter IX (pages 22–26)

New Character:

Mademoiselle Reisz: *a loner at Grand Isle; a gifted pianist who becomes very close to Edna*

Summary

It is now Saturday night, a few weeks after the conversation between Robert and Adèle. The main house is all lit up and decorated, and all the guests are there for relaxation and entertainment. Even the children are permitted to stay up later than usual, until after ice cream and cake are served. The Farival twins perform the same songs as always on the piano, a little girl performs a dance, and a brother and sister give recitations. Then everyone dances while Adèle plays the piano.

While Adèle is playing, Edna conjures up an image of a naked man standing alone and hopeless on the beach, watching a bird fall from the sky.

Robert leaves to get Mademoiselle Reisz, who agrees, to everyone's happiness, to play the piano. Edna is very fond of music; if it is well played, it evokes pictures in her mind. This time, however, she sees no pictures. Instead, the music invokes great passion, and she finds herself shaking and crying. Mademoiselle Reisz finishes playing and leaves, happy with Edna's response.

The party breaks up shortly after Mademoiselle Reisz leaves, although many of the guests decide to go bathing at Robert's suggestion.

Analysis

The chapter opens with entertainment being provided for the guests, by the guests. The Farival twins repeat their earlier performance, reminding us again of Zampa's romantic death at sea.

Adèle plays piano while everyone dances. She plays only

because it was a "means of brightening the home and making it attractive." Everything Adèle does is for others. She is in direct contrast to Mademoiselle Reisz who is a true artist but has no family or love in her life. These are the two extremes surrounding Edna. Mademoiselle Reisz, physically, is the extreme opposite of Adèle. She is short, thin and ugly, and nobody really likes her. This is what happens to women who forsake marriage and motherhood.

Adèle plays a piece that Edna names "Solitude." While listening, Edna finds herself conjuring up an image of a solitary naked man by the seashore. His attitude was one of "hopeless resignation" as he watches a bird in flight. This is how Edna feels: alone, lonely, unable to fly away and be free. It can also be seen as foreshadowing of Edna's fate. The same image comes up in Chapter XXXIX, only it has a slightly different feel to it there.

When Mademoiselle Reisz plays the piano, Edna is stirred by a whole new set of emotions, notably passion. She is so moved she sobs. Edna has never felt that sort of passion before but will now long to feel it again.

Study Questions

1. Why is the hall lit up and decorated?
2. Why are the Pontellier children exerting authority over the other children?
3. What songs do the Farival twins play?
4. Why does Adèle keep up with her music?
5. What is Edna looking at when she sat on the windowsill?
6. What does Mademoiselle Reisz look like?
7. What does Edna think of when she hears the song Adèle plays that she calls "Solitude"?
8. What is different about Edna as she hears Mademoiselle Reisz's first chords on the piano?
9. What is Edna's reaction to Mademoiselle Reisz's music?
10. Why does Mademoiselle Reisz think Edna is the only one worth playing for?

Answers

1. It is Saturday night, and all the guests are gathered for an evening of entertainment.
2. Léonce had brought them colored sheets of the comic papers, and all the children want to see them.
3. They play the duet from *Zampa* and the overture from *The Poet and the Peasant.*
4. She and her husband considered it a means of brightening their home and making it attractive.
5. She is looking at the moon casting its light across the restless sea.
6. She is small and ugly, with a weazened face and body.
7. She thinks of a naked, lonely man standing on the seashore, looking at a distant bird with hopeless resignation.
8. It is the first time she is truly ready to hear an artist and for Edna, this means to hear the truth.
9. She feels stirred by passion, as if waves are beating against her body.
10. She thinks Edna is the only one who is visibly and genuinely moved.

Suggested Essay Topics

1. What is the difference between the way Adèle and Mademoiselle Reisz play the piano? How does each one's style affect Edna?
2. What is the similarity between Edna and the image of the lonely man she conjures up while listening to Adèle play?

Chapter X (pages 26–30)

Summary

The guests walk in little groups down to the beach, but Robert lingers behind with the lovers. Edna wonders why he is not coming; she misses him when he is not around her. The sea is quiet and the moon is bright.

Edna had been trying all summer to learn to swim, but tonight she finally is able to swim. She is so happy she shouts for joy and swims out by herself as far as she can go. While out there, she feels a momentary twinge of panic, but manages to swim safely back in. After that she changes into dry clothes and leaves, despite protestations from the other guests.

Robert overtakes her as she is walking home, and they chat about spirits and the dreamlike quality of the night. At one point Edna becomes offended, thinking Robert is mocking her feelings. When they reach her cottage, Edna stretches out in the hammock to wait for Léonce. Robert waits until he thinks she is asleep and then leaves. She watches him walk away.

Analysis

Edna is beginning to realize how much she misses Robert when he is not around. The imagery continues to get more romantic, erotic, and poetic as her feelings get stronger. At the beach she smells "a tangle of the sea smell and of weeds and damp, new-plowed earth, mingled with the heavy perfume of a field of white blossoms."

Edna swims for the first time tonight and revels in the power she suddenly has over her body and soul. This is another awakening. She wants to swim far out, "where no woman had ever swum before." She feels intoxicated, as she did in Chapter VII when she opened up to Adèle. This feeling of intoxication is repeated throughout the novel, whenever Edna feels a surge of personal power. It is contrasted with the numerous periods of languor or stupor, which come over her when she feels powerless or hopeless.

Edna feels a moment of panic and sees a quick vision of death when she sees how far out she has swum, but she rallies her strength and swims back. She is still unsure of and frightened by her new sense of freedom and power, despite the joy she feels.

The story about spirits that Robert tells Edna as he walks her home is important because, although he does not know it, a new spirit has truly entered into Edna; she has had her first real taste of freedom. This sense of magic also sets the stage for Edna's "first-felt throbbings of desire" for Robert.

Study Questions

1. How does Edna feel when Robert is not around?
2. What is the odor Edna smells down by the sea?
3. Why had Edna not been able to learn to swim?
4. What is different about this night?
5. How does Edna feel when she starts swimming?
6. What is she looking for when she swims out?
7. What does Edna experience after she swims a certain distance?
8. How does Edna describe the night to Robert when he walks her home?
9. How does Robert describe it?
10. What happens in the silence when Edna is in the hammock and Robert is sitting by her?

Answers

1. She misses him and wonders why he is not with her.
2. She smells a tangle of the sea, weeds, damp, new-plowed earth and the heavy perfume of a field of white blossoms.
3. She feels an ungovernable dread in the water unless someone is nearby.
4. Edna is realizing her power.
5. She feels exulted, as if she had been given power finally over her body and soul. She wants to swim far out, where no woman has swum before.
6. She is looking for space and solitude, reaching out for the unlimited in which to lose herself.
7. She has a quick vision of death that makes her temporarily weak.
8. She feels as if it is a dream.

9. Robert tells Edna that there is a spirit out, who searches for someone worthy to inhabit and that tonight the spirit found Edna.
10. They feel the throbbings of desire for one another.

Suggested Essay Topics

1. How does learning to swim contribute to Edna's awakening?
2. What is the significance of Robert's story about the spirit that haunts the shores and his statement to Edna that tonight the spirit found her?

Chapter XI (pages 30–32)

Summary

When Léonce returns to the cottage, he finds Edna lying in the hammock and asks, then demands, that she come inside. Edna refuses, realizing that this is the first time she has ever done so.

Léonce had prepared for bed already, but he goes outside and sits in the rocker with a glass of wine and a cigar. After a while, Edna feels her will leaving her; she begins to feel helpless again. She arises and goes inside and asks Léonce if he is joining her. He tells her he will come in after he finishes his cigar.

Analysis

Edna's refusal to go inside at Léonce's command marks her first rebellion, powered by her swim and the spirits of the night. She realized that her will had "blazed up," and that she could have not done other than refuse him. Her "awakening" is powerful and has more control of her than she has of it at times.

Unfortunately, Léonce still wins this first round. As he sits smoking on the porch, Edna again begins to feel "the realities pressing against her soul." This is the reality of convention that Edna is fighting against, the convention that gives the husband control over the wife. Her feeling of exuberance turns to one of helplessness and weakness, and she has to yield.

Study Questions

1. Where does Léonce find Edna when he returns to the cottage?
2. What does Léonce say to her?
3. What would Edna normally have done in this situation?
4. What is different about this night?
5. How does Léonce respond to Edna's refusal to obey him?
6. How long is Léonce preparing to stay outside.
7. How does Edna feel when she realizes Léonce is staying outside with her?
8. Why does Edna go back inside?
9. What does Léonce do after Edna goes inside?
10. Who is the winner in this battle between Edna and Léonce?

Answers

1. She is lying in the hammock on the front porch.
2. He demands that she come inside.
3. She would have given in to Léonce out of habit.
4. Edna's will had blazed up, stubborn and resistant.
5. He put something on over his pajamas and went outside with a cigar and a glass of wine.
6. He is prepared to stay outside as long as Edna does.
7. She feels like she had awakened from a delicious dream to the ugly realities of her life.
8. The exultation she felt is gone, and she feels helpless and tired.
9. He stays outside to finish his cigar.
10. Léonce wins because Edna feels forced by her crushed spirit to finally go inside.

Suggested Essay Topics

1. What are the realities that Edna is talking about when she says she feels again "the realities pressing into her soul"? Why do these realities cause her to go inside?
2. Put yourself in Léonce's place. Describe your reaction to Edna's refusal to come inside.

Chapter XII (pages 32–35)

New Characters:

Mariequita: *a "mischievous," carefree Spanish girl who works at Grand Isle*

Baudelet: *an old sailor who takes people by boat to Mass at Chênière Caminada*

Summary

Edna sleeps badly and is up and dressed early. Only a few others are up, those who intend to go to mass at the Cheniere. Edna sends Madame Lebrun's servant to wake up Robert, to tell him to come to mass with her. They each have coffee and a roll, and then join the others at the wharf. The lovers are there, the lady in black, old Monsieur Farival, and a young girl named Mariequita whom Robert knows and speaks to in Spanish.

Edna stares at Mariequita, and Mariequita asks Robert if Edna is Robert's lover. Robert answers that she is married.

Edna feels light and free again sailing on the bay, and Robert asks her to go with him to Grand Terre the following day. They chat about it for a while in an intimate manner, and then everybody goes to the church except Baudelet and Mariequita.

Analysis

Here Chopin shows us how Edna's "awakening" has taken hold of her; she is not acting with purpose so much as "blindly following whatever impulse moved her." Edna has moved forward from feeling "aimless" and "unguided" in Chapter VII to feeling as if "alien hands" were directing her. She asks Robert to join her for mass without thinking about it, without even noticing that she had never done that before.

Mariequita, who is very open, points out the truth and the irony about Edna and Robert's relationship, although nobody realizes it. When she asks Robert if Edna is his lover, and Robert answers that she is married, Mariequita responds with a story about a man who ran away on a boat with a married lady. Obviously, Edna's marriage is not going to protect them from their feelings. In fact, Edna and Robert are on a boat together as the story is being told, and they make plans to go sailing together again the following day. Mariequita and Robert also share a laugh about the lovers not being married; obviously it is not just Edna for whom marriage and romance are separate.

Study Questions

1. How does Edna sleep after finally going inside?
2. What is the something Edna feels is unattainable?
3. Was it usual for Edna to invite Robert to mass?
4. What does Robert note about Edna when they are drinking their coffee?
5. What does Mariequita look like?
6. What does Mariequita ask Robert?
7. Does Robert deny it?
8. What does Mariequita think of the fact that Edna is married?
9. Why is it understood that the lovers aren't married?
10. What do Robert and Edna talk about on the boat?

Answers

1. She sleeps badly, disturbed by dreams that leave her with a sense of something unattainable.
2. She feels that her freedom is unattainable.
3. No. She had never done it before, although neither one of them realize how unusual it was.

4. He says that she often lacks forethought.
5. She has a round face and pretty black eyes, but her feet are broad and coarse.
6. She asks if he and Edna are lovers.
7. No. He only answers that Edna is married and has children.
8. Mariequita knows that fact would not stop two lovers from being together and tells a story to Robert about a man and a married woman who ran off together in a boat.
9. People think that marriage and romance don't go together.
10. They plan some trips together alone on the boat.

Suggested Essay Topics

1. What other examples do we see of Edna's lack of forethought?
2. How does Edna feel about marriage and romance and why?

Chapter XIII (pages 35–39)

New Characters:

Madame Antoine: *a village woman at Chênière Caminada whose house Edna stays in when she feels ill*

Tonie: *the son of Madame Antoine*

Summary

Edna begins to feel tired and sick during the service and leaves before it is over. Robert follows her outside and suggests they go to Madame Antoine's. Madame Antoine welcomes them in and brings Edna to a room with a large, white four-posted bed. Robert sits outside with Madame Antoine to wait for Tonie. Edna bathes in the basin, undresses, and luxuriates in the smell of the bed and the feel of her body. Eventually she falls asleep.

When Edna awakes, she feels as if she has been asleep a long time. She washes again and walks into the adjoining room where she enjoys the food and drink Madame Antoine has set out for her. When she finds Robert, they joke that she slept for 100 years, and they are the only two people left.

Robert prepares more food, and they eat a hearty meal, deciding that since the others have already returned to Grand Isle they will wait till the sun goes down to return. Madame Antoine returns and tells them stories under the night moon. Then they leave in Tonie's boat.

Analysis

We see for sure here that Edna's awakening is not religious in nature; in fact her strict religious upbringing was one of the causes of her repression. Now free to come or go, she gets sick while in church and has to leave. This sickness also gives her more time to be alone with Robert. Away from the stodgy church, Edna can again hear the voice of the sea and continue with her romantic getaway.

Alone and partially undressed in Madame Antoine's bed, Edna experiences an erotic enjoyment of her own body. This growing sexuality is part of her awakening.

When Edna wakes up, she and Robert continue the fairy tale fantasy they have been sharing. Edna asks Robert how many years she has been asleep, and he answers, "one hundred." He then tells her that he has been guarding her slumber since they are the only people left on earth. Later when the sun goes down, Edna can hear "the whispering voices of dead men and the click of muffled gold." When she and Robert finally leave in Tonie's boat, "misty spirit forms were prowling in the shadows."

Edna eats when she first wakes up, and she eats again with Robert. Her appetite, her pleasure in food and drink, is part of the sensuousness that is beginning to surround her.

Study Questions

1. What happens to Edna during the mass?
2. What is the only sound Edna hears after she leaves the mass?
3. Where does Robert take Edna to rest?
4. What does Edna do when she is alone in the bedroom?

5. How does Edna feel laying in the bed?
6. How does Edna feel when she awakes?
7. How does Edna turn their trip into a romantic fairy tale?
8. What is Robert's response?
9. What does Robert do for Edna after she awakes?
10. How is the fairy tale quality continued when Robert and Edna leave?

Answers

1. She is overcome with a feeling of oppression and drowsiness, and her head begins to ache.
2. She hears the voice of the sea whispering through the reeds.
3. He takes her to Madame Antoine's house at the far end of the village.
4. After she bathes her face, neck, and arms, she takes off her shoes and stockings and stretches herself out on the bed.
5. She feels luxurious and sensuous, enjoying the way her body feels in the bed.
6. As if she had been asleep a very long time. Additionally, she is very hungry.
7. She asks Robert how many years she has been asleep and if they are the only two people left on earth.
8. Robert plays along, saying she was asleep for 100 years, and he had been guarding her sleep.
9. He cooks a meal for her.
10. They are alone together in the boat in the dark, with spirit forms lurking in the shadows and phantom ships upon the water.

Suggested Essay Topics

1. How does the idea of fairy tale fit in with Edna's awakening and her relationship with Robert?

2. What is Edna's attitude about food and eating? What does this tell us about her personality?

Chapter XIV (pages 39–40)

Summary

When Edna returns to her cottage at nine o'clock, Adèle, who has been watching the children, tells Edna that Etienne, the younger of Edna's sons, would not go to sleep. Edna sits in the rocker with him and soothes him to sleep. Léonce, after being dissuaded from fetching Edna back earlier, has gone to Klein's.

Robert leaves and goes for a solitary walk after Edna points out that they have been together the whole day. Edna, too, stays alone, in the cottage, rather than join the others. She realizes that she has changed since last summer and that in fact she is different than she has ever been before.

She wonders why Robert has not stayed, and wishes that he had. She begins singing a song that he had sung to her on the boat.

Analysis

Edna is very loving and attentive to her children when she returns from *Chênière Caminada* because she is feeling good about herself. This is part of her central conflict. She can love them when she's not feeling repressed by them.

Léonce, as usual, is not around. His role as husband is merely that of provider. He feels no responsibility to help around the house or spend time with his wife.

While Edna is awaiting Léonce's return, she realizes that she is beginning to change; she just doesn't understand the significance of the change yet. Although she is waiting for Léonce, she spends the time thinking about Robert.

Study Questions

1. Why is Etienne still up when Edna returns?
2. How does Edna act with Etienne when she returns home?

3. Why is Edna so loving toward Etienne at this time?
4. Why is Adèle staying with the children?
5. Why does Adèle leave immediately after Edna returned?
6. How does Robert show his feelings as he says goodnight to Edna?
7. What does Robert do after he left Edna?
8. What does Edna realize about this summer at Grand Isle?
9. How does Edna feel about Robert's leaving?
10. What does Edna do while waiting for Léonce to return?

Answers

1. He had refused to go to bed and had made a scene.
2. She coddles and caresses him and is very loving and tender.
3. She is feeling good about herself.
4. Léonce left to go to Klein's for the evening.
5. Monsieur Ratignolle hates to be alone.
6. He presses her hand.
7. He goes for a solitary walk by the sea.
8. She realizes that she is somehow different than she had been in previous years.
9. She regrets that he left; it has become natural to have him around.
10. She sings the song that Robert sang to her on the boat.

Suggested Essay Topics

1. Describe Edna's relationship with her children and why it changes based on her feelings about herself.
2. What are some of the ways Edna has changed already?

Chapter XV (pages 40–45)

Summary

A few days later, Edna enters the dining room a little late and learns from several people at once that Robert is going away to Mexico, and he is leaving for New Orleans that very evening. This comes as a surprise to her, and she shows it. Robert looks embarrassed and uneasy. He explains to everyone at the table, in a defensive voice, that he is going to meet someone in Vera Cruz and that he just decided that afternoon to go.

The lovers, as usual, speak only to each other. Everyone else is buzzing about the trip. Adèle warns him about the Mexicans, whom she does not trust. Edna asks him what time he is leaving and then leaves the room.

She goes back to her cottage where she busies herself with little things and then tells the children a story. The little black girl comes by to invite Edna to Madame Lebrun's to sit until Robert leaves, but Edna feigns illness. Adèle stops by and Edna expresses her shock, with which Adèle agrees. Then Adèle leaves to join the group.

Robert finally stops by, and Edna berates him for not telling her of his plan. She tells him how she looks forward to seeing him and spending time together. Robert agrees and intimates that this is the reason he is leaving. He holds out his hand, and Edna clings to it, entreating him to write to her. Robert agrees and leaves rather stiffly. Edna tries to hold back her tears and her feelings, but she is forced to recognize her feelings of infatuation.

Analysis

Robert's announcement that he is leaving for Mexico takes Edna completely by surprise. Because she feels controlled by outside forces to some extent, she never thinks about the future. Additionally she is very self-absorbed. It does not occur to her that Robert might have plans of his own that don't include her.

We see another side of Adèle here. She is a beautiful mother-woman, but she is also a bigot and clearly not very intelligent. It is clear that her opinions come from somewhere outside her. This is just one of the characteristics of the mother-woman.

Edna refuses to go to the Lebruns because she is hurt and angry. She is experiencing a childish temper tantrum. Robert makes it clear that he is leaving because of what is happening between him and Edna. He is a man of honor, and if he cannot have her, then he wants to leave. Edna has no concept of what he is feeling. She cannot see past her own feelings, which she finally recognizes as infatuation of the type she used to feel before she married Léonce.

Study Questions

1. How does Edna learn that Robert is going to Mexico?
2. What does Edna do with her feeling of bewilderment?
3. How does Robert look when he sees Edna's face?
4. How does Robert explain his sudden departure?
5. How does this news affect Edna's appetite?
6. What does Adèle warn Robert about?
7. What does Edna do when she goes back to her room?
8. Why does Edna refuse to go to the Lebruns?
9. What does Robert make clear to Edna before he leaves?
10. What does Edna realize after Robert leaves?

Answers

1. Several people tell her at once when she enters the dining room late for dinner one afternoon.
2. She lets it show on her face.
3. He looks embarrassed and uneasy.
4. He was meeting his mother's friend in Vera Cruz, and he needed to get to New Orleans to pack in time to make the ship that would take him there by the appointed day.
5. She forces herself to finish her soup but can't eat her stew.
6. She tells him that Mexicans are not to be trusted.

7. She busies herself with little odds and ends and helps put the boys to bed.
8. She claims she is tired, but the truth is she can't bear to watch Robert go.
9. He is leaving because of his strong feelings for Edna.
10. She realizes that she loves him.

Suggested Essay Topics

1. Why does Robert feel the need to leave?
2. How does Edna's realization of her love for Robert contribute to her awakening?

Chapter XVI (pages 45–49)

Summary

Mademoiselle Reisz asks Edna if she misses Robert. In fact she misses him greatly and feels that her life has been dulled. She talks about him constantly and looks at old family pictures with Madame Lebrun. She wishes there were a recent picture for her to look at. Madame Lebrun shows her a letter Robert had written, and Edna feels jealous that he wrote to his mother rather than her.

Even Léonce assumes that Edna misses Robert. Léonce saw Robert in the city before he left for Mexico, and Edna pesters him with questions. She does not find it at all "grotesque" that she is making so much of his absence; in fact, she does not think much about it at all and does not feel the need to voice her feelings.

Edna prefers to keep her thoughts and emotions to herself. She once told Adèle that she would never sacrifice herself for her children, although she would give up her life. The two women argued about it, and Edna felt like they were speaking two different languages; Adèle did not understand.

Nonetheless Edna answers Mademoiselle Reisz's question honestly, if lightly. Then they chat about the Lebruns, and Mademoiselle Reisz has nasty things to say about both Madame Lebrun and Victor. Edna feels depressed by Mademoiselle Reisz's venom and leaves her to go bathing, although she had not planned to. She swims for a long time, feeling thrilled and invigorated. She hopes that Mademoiselle Reisz won't wait for her, but she does. Mademoiselle Reisz gives Edna her city address and invites her to come visit as the summer is nearly over, and they will both be leaving Grand Isle within the next two weeks.

Analysis

Edna says that swimming is the only pleasure she has. This is because when she is swimming she feels powerful, like she is in control of her body and soul. The rest of the time she feels the reality of her constraint and the reality of Robert's absence. Swimming is also a sensuous experience for Edna, as she feels a longing for Robert.

Edna feels jealous that Robert wrote to his mother rather than her. This shows the immaturity and the intensity of her feelings. The fact that everybody assumes she misses him shows how nobody, including Léonce, takes the relationship seriously—nobody but Robert and Edna, and Edna doesn't even realize how seriously she takes it.

Adèle does not understand Edna's statement that she would die for her children but would never sacrifice herself, which brings back a theme from the parrot in the first chapter. As long as Edna mimics everyone else, she can get along and be understood. As soon as she starts becoming her own person, she is suddenly speaking a different language that only she understands. Thus, it is clear right here that Edna cannot have her awakening and continue to live in her old world.

Edna gets depressed by Mademoiselle Reisz's mean talk, but she is drawn to her nonetheless, because she is an artist and stirs the passion in Edna that Edna longs to feel.

Study Questions

1. What does Edna consider to be the only pleasurable moments she has?
2. How does Edna keep close to Robert after he leaves?
3. How does Léonce feel about Edna's missing Robert?

4. Why is Edna jealous when she read's Robert's letter?
5. What does Edna tell Adèle about her children?
6. Why can't Adèle understand what Edna is talking about?
7. What does Edna mean when she says she wouldn't sacrifice herself for her children?
8. What do Edna and Mademoiselle Reisz talk about as they walk to the beach?
9. Why does Edna spend time with Mademoiselle Reisz if the woman's meanness depresses her?
10. How does Edna swim now?

Answers

1. She feels pleasure only when she is swimming.
2. She keeps close to him by talking about him to everyone who knows him and by looking at Madame Lebrun's family photographs.
3. He doesn't give it a second thought; it would never occur to a Creole man that his wife could be unfaithful.
4. He wrote to his mother and not to her.
5. She said that she would die for her children, but she would not sacrifice herself.
6. Edna is becoming her own person and speaking a new language.
7. She won't let her life be controlled by her responsibility to her children. She needs to be her own person, apart from her role as mother.
8. They talk about the Lebrun family and how Robert and Victor had a big fight the previous year over Mariequita.
9. She needs to be with an artist, someone who can inspire passion.
10. She swims with an abandon that thrills and invigorates her.

Suggested Essay Topics

1. Describe the gulf that has grown between Edna and Adèle. Why doesn't Adèle understand what Edna is telling her?
2. What is considered essential by Edna compared to what would be considered essential by other women of her time?

Chapter XVII (pages 49–53)

Summary

The story has now moved to New Orleans. There is a description of the Pontelliers' house on Esplanade Street, which is very beautiful and luxurious. Léonce is very fond of walking around the house and taking pleasure in his possessions.

Since her wedding six years earlier, Tuesday has been a reception day for Edna. There is a constant stream of female callers all afternoon, and sometimes at night the men would join their wives. One Tuesday night at dinner, several weeks after their return to the city, Léonce notices that Edna is not in her reception dress but is wearing an ordinary housedress. Edna tells him she went out for the day and thus was not home to receive the callers.

Léonce reprimands her, reminding her that they have to observe convention. Then he asks to see the cards that were left, so he would know who called. He begins to read the names aloud, commenting on each one as he reads. He is upset when one of the ladies' husbands is a wealthy man whom he is afraid to snub. Edna gets angry, and Léonce, saying the food is a disaster and claiming it is Edna's fault for not looking after the cook, leaves to eat at the club. Although this scene was not unfamiliar, Edna's reaction is. She sits and eats her dinner by herself and then goes up to her room, still not bothering with the cook.

When Edna gets to her room, she stands by the open window to look at the garden below, which seems full of mystery. She contemplates that she is seeking and finding herself but feels devoid of hope. This makes her angry. She tears up the handkerchief in her hands and then throws her wedding ring down and stomps on it. Then she shatters a glass vase, feeling the need to destroy something.

A maid, hearing the noise, comes in and Edna explains that the vase had fallen. The maid picks up Edna's ring and hands it to her. Edna slips it back on her finger.

Analysis

We see again Léonce's view of the world. It is based on finance and ownership. He likes to walk through his house examining his possessions, which he enjoys because they belong to him. Unfortunately, he includes Edna among his possessions.

Léonce cannot understand why Edna abandoned her Tuesday reception, but his concern is only economic. He is afraid Edna will snub someone who is important to him in the business world. He is not at all concerned with her personally.

After their little fight, Léonce leaves to have dinner at the club. It is his constant escape, and he goes there whenever things are not to his liking.

Edna responds differently to the fight than she used to. "Her eyes flamed with some inward fire," and she finished her dinner alone and didn't run to fix things with the cook. She is no longer running to please Léonce, no longer intimidated by his disapproval.

However the fight does leave her feeling hopeless, and this makes her angry. "She wanted to destroy something." What she really wanted to destroy was her marriage, and in yet another attempted rebellion, she throws off her wedding ring and tries to crush it. In the end, however, she is defeated because she puts the ring back on her finger.

Study Questions

1. How does Léonce feel about his house in New Orleans?
2. What do Tuesdays mean for Edna?
3. What is Léonce angry about on this particular Tuesday?
4. Why is it so important to Léonce that Edna be home for her receptions?

5. Who does Léonce blame for the poorly cooked meal?
6. How does Edna react to Léonce's reprimand and departure for the club?
7. What does Edna seek in the garden that night?
8. What does Edna find in the garden?
9. How does Edna act out her anger?
10. How do we know that this rebellion ends in defeat as her first one did?

Answers

1. He likes to walk around admiring his possessions.
2. Tuesday is her traditional reception day, where other society women call on her during the afternoon.
3. Edna went out instead of being home to receive her guests.
4. It is important because it is the proper thing to do, and it would look bad for him if Edna didn't go along; ultimately it might affect him financially.
5. He blames Edna for the poorly cooked meal. He feels it is her job to keep watch over the cook.
6. Instead of her usual reaction, Edna finishes her meal by herself and says nothing to the cook.
7. She is looking for herself and for signs of hope.
8. The voices she hears are mournful and devoid of hope.
9. She tears up a handkerchief, breaks a glass vase, and throws off her wedding ring and tries to crush it with her shoe.
10. She puts her wedding ring back on after the maid picks it up.

Suggested Essay Topics

1. What is the real cause of Edna's anger? Why does she put her wedding ring back on?
2. How does Chopin use natural imagery to help the reader understand Edna's moods?

Chapter XVIII (pages 53–56)

Summary

The next morning Léonce asks Edna to meet him in the city to go shopping; she does not want to go shopping. He notes that Edna is not looking well; she is pale and very quiet. Edna watches him leave and watches the children playing. She feels no interest in anything around her. In fact she feels the outside world, including her children, has suddenly become alien and antagonistic.

Although Edna criticizes most of her sketches, she gathers up some of them and leaves the house to go visit Adèle. She is thinking about Robert, feeling an "incomprehensible longing."

The Ratignolles live not far from the Pontelliers, in spacious apartments over Monsieur Ratignolle's drugstore. Every two weeks the Ratignolles give a musical party, and they were very popular. Edna considers their lifestyle to be very French and very foreign.

Adèle looks more beautiful than ever, and Edna hopes she might someday paint her. She shows Adèle her sketches. She knows her opinions are valueless but wants to hear the encouragement. Adèle, of course, praises them highly and even shows them off to her husband when he comes in for his midday lunch. Monsieur Ratignolle is a good man, and he and Adèle have a close relationship where they understand each other perfectly. When he speaks, Adèle listens attentively, even laying down her fork so as to listen better.

Edna feels a little depressed after leaving them, finding nothing worthwhile in their domestic harmony. She feels some pity for Adèle, who would never know a moment of anguish, never have a taste of "life's delirium."

Analysis

Edna, immersed in her defeat of the night before, feels hopeless and depressed. Her home does not interest her, and her children become antagonists who are trying to enslave her. They have become antagonists because if it were not for them, she could leave.

Edna tries to forget Robert, but she cannot. She is "under a spell," continuing the mystical and fairy tale terminology. Whenever she thinks of him, she feels an "incomprehensible" longing; it is incomprehensible to her because she has never felt anything like it before.

Edna has no confidence in herself as an artist; after all, wives and mothers cannot be artists. She goes to Adèle's for encouragement and validation even though she knows Adèle's opinion is worthless. Edna's awakening to beauty is shown here in her response to Adèle, who looks "more beautiful than ever." She looks so beautiful that Edna wanted to paint her.

The narrator tells us that the Ratignolles understand each other perfectly and have fused into one being. This is supposed to be the goal of marriage. However, we know that the reason they have fused is because Adèle has given up her identity. Even here she listens attentively to him, putting down her fork so as to listen better. We don't hear anything about him listening to her.

Witnessing this domestic bliss leaves Edna depressed and sad for Adèle. Adèle will never know the highs and lows of life, which Edna believes are signs that one is truly alive. Although she says she is not sure what she means by "life's delirium," it seems to be the fusion of true love with sexual passion. Adèle's life is one of "blind contentment," not passion.

Study Questions

1. How does Edna feel about her children the morning after her fight with Léonce?
2. Why does Edna always find fault with her sketches?
3. Why does Edna take her sketches to Adèle's?
4. What is Edna thinking about as she walks to Adèle's?
5. What is symbolic about Edna considering the Ratignolles' life French and foreign?
6. What are Edna's first thoughts about Adèle when she sees her?
7. What is one example given of the "fusion" the Ratignolles have accomplished in their marriage?

8. Why does Edna pity Adèle after witnessing this marital bliss?
9. What does Edna mean by "life's delirium"?
10. Why is it important for Edna to feel both anguish and passion?

Answers

1. She considers her children part of "an alien world that has suddenly become antagonistic."
2. She has no confidence in herself as an artist.
3. She needs validation and encouragement.
4. She is thinking about Robert and how much she misses him.
5. The concept of their domestic bliss, of any marriage, has become foreign to her.
6. Edna thinks that Adèle looks more beautiful than ever, and she would like to paint her picture.
7. Adèle listens attentively to everything her husband says, even putting down her fork to listen better.
8. Edna pities Adèle because Adèle will never feel true anguish nor would she ever know "life's delirium."
9. Life's delirium is the combination of true love and sexual passion.
10. These feelings show her that she is truly alive, truly her own person.

Suggested Essay Topics

1. How is the Ratignolles' marriage different from the Pontelliers'?
2. What is it about Adèle's and Edna's marriages that prevents them from knowing "life's delirium"? Why is Adèle content with this while Edna is not?

Chapter XIX (pages 56–58)

Summary

Edna realizes that her outburst with the ring and vase had been childish and futile. Instead she begins to do and feel exactly as she pleases, including more painting. She completely abandons her Tuesday receptions and makes no efforts toward running the household. Léonce, who had always been courteous as long as Edna had been submissive, now grows angry at her insolence. He compares her to Adèle, who keeps up with her music but also with all her responsibilities. Edna tells him to leave her alone, and he does. However he wonders if Edna is growing mentally unbalanced. He cannot see that she is actually becoming her true self.

Edna goes to her atelier at the top of the house to paint. She is working a lot, using everyone in the house as models. However none of her work satisfies her. Sometimes as she works she sings the song Robert had sung to her, and she would feel desire sweeping through her.

There are days when she is very happy, especially when she is alone and able to dream. There are also days when she is very unhappy and despairing, and she cannot work on those days.

Analysis

Edna realizes the futility of her temper tantrums and finds a better way to express her displeasure with Léonce and her desires for herself; she will simply abandon her pretense of being a good wife and do exactly as she pleases.

Léonce, as earlier described, was a good husband by societal standards. We find out here that he was courteous only because Edna was submissive. Now that she is defying him he becomes angry and rude. However, this only serves to strengthen Edna's resolve.

Léonce doesn't understand Edna's need to be alone in her atelier painting. He doesn't equate it with his constant need to escape to the club because only he is allowed to have such needs. He believes all of Edna's time should be spent on the advancement of her family's welfare. He wants her to be more like Adèle, who plays music only for her family to enjoy, not out of any thought for her own pleasure.

Léonce thinks that Edna is not herself; he does not realize that she never had a self to be before. It is only now that she is developing a sense of self, and it is threatening to him. Chopin's language is a romantic image of rebirth. Edna is "daily casting aside that fictitious self which we assume like a garment with which to appear before the world." The "casting aside" brings to mind the shedding of old skin. Edna is crawling out of her cocoon and turning into a butterfly; Léonce wants to clip her wings.

Whenever Edna thinks of Robert, Chopin's language becomes romantic and sensual. Edna hears the "ripple of the water," sees the "glint of the moon on the bay," and feels the "soft gusty beating of the hot south wind."

Edna likes to be alone, where she can dream. It is important to her awakening that she is away from the realities of life enough to keep her hope alive.

Study Questions

1. Why is it more powerful for Edna to neglect her household than to have temper tantrums?
2. Why had Léonce always been a courteous husband?
3. How does Léonce's anger contribute to Edna's awakening?
4. How does Léonce feel about Edna's painting?
5. Why is Adèle's piano playing different from Edna's painting?
6. What can't Léonce see about Edna when he says she's "not herself"?
7. Why does Edna notice the housemaid's back and shoulders?
8. How does Edna feels when she thinks of Robert?
9. When does Edna feel really happy?
10. What contributes to Edna's days of unhappiness?

Answers

1. Neglecting her household will get more of a reaction from Léonce than a temper tantrum and also gives her more of a sense of freedom.
2. Edna had always been submissive.
3. Léonce's anger makes her resolve never to take another step backward.
4. He thinks her time would be better spent working for the comfort of her family.
5. Adèle plays piano for her family; Edna paints for herself.
6. He can't see that she had no self before; it is only now that she is actually becoming her true self.
7. She is becoming more of an artist and is noticing beauty more.
8. She feels filled with desire.
9. She feels really happy when she is alone in the sun dreaming.
10. She feels unhappy when feelings of hopelessness come over her, when she believes that her situation will never change.

Suggested Essay Topics

1. Why is Edna's painting important to her awakening and her sense of independence?
2. What does Edna mean when she says that Adèle is not a musician and she is not a painter?

Chapter XX (pages 58–61)

Summary

Edna decides to visit Mademoiselle Reisz, despite the bad feeling she had gotten from their last conversation. She feels the need to hear her play the piano. Unfortunately, Mademoiselle

Reisz has moved, and Edna has some trouble locating her. She decides to go to the Lebruns to ask Madame Lebrun. Victor answers the door, and after having an argument with his servant, he sends her to fetch Madame Lebrun.

Edna waits on the porch, and Victor sits down with her and amuses her with a story about a woman he had met the night before. Mrs. Lebrun comes out just as Victor is about to get into sordid details. She sends Victor in to get two letters from Robert to read to Edna. The letters are about his life in Mexico with no mention of Edna. She begins to feel despondent again and asks Madame Lebrun for Mademoiselle Reisz's address.

As she leaves, Edna banters a bit with Victor again and then regrets it, thinking she should have been more dignified and reserved. Mrs. Lebrun comments on how well she looks, and Victor notes that she seems like a different woman.

Analysis

Edna needs to see Mademoiselle Reisz, because she gives Edna inspiration and stirs her to feel passion, both of which Edna needs to keep going. Unfortunately she has a hard time finding her. Again we hear how unpleasant and unpopular Mademoiselle Reisz is, and this is because she is an artist who does not conform to society's rules and dictates. Her worst crime is that she is unmarried and childless. Adèle naturally doesn't like her, because she is the polar opposite of Adèle, who strictly conforms to society's standards and lives only for and through her family.

Victor's attitude is typical of his time. He can't tell Edna about his presumably raunchy adventures of the evening before because she is a woman and wouldn't understand. However, Edna has come a long way from the woman who blushed when Robert spoke of Adèle's pregnancy. Her awakening sexuality and passion has taken over her inborn prudery, and she is interested and amused by Victor's story.

Edna begins to feel good until she reads Robert's letters, which make no mention of her. Then the feeling of despondency takes over, and she is reminded of her need to see Mademoiselle Reisz. Before she leaves, she banters with Victor again, before remembering that the proper thing would have been to look disapproving. But she is beyond such artifice and can respond only naturally now. Victor notices the change. He remarks that in "some way she doesn't seem like the same woman."

Study Questions

1. Why does Edna want to visit Mademoiselle Reisz?
2. Why does Edna have such a hard time finding Mademoiselle Reisz?
3. Why does it make sense that Adèle wouldn't like Mademoiselle Reisz?
4. What does the Lebrun house remind Edna of?
5. Why is Victor fighting with the servant when he opens the door?
6. Why doesn't Victor want to tell Edna about the time he had the evening before?
7. Why does Victor grow more daring in the telling of his story?
8. Why do Robert's letters fill Edna with despondency?
9. What does Edna remember after she leaves Victor?
10. What does Victor perceive about Edna?

Answers

1. She wants to hear her play the piano; she wants to feel passion.
2. Mademoiselle Reisz moved, and since nobody liked her, nobody cared where she moved to.
3. Mademoiselle Reisz is the opposite of everything Adèle believes in; she is unmarried, childless, and ugly.
4. It is like a prison because of the iron bars on the doors and lower windows.
5. The servant thought it was her job to open the door.
6. She is a woman and wouldn't comprehend such things.
7. Edna is showing interest in his story.

8. There is no message for her.
9. She remembers that she was supposed to be dignified and reserved.
10. He perceives that she has changed; he says she doesn't seem like the same woman.

Suggested Essay Topics

1. Describe the different influences Adèle and Mademoiselle Reisz have upon Edna.
2. Describe the significance of Edna's bantering with Victor and how Edna has changed since she blushed at Robert's story in Chapter IV.

Chapter XXI (pages 61–64)

Summary

Mademoiselle Reisz lives in an apartment under the roof with open windows that let in soot and dirt along with the light and air. Everything is fairly dingy except for a "magnificent piano" that crowds the apartment.

Mademoiselle Reisz is glad to see Edna and expresses her surprise that Edna has actually come. As Mademoiselle Reisz pours coffee for them, she tells Edna she has a letter from Robert in which he writes of nothing but Edna. Edna asks to see it, but Mademoiselle Reisz refuses at first. Edna asks her to play the piano and tells her she has been painting, that she is becoming an artist. Mademoiselle Reisz replies that one must have more than talent to be a true artist; she said one must have a "courageous soul."

Mademoiselle Reisz finally agrees to let Edna see the letter, and she plays love songs on the piano while Edna reads. Edna begins to cry, just like the time Mademoiselle Reisz played at Grand Isle. When she leaves, she asks if she can come again.

Analysis

Mademoiselle Reisz's apartment, like her, is old and dingy and unkempt. However in the center of the apartment, crowding everything else, is a magnificent piano. True to her calling, nothing is important except her music.

Mademoiselle Reisz is pleased with Edna's honesty. There was a time when Edna would not have been so honest, but now she is not so afraid. It is part of her awakening, and in Mademoiselle Reisz's eyes, it is imperative if Edna is to become an artist.

When Edna tells Mademoiselle Reisz that she is becoming an artist, Mademoiselle Reisz is skeptical. She tells Edna that an artist must have a "courageous soul," one that is not afraid to defy convention. This Mademoiselle Reisz clearly has, and Adèle clearly has not. Edna is beginning to develop a courageous soul but will never go so far as Mademoiselle Reisz.

Chopin again uses music and mysticism to set a romantic mood for Edna to read Robert's letter. Mademoiselle Reisz's music ranges from "quivering love notes" to "soulful and poignant longing." Then it becomes "strange and fantastic," spilling out from the deeply shadowed apartment up to the sky. Just as she did that night at Grand Isle, Edna bursts into tears.

Study Questions

1. What is the centerpiece of Mademoiselle Reisz's apartment?
2. How is Mademoiselle Reisz described when Edna sees her?
3. Why did Mademoiselle Reisz think that Edna would never come to visit?
4. Why is Mademoiselle Reisz pleased when Edna admits that she's not sure if she likes her?
5. What does Mademoiselle Reisz tell Edna about Robert's letter?
6. How does Edna describe herself to Mademoiselle Reisz?
7. What does Mademoiselle Reisz tell Edna about being an artist?
8. What did Mademoiselle Reisz play for Edna while Edna was reading Robert's letter?

9. What is Edna's reaction to the letter and the music?
10. How does Chopin set the mood for Edna's emotions?

Answers

1. She has a magnificent piano crowding everything else in the apartment.
2. She hasn't changed; she is the "little musician," still ugly, still wearing the same ugly dress.
3. Edna is a "society" woman, and those women generally have no use for artists such as Mademoiselle Reisz.
4. It is an honest answer and honesty takes courage.
5. The letter is all about Edna.
6. She says that she is becoming an artist.
7. She says that to be an artist one must have a courageous soul, a soul that dares and defies.
8. She starts with a song about longing, moves into a song about love, and then back into longing.
9. She begins to cry.
10. The music grows "fantastic" and fills the room, and the shadows deepen. There is a magical feeling.

Suggested Essay Topics

1. Why does an artist need a courageous soul? Why is it hard for women of that era to have that kind of courage? What is Edna doing to achieve a courageous soul?
2. How does Chopin use music to set the mood? How does the music interact with Edna's discovery of passion?

Chapter XXII (pages 64–67)

New Character:

Dr. Mandelet: *good doctor who tries to help Edna*

Summary

One morning Léonce decides to visit Dr. Mandelet, the family physician. He wants to talk about Edna, explaining that she is acting odd. He says that her whole attitude has changed and hints that they were no longer having sex. Dr. Mandelet inquires if Edna is spending time with a certain group of pseudointellectual women. Léonce explains that she has been isolated, not spending time with anyone. At this Dr. Mandelet grows concerned. Léonce tells him about Edna's sister's upcoming wedding and how Edna refuses to attend.

Dr. Mandelet advises Léonce to let Edna alone for a while, assuring him that this peculiarity would pass. He also agrees to come for dinner so he can observe Edna firsthand.

When Léonce leaves, Dr. Mandelet wonders to himself if there is another man in the picture.

Analysis

Dr. Mandelet is clearly a wise man. He is "known more for his wisdom than his skill," and his eyes "had lost none of their penetration." However, he is still a man of his time and can understand only so much about Edna's awakening. When Léonce first explained Edna's strangeness, including that she refused to sleep with him, Dr. Mandelet thought she was mixed up with a group of "pseudointellectual women." It is only when Léonce tells him that Edna has been isolating that Dr. Mandelet becomes worried. This was very unnatural for a society woman. But even then he attributes it to the "moody and whimsical" nature of women and advises Léonce to ignore it until it has passed.

Dr. Mandelet secretly does wonder if Edna is having an affair. He knows, however, that this is something unheard of in the Creole culture so he wisely keeps quiet about it.

Study Questions

1. What kind of doctor is Dr. Mandelet?
2. Why does Léonce go to see Dr. Mandelet?
3. What is Edna's problem as Léonce describes it?

4. How is this most affecting Léonce?
5. What are Dr. Mandelet's first thoughts on Edna's problem?
6. Why does he finally get concerned?
7. Why won't Edna go to her sister's upcoming wedding?
8. What does Dr. Mandelet attribute Edna's problem to?
9. Why does Léonce invite Dr. Mandelet to dinner?
10. What is Dr. Mandelet's fear about Edna?

Answers

1. He is a semi-retired physician, known more for wisdom than skill.
2. He is worried about Edna.
3. She is suddenly concerned with women's rights and is therefore neglecting her family.
4. Edna has stopped sleeping with him.
5. He wonders if she has been associating with a certain group of pseudointellectual women who might be putting ideas in her head.
6. Léonce tells him that she has been isolating, giving up her social ties.
7. She says that weddings are "one of the most lamentable spectacles on earth."
8. He says that women tend to get moody and whimsical and that this latest "mood" would probably pass.
9. He wants Dr. Mandelet to observe Edna firsthand.
10. He is afraid that there is another man involved in the picture.

Suggested Essay Topics

1. How are Dr. Mandelet's attitudes toward Edna's problem similar to Léonce's attitude?
2. How has Edna's awakening contributed to her refusal to

sleep with her husband? How is this related to her comment that weddings are "one of the most lamentable spectacles on earth"?

Chapter XXIII (pages 67–71)

New Characters:

Alcée Arobin: *a young man-about-town with whom Edna has an affair*

The Highcamps and the Merrimans: *society people who are social friends of Edna's*

The Colonel: *Edna's father*

Summary

Edna's father is in the city to purchase a wedding gift for Edna's sister Janet. He is a retired colonel and still has his military bearing. Edna and her father are not very close but are companionable. He sits still for a sketch, happy to sit rigidly for hours.

Edna takes her father to a party at the Ratignolles' where Adèle flirts with him. Edna notes that she is unable to do that. Léonce does not attend these parties; he prefers to be at the club. Adèle expresses disapproval of this, but Edna is happy that they don't spend much time together. She wonders what they would talk about if they did.

One afternoon Edna and her father go to the racetrack, and win, and that is the main topic of conversation at dinner. At the track, they had met Mrs. Merriman, Mrs. Highcamp, and Alcée Arobin. Léonce, of course, disapproves of gambling. After dinner everyone tells stories. Edna tells one about a woman who had paddled away with a lover one night and never returned.

Dr. Mandelet is at dinner that night observing Edna, and he thinks Edna seems radiant. He notices a subtle change in her, a liveliness he had not seen before.

Analysis

The Colonel allows a glimpse into the other male influence on Edna. Her father is stern, rigid, and rugged; he wears padded jackets to make himself look bigger. When Edna is sketching him, he gets angry at the children for interrupting and disturbing his "fixed lines." In today's terms he would be called macho. He is certainly not someone who would be sympathetic to Edna's feelings.

Edna marvels at Adèle's ability to flirt, noting that she cannot do so. This is because flirting is a feminine art, and Edna is consistently described as more masculine than feminine.

The sad truth of the Pontelliers' relationship is revealed when Adèle says that Léonce should stay home more, and Edna is horrified, knowing that they would have nothing to say to one another. This is contrasted with the ease in which she converses with Robert and later Alcée Arobin.

Dr. Mandelet notices the change in Edna and uses very sexual terms to describe her. Although she used to be listless, she now seemed "palpitant with the forces of life" and like "some beautiful, sleek animal waking up in the sun." He becomes even more convinced that she is having an affair.

When Edna makes up the story about the woman who runs away with her lover, she is so passionate that it seems real to those who hear it; they could actually picture it in their minds.

Study Questions

1. What is the nature of Edna's relationship with her father?
2. Why is she glad he is visiting?
3. What does Edna's father look like?
4. Why can't Edna flirt like Adèle?
5. Why does Léonce not attend the Ratignolles' parties?
6. How does Edna respond to Adèle's suggestion that it would help the Pontelliers' relationship if Léonce stayed home more?
7. Why do Edna and her father have such a good time at the racetrack?
8. What does Dr. Mandelet think of Edna when he comes to dinner?

9. Why is Edna's story significant?
10. What does Dr. Mandelet think about Edna's problem after observing her?

Answers

1. Edna is not warmly attached to her father, but they are companionable because they have certain tastes in common.
2. He provides a distraction and a new outlet for her emotions.
3. He is tall and thin, with silky white hair and moustache. He still has his military bearing and wears jackets that exaggerate the breadth of his chest.
4. Edna has been too repressed to play such games. She is also too masculine for such "girlish" games.
5. He would rather spend his time with the men at the club.
6. Edna would be very unhappy if Léonce were home more often. She says that they would have nothing to talk about.
7. They won money and met some charming people, including Alcée Arobin.
8. He notices that she seems to have come to life, and she reminds him of a sleek animal waking up in the sun.
9. She is hinting at her inclinations, perhaps looking for a response to the idea.
10. He is even more sure that another man was involved.

Suggested Essay Topics

1. How does Dr. Mandelet's description of Edna fit in with her awakening? How does this imagery compare with other natural imagery Chopin uses?
2. Why doesn't Adèle understand Edna's contentment with Léonce's spending time away from her?

Chapter XXIV (pages 71–73)

Summary

Edna and her father have a fight over Edna's refusal to attend her sister's wedding. Léonce, on Dr. Mandelet's advice, stays out of it, but he plans to go himself to atone for Edna. Edna's father disapproves of the way Léonce is handling the situation. He advises him to put his foot down, asserting that "authority and coercion" were necessary to handle a wife. Even Léonce realizes that the Colonel had probably coerced his own wife into an early grave. Edna is very glad when he leaves.

Just before Léonce leaves for New York shortly thereafter, Edna grows affectionate and feels she will miss him. The children leave, too, off to stay with their grandmother in the country. When Edna is finally alone, a "radiant peace" settles over her. She feels a new and "delicious" feeling. She walks through the house as if she is seeing it for the first time. She enjoys a solitary dinner and then reads Emerson in the library until she grows sleepy. When she finally snuggles beneath her covers, she feels a restfulness she had not known before.

Analysis

In the preceding chapter, we learned a bit about Edna's father. Now we learn something about her mother. When the Colonel advises Léonce that "authority and coercion" are needed to manage a wife, we are told that the Colonel was "perhaps unaware that he had coerced his own wife into her grave." This could mean either that she became sick and died or, more portentiously, maybe she committed suicide. In any event it becomes more and more clear what Edna has been up against all her life and how difficult her journey is.

Edna grew somewhat sentimental before Léonce left, acting like a true wife for a while. However, once he and the children were gone, she felt a "radiant peace" and a feeling of relief. She views her house as if for the first time. In a way it is the first time because she is a different person. She is looking at the house as if it were hers instead of Léonce's, and therefore she is enjoying it.

As always, Edna enjoys her food. This is another sensual image: Edna's constant satisfying of her physical appetite. It is also something that sets her apart from other women who usually pretend not to enjoy their food.

Study Questions

1. What is Léonce's position in Edna's fight with her father over her sister's wedding?
2. What is the Colonel's advice to Léonce about Edna?
3. What is hinted at about the Colonel's wife?
4. How does Edna feel right before Léonce leaves for a long trip to New York?
5. How does she actually feel after Léonce and the children have gone?
6. What does she do when she is finally alone?
7. What is Edna's first meal alone like?
8. What does Edna do after dinner?
9. What does Edna plan to do now that she is on her own?
10. How does Edna feel as she snuggles in her bed at night?

Answers

1. Léonce, on Dr. Mandelet's advice, stays out of it.
2. He says that authority and coercion are needed to manage a wife.
3. It is hinted that maybe she had committed suicide.
4. She feels almost affectionate and thinks that she will miss him.
5. A radiant peace settles over her, a feeling of relief.
6. She walks through the house as if it were the first time, enjoying everything as never before.
7. She enjoys a tasty meal with good wine and the comfort of being able to dine in a peignoir.

8. She reads in the library until she grows sleepy.
9. She wants to embark on a course of intellectual self-improvement.
10. She feels a sense of restfulness that she has never known before.

Suggested Essay Topics

1. Imagine that you are Edna but are allowed to speak freely. How would you respond to the Colonel's statement that authority and coercion are needed to manage a wife?
2. Why does Edna walk through the house as if it were the first time? How is the house different for her now?

Chapter XXV (pages 73–77)

Summary

Edna cannot work when it is dark and cloudy; she needs the sunlight to inspire her. On rainy days she goes out to see friends or sits home alone feeling as if her life is passing her by.

She begins frequenting the racetrack. One afternoon, Mrs. Highcamp and Alcée Arobin invited her to the track. She plays for very high stakes and wins; she feels intoxicated.

After dinner at the Highcamps, Alcée drives Edna home, and she agrees to go to the races with him again. After Alcée leaves, Edna feels hungry, restless, and excited. She wants something exciting to happen and regrets she did not ask Alcée to stay and talk for a while.

A few days later Alcée calls on Edna to go to the races, and this time they go alone. She feels excited again and becomes easily intimate with Alcée, who is good at initiating such intimacy. He stays for dinner, and afterward they sit by the fire. He shows Edna a scar on his wrist, and she touches his hand as she looks at it. Then she jumps up and walks away, agitated.

Alcée walks back over to her, and she feels an awakening sensuousness as she looks at him. He sees it and feels emboldened to take her hand when he says goodnight.

However, when Alcée asks if she will go to the races again, she says no and tells him to leave, saying that she doesn't like him; they both know she is lying. He kisses her hand, and she explains that she was excited from the track and hopes she hadn't misled him. He also apologizes and finally leaves.

After Alcée left, Edna stares at her hand where he kissed her. She feels like she had already been unfaithful and wonders what Robert would think of it. She knows she doesn't really care for Alcée, yet his presence and his touch act as a "narcotic" upon her. She falls into a deep sleep.

Analysis

As Edna becomes more independent, she grows more confident in herself as an artist. Yet it is not enough, and there are days when she feels her life is passing her by.

Mrs. Highcamp is a married woman who has affairs with young men. She attracts them through her young daughter and then seeks them for herself. She is a route Edna will later choose not to go.

One place Edna feels young and alive is at the racetrack. She wins a lot of money and feels intoxicated. Chopin often describes Edna as feeling intoxicated when she feels powerful.

After spending the whole day with the purposefully charming Alcée, Edna feels restless and excited. She wants something to happen. She doesn't realize it yet, but Alcée stirred a passion in her. When they finally spend some time alone together, it becomes more clear. Alcée, who is used to seducing women, gets Edna to touch his hand by showing her a scar on his wrist. Her own response flusters her though, and she walks away from him. She tries to send him away, telling him she doesn't like him, but it is too late. After he leaves, she stares at her hand where he kissed it good-bye and feels like she was already unfaithful. This is because of what she is thinking and feeling about Alcée.

Study Questions

1. Why can't Edna work when it's dark and cloudy?
2. How does Edna feel on her melancholy days?

3. What does Alcée look like?
4. Why does Edna enjoy the racetrack so much?
5. How does Edna feel while she is at the track?
6. How does Edna feel after Alcée takes her home?
7. What happens between Edna and Alcée at the track?
8. Why does Edna touch Alcée's hand?
9. What happens when Alcée looks into Edna's eyes?
10. What is Edna's reaction to Alcée after he has gone?

Answers

1. She needs the sun to mellow her mood.
2. She feels as if her life is passing her by, leaving her with broken and unfulfilled promises.
3. He has a good body, a pleasant face not burdened with any depth of thought or feeling, a perpetual smile in his eyes, and hc dresses in the height of fashion.
4. It reminds her of happy times in her childhood stables. Also, she wins a lot of money.
5. She feels intoxicated.
6. She wanted something exciting to happen and regretted that she had not asked him to stay a while.
7. They develop a certain intimacy.
8. He is showing her a scar on his wrist.
9. He draws out all her latent sensuality.
10. She stares at her hand where he kissed her goodnight and feels like she has already been unfaithful.

Suggested Essay Topics

1. How does Edna's experience at the track compare with other experiences where she felt intoxicated? What is the meaning of this intoxication?

2. Why does Edna allow Alcée to kiss her hand? Why does she then feel like she has been unfaithful?

Chapter XXVI (pages 78–82)

Summary

Alcée writes Edna a note of apology, and Edna feels silly for having made a fuss over a kiss on the hand. Soon they are spending time together again, growing closer and more intimate. Sometimes he talks in a way that makes her blush, but after a while she enjoys it; there is something in her that responds to it.

When Edna needs a lift, she visits Mademoiselle Reisz; her music "seemed to reach Edna's spirit and set it free." Upon arriving at Mademoiselle Reisz's apartment, Edna informs her that she is moving out of her house to a smaller one around the corner. When pressed for a reason, Edna says it is because she wants a place of her own. She has her own money now because of her winnings at the track and from sales of her paintings. She has resolved never to "belong" to anyone again. Edna also tells Mademoiselle Reisz that she is giving a dinner party the night before she leaves the old house.

Mademoiselle Reisz gives another of Robert's letters to Edna to read. She tells Edna that the reason he doesn't write her is because he is in love with her and is trying to forget her because she is not free. Edna reads as Mademoiselle Reisz's music brightens her soul, "preparing her for joy and exultation"; the letter says Robert is coming home soon.

Edna finally admits to Mademoiselle Reisz that she is in love with Robert, although she can't explain why. She feels suddenly happy, knowing he is coming home. On her way home, she stops at a confectioners to send a box of candy to her children. Then she writes a cheerful letter to Léonce, telling him of her intention to move out.

Analysis

Alcée has wormed his way into Edna's life, and they are growing more and more intimate. She is getting used to having him around the way she got used to having Robert around, although she doesn't feel the same way about Alcée. Edna likes having adoring men around her. In Chapter VII she says of Léonce that "his absolute devotion flattered her." So although she is seeking and gaining independence, she does not want to be totally alone. It is important to her to have a man around, which is why she cannot become like Mademoiselle Reisz.

Alcée continues to bring out Edna's sexuality, talking to her in ways that make her blush at first, but soon please her, "appealing to the animalism that stirred impatiently within her."

Edna visits Mademoiselle Reisz and tells her that she is moving from her house into a smaller one around the corner because she wants it to be hers completely. She has been gaining not only emotional independence but financial independence through her winnings at the track and sales of her paintings. This financial independence can buy her physical independence. It also takes her farther away from being a traditional woman; financial independence was usually reserved for men.

Mademoiselle Reisz tells Edna that Robert is coming home and that he is in love with her. Then Edna admits her own feelings for him. One wonders why Mademoiselle Reisz is so interested in Robert and Edna; perhaps it is because she has no love in her own life.

When Edna leaves Mademoiselle Reisz's, she sends her children a box of candy along with a loving note. As usual she feels loving toward her children when she feels happy and fulfilled with her own life.

Study Questions

1. Why does Edna deliberate over how to answer Alcée's apology?
2. Why is it so easy for Alcée to become intimate with Edna?
3. Why does Edna visit Mademoiselle Reisz?
4. Why do you think Mademoiselle Reisz is always eating or drinking chocolate?
5. What reason does Edna give for moving out of her house?
6. How does Edna have the money to be on her own?

7. What is Edna's big resolve?
8. Why does Edna sigh after announcing her farewell dinner party?
9. What good news does Edna find out from Mademoiselle Reisz?
10. Why does Edna send a box of candy to her children?

Answers

1. Edna doesn't want to give it undue importance, and she doesn't want him to think she took it seriously.
2. He appeals to the sexual self that is awakening inside her.
3. Mademoiselle Reisz, through her music, touches Edna's spirit and makes her feel free and hopeful.
4. Her life is bitter and alone, and chocolate is sweet.
5. She wants a place that is her own, not provided for by her husband.
6. She has been winning a lot of money at the track and selling some of her paintings. Additionally, she has a small inheritance from her mother.
7. She vows that she will never again belong to another person.
8. It is clear to her that she has never really been happy.
9. She learns that Robert loves her and that he is coming home soon.
10. When Edna is happy, she feels more loving toward her children.

Suggested Essay Topics

1. What is the significance of Edna's moving into her own house? Why is it so important for her to have this physical separation?
2. Why is it that Edna feels more loving toward her children when she feels happy with herself? How do the children affect her desire for independence?

Chapters XXVII and XXVIII (pages 82–84)

Summary

That evening, in Chapter XXVII, Alcée says he has never seen Edna in such a good mood. He sits close to her, letting his fingers lightly touch her hair, which she enjoys. Then she tells Alcée she needs to figure out what kind of woman she is; she feels wicked but doesn't really think she is. Alcée responds that she needn't think about it because he can tell her what kind of woman she is.

Then Edna recounts something Mademoiselle Reisz had said to her about how birds that want to soar above tradition and prejudice must have strong wings. Alcée responds that Mademoiselle Reisz must be demented, but Edna argues that she seems wonderfully sane to her.

Alcée notes that Edna's thoughts seem far away, then leans over and kisses her on the lips. She clasps his head, holding his lips to hers. It is the first kiss of her life that arouses her.

Chapter XXVIII is the second narrative break of the novel. Chopin tells us that Edna cried a bit after Alcée left. She felt irresponsible, and she felt the reproaches of Léonce and Robert. However, she also felt that she understood the world a little better. She did not feel any shame or remorse, only regret that it was not the kiss of love that had inflamed her.

Analysis

In Chapter XXVII, Edna knows that by society's standards she is wicked because she is in love with another man and wants to leave her husband. Yet she doesn't feel wicked because, for the first time in her life, she is following her heart and being true to herself. We see here how Alcée is no different from Léonce or any other man. He tells Edna he can tell her about herself better than she can. He is already assuming a proprietary "I know best" air with her.

He also clearly doesn't understand what she is trying to do with her life; his only response to Mademoiselle Reisz's comment is that he heard she was demented. Mademoiselle Reisz is the only one who truly understands Edna and the only one who understands how difficult her journey is; even Edna doesn't quite get that yet. Mademoiselle Reisz knows how difficult it is to defy convention and rise above prejudice.

When Alcée kisses Edna, she feels aroused for the first time in her life.

In Chapter XXVIII, Edna is filled with emotion after being with Alcée. She knows that Léonce would feel betrayed because of all the material things he has provided her with. She thinks Robert would feel betrayed because she gave herself for less than true love. However, Edna now understands the difference between lust and love and does not feel ashamed of her lust. It is crucial that she does not feel shame or remorse; this is because she is responding to her true nature, one she has denied her whole life. She feels that anything she does now is acceptable. The only regret she has is that it was Alcée and not Robert who is her true love.

Study Questions

1. Why does Edna say she is a wicked woman?
2. Why does she think at the same time that she is not?
3. What is Alcée's response to Edna's question?
4. What is significant about Alcée's response?
5. What does Mademoiselle Reisz tell Edna about courage?
6. How does Edna feel after kissing Alcée?
7. What is the significance of the reproach Edna imagines from Robert?
8. What does Edna understand about life after being with Alcée?
9. What specifically does Edna not feel?
10. Why does Edna feel a pang of regret?

Answers

1. Edna knows she would be perceived as wicked because of her move toward independence and because of the sexual feelings she has.

2. She is following her true nature.
3. He says she shouldn't bother thinking about it because he can tell her what kind of woman she is.
4. He is acting just like any other man, presuming to know better than she does, not letting her be independent.
5. She says that Edna must have a lot of strength and courage if she is going to defy convention and prejudice.
6. It is the first kiss of her life that truly arouses her.
7. It is because she is giving herself for less than true love.
8. She realizes that there is a difference between lust and love.
9. She does not feel either shame or regret.
10. She wishes that it was love, rather than lust, that had opened her up.

Suggested Essay Topics

1. Why doesn't Edna feel shame or regret? In Chapter VI, Chopin talked about wisdom that is usually denied to women. What is Edna learning from being with Alcée, and why is that usually denied to women?
2. Describe the reactions that Léonce, Robert, Mademoiselle Reisz, and Adèle would have to Edna's actions.

Chapter XXIX (pages 84–86)

Summary

Without waiting for an answer from Léonce regarding her decision to move, Edna hastens her plans. There is no thought involved, she just moves. She takes only what is hers. Alcée arrives in the afternoon, walking in unannounced, and finds Edna on a stepladder taking a picture off the wall. He then helps out. She tells him the dinner party will be two days later with the very finest of everything; she is going to let Léonce pay for it. She says goodbye to Alcée, and he is dismayed that he can't see her again before the party.

Analysis

Edna hastens her preparations to move out after spending the night with Alcée. She realizes now more than ever her need for independence. Now that she's experienced such pleasure she wants to be able to continue, and she can't do that in the old house. In fact the old house now seems forbidden, as if she had desecrated an altar.

Edna is determined to be completely independent, and so she takes nothing that belongs to Léonce. Her independence is underscored by Alcée's reflection that she never looked more handsome. She is more masculine because she is freer.

Alcée continues to act in a proprietary manner. He walks in the house unannounced as if he lived there. Being such a womanizer, he probably expected Edna to be either tearful or ashamed. He has no idea who or what he's dealing with.

Edna's allowing Léonce to pay the bills for the party seems a bit out of character, but it's probably a final bit of revenge.

Study Questions

1. How does Edna go about her preparations to move?
2. What is causing Edna to be in such a rush?
3. What does Edna mean when she says the old house seems like a forbidden temple?
4. What does Edna take from the old house to the new?
5. How does Alcée enter the house?
6. How does Alcée expect to find Edna after their night together?
7. What is Edna doing when Alcée walks in the house?
8. How is Edna described when she is up on the stepladder?
9. What is significant about this description of Edna?
10. Why does Alcée call Edna's dinner a coup d'état?

Answers

1. She moves feverishly, with no deliberation before action.
2. Her night with Alcée increases her desire to be on her own.
3. It is someplace where she is an intruder and no longer has a right to be.
4. She takes only what belongs solely to her, not bought by Léonce.
5. He rings but then walks right in.
6. He expects her to be either angry or sentimental, not indifferent.
7. She is on a stepladder unhooking a picture from the wall.
8. She never appeared more handsome.
9. It can be taken to mean she never looked more masculine, in the sense of what she is doing rather than how she actually looks.
10. He means that it is her farewell dinner from Léonce's house, and she is letting Léonce pay the bills for it.

Suggested Essay Topics

1. What does it say about Edna that she is letting Léonce pay the bills for her dinner? Is this consistent with her character so far?
2. What is the significance of Alcée's walking in the house, unannounced?

Chapter XXX (pages 86–91)

Summary

Edna's dinner party and its guests are described in detail. There are nine guests, and Edna seats herself between Alcée and Mademoiselle Reisz. The table is set lavishly, with satin, lace, silver, gold, and crystal. There are fresh red and yellow roses on the table.

The conversation is lively and loud, and the food is abundant. Mrs. Highcamp, seated next to Victor Lebrun, spends the evening trying to capture his attention.

Edna is dressed in satin and is wearing a diamond tiara, a birthday present from Léonce which had arrived that morning. Edna is 29 years old. Seated at the head of the table, her bearing is regal. Yet she feels her old ennui creeping in, and seeing Robert's picture before her eyes, feels overwhelmed with helplessness.

Monsieur Ratignolle is the first to leave; Adèle was at home, anxious about her impending birth. Mademoiselle Reisz goes with him.

Mrs. Highcamp begins increasing her attention to Victor, draping him first with a garland of roses and then a white scarf. Victor, a bit drunk from the wine and the attention, agrees to sing. However, the song he chooses was the one his brother Robert had sung to Edna on the boat. Edna shouts out for him to stop. In the process, she spills a glass of wine on Alcée and Mrs. Highcamp. Victor, unfortunately, doesn't take her seriously at first, and Edna has to get up and cover his mouth with her hand. After this incident, everyone leaves except Alcée.

Analysis

Edna plans her farewell dinner party to be her moment of glory. She spares no expense with the food or the table setting. In fact, she looks like a queen sitting at the head of her table. By all accounts her party is a smashing success. The irony is that Edna becomes miserably unhappy during the meal, realizing that all she wants is Robert and nothing else matters.

Mrs. Highcamp's attempted seduction of Victor is important to Edna's decision to kill herself. Mrs. Highcamp is seen as pathetic, using her daughter as a pretext to seduce young men. Edna knows that if she stays married to Léonce for the sake of her children, she could end up like Mrs. Highcamp. That thought is horrifying and degrading to her.

Edna is so absorbed in her newfound sexuality that even as she forces Victor to stop singing because it reminds her of Robert, she still notices how good his lips feels on her hand.

Study Questions

1. Why is Adèle unable to attend Edna's dinner party?
2. Describe the splendor of the dinner table.
3. How does Edna appear, sitting at the head of the table?
4. Why is the occasion doubly special for Edna?
5. Despite all the glamour, how does Edna feel?
6. Why is Alcée's name on the letterhead of a law firm?
7. What does Mrs. Highcamp do to Victor, and what does she want?
8. What song does Victor sing at the table?
9. What is Edna's reaction?
10. What does Edna have to do to get Victor to stop singing?

Answers

1. She is close to giving birth and in a lot of pain.
2. The tablecloth is pale yellow satin under strips of lace. There are candles in brass candelabra, fresh roses, silver, gold, and crystal.
3. With her dress of satin and lace and her diamond tiara, she appears regal, in control, alone.
4. It is her twenty-ninth birthday.
5. She feels tired and hopeless, thinking about Robert with longing.
6. He finds it necessary to "assume the virtue of an occupation" to satisfy other people's inquiries.
7. She weaves a garland of roses and places it on his head, then drapes his shoulders with a white silk scarf. She is trying to seduce him.
8. He sings the song that Robert sang to Edna on the boat.
9. She cries out for him to stop and is so upset that she spills a glass of wine.
10. She walks behind him and puts her hand over his mouth.

Suggested Essay Topics

1. What does Mrs. Highcamp's behavior tell Edna about her choices in life? Knowing what you know about Edna so far, do you think she would want to stay married to Léonce and have affairs?
2. Why does Chopin take such great pains to describe the splendor of the party? Explain Edna's sadness.

Chapter XXXI (pages 91–93)

New Character:

Celestine: *the Pontelliers' servant*

Summary

After everyone leaves, Edna and Alcée lock up and leave for the new house. Celestine, the Pontelliers' servant, is moving in with Edna into the new house but will go back and clean up at the old house in the morning. Edna is quiet and seems disheartened.

When they arrive at the new house, it feels homey and hospitable; Edna had been working on it already. It is also filled with flowers that Alcée had sent over earlier.

Edna tells Alcée that she feels tired and miserable and that she just wants to rest. She puts her head down on the table, and Alcée begins stroking her hair, then moves to her shoulders. Finally, he sits down and kisses her. When she says she thought he was leaving, he replies that he will after he says good night. However, he does not leave until after they make love.

Analysis

Edna feels disheartened after her party, wanting nothing but to be alone (since Robert is not available). She is happy to go to her new house, which she has already made homey and hospitable. This is in direct contrast to the old house, which was telling her to go away.

Despite Edna's stated intention to be alone, Alcée's magnetic hands draw her in and she follows the desires of her body. It is as if she no longer cares, and for the moment, she is willing to settle for second best. Her desire to feel *something*, to experience whatever life has to offer, outweighs the emptiness she feels with Alcée.

Study Questions

1. Where does Edna go after her party?
2. How does Alcée act around Edna now?
3. What does Edna mean when Alcée offers her a spray of jessamine, and she says she doesn't want anything?
4. What does Edna notice as she and Alcée walk to the new house?
5. What is the surprise waiting for Edna at her new house?
6. How does the parlor in the new house look when they enter?
7. How does Alcée's touch on Edna's hair feel?
8. Why does Edna say the party was stupid?
9. What does Alcée notice when he touches Edna's shoulder?
10. How does the evening end for Edna and Alcée?

Answers

1. She goes over to her new house.
2. He acts like a husband.
3. All she wants is Robert, and nothing else is really important.
4. She notices the way his leg moves so close to her and how the black of his pants looks against the yellow of her gown.
5. Alcée has filled the house with fresh flowers.
6. It looks homey and hospitable.
7. It is magnetic, and it draws her in.

8. She now thinks it was stupid because it didn't make her happy like she thought it would.
9. Alcée notices that her body is responding sexually.
10. They spend the night together.

Suggested Essay Topics

1. Why does Edna sleep with Alcée when she's longing for Robert?
2. Explain the irony of the term "pigeon-house." What makes the new house seem so homey and hospitable, and why is that so important to Edna?

Chapter XXXII (pages 93–95)

Summary

Léonce, who is too late, sends word to Edna that he disapproves of her move, mainly because he is afraid that people will think their finances have taken a turn for the worse. He takes care of it in a businesslike manner, immediately planning reconstruction of the old house so that it will seem like they had no choice but to move.

Edna is very happy in her new home. She feels that although she may have descended the social scale, she has moved up on the spiritual scale and is able to see and understand things with her own eyes.

Edna goes to visit her children who are staying with Léonce's mother on the farm. She weeps with joy to see them and truly enjoys their company for the whole week. When she leaves, she carries the sound of their voices all the way home. However, once she gets home, she forgets it, because she is alone again.

Analysis

As always, Léonce's concerns are financial, not personal. His only thought over Edna's moving out is how it might affect his reputation and his business.

Edna enjoys her new home and feels as if she has grown spiritually. She is seeing the world with new eyes—with her own eyes—and she is thinking rather than blindly accepting. She is understanding things in a whole new way, gaining wisdom that most women never gain (see Chapter VI). Maybe she had to descend socially to do this because in her old social world it would not be possible. In her old social world, one had to conform to be accepted.

Because Edna is feeling spiritually fulfilled and independent, she feels loving toward her children and can't get enough of them. Continuing with the theme of fulfilling appetite, Edna feels "hungry" for her children. Of course as soon as she returns home, she forgets them again.

It becomes clear that, as she has been accused of before, Edna has not thought out her future. What will she do when it is time for Léonce and the children to return? She tells the children that "the fairies would fix it all right," but that is part of her fantasy. She thinks everything will work out if she just keeps on her present course. She does not yet realize the full implications and possible consequences of her actions.

Study Questions

1. What is Léonce's main concern with Edna's moving out of the house?
2. What specifically is Léonce not concerned about?
3. How does Léonce handle Edna's move?
4. How does Edna feel about her new home?
5. What does Edna's "spiritual awakening" feel like to her?
6. How does Edna feel when she goes to visit her children?
7. What does Edna give to her children?
8. How does Edna respond to the children's concerns about their place in the new house?
9. How does Edna feel when she leaves the children?
10. How does she feel when she returns home?

Answers

1. He is afraid people would think the Pontelliers' finances had taken a turn for the worse, and this could hurt him financially.
2. He is not concerned about scandal. It never occurs to him that Edna might have another man.
3. He takes care of it in a businesslike manner, hiring an architect to remodel his home so that it would look like Edna had no choice but to move out for a while. He also puts a notice in the paper to that effect.
4. She is very happy there and feels that although she may have descended on the social scale, she has clearly risen on the spiritual scale.
5. She begins to see things with her own eyes, and to have a deeper understanding of life.
6. She is so happy she weeps for joy. She feels hungry for them and is happy to listen to their stories.
7. She gives them all of herself, for the first time ever.
8. She tells them the fairies will fix everything all right.
9. Edna feels sad when she leaves the children and carries away with her the sound of their voices and the touch of their cheeks.
10. As soon as Edna is alone in her new house again, she forgets once more about her children.

Suggested Essay Topics

1. What is the significance of Edna's telling her children the fairies will fix everything all right? What does this say about Edna's plans for the future?
2. Why is it that to rise on the spiritual scale Edna needs to descend on the social scale? Give examples of both her social descent and her spiritual ascent.

Chapter XXXIII (pages 95–100)

Summary

One day, Edna sets out for Mademoiselle Reisz's to rest and talk about Robert. She had a talk with Adèle earlier in the day, and Adèle had noted that Edna seemed to act without reflection—like a little child. She worried what people would think about Alcée's visits. Then she made Edna promise that she would come when Adèle gives birth.

Edna is waiting in Mademoiselle Reisz's apartment for the lady to come home and begins to softly play the piano. There is a knock on the door, and Edna says to come in. It is Robert; he clasps her hand. Then Edna sits by the window, and Robert sits on the piano stool. He tells Edna he has been home for two days. She is very upset and wonders if he really loves her, as Mademoiselle Reisz had said. He stammers some excuse about why he hasn't been to see her.

Edna sees in Robert's eyes the same feelings that had always been there, but neither one say anything. He is surprised that Edna is not away with her husband or her children.

They leave together without waiting for Mademoiselle Reisz to return, and Edna asks him to stay for dinner. He tries to get out of it but ends up staying. At the house he sees a picture of Alcée and asks a lot of questions; he clearly disapproves of Edna spending time with him. Robert reports that he has been feeling like a lost soul; Edna echoes the feeling. Then they become silent and wait for Celestine to serve dinner.

Analysis

Adèle's pregnancy has been a theme throughout the novel, and it is no surprise that it will end up having a major impact on Edna. Here Edna promises Adèle that she will go to her at any hour of the day or night, and the reader should guess by now that something important will happen there.

Edna's and Robert's meeting takes place in Mademoiselle Reisz's apartment, the place where Edna found out Robert loved her and admitted that she loved him. However, the meeting is not as Edna fantasized it. Again she does not think about reality at this point, only about what she wants. She does not think at all about how Robert, an honorable Creole man, would feel about taking a married woman away from her husband.

Edna is glad that Robert did not know her in her old house because that was her fake self; she wants Robert to know her as she truly is, a woman free to love.

Robert has no sense of Edna's awakening, which is why he thinks she is mocking him when she mimics his answer. To his mind, she is not a free woman and therefore should not be having feelings for him. He still doesn't know that she loves him.

Study Questions

1. Why does Edna want to visit Mademoiselle Reisz?
2. What does Adèle make Edna promise before she leaves her?
3. What does Adèle warn Edna about?
4. Why is Edna caught off guard when Robert tells her he has been home for two days?
5. What reason does Robert give for coming home?
6. What does Edna see when she looks into Robert's eyes?
7. Why is Edna glad that Robert never knew her in her former home?
8. What does Robert mean when he said he's been "seeing the waves and the white beach of Grand Isle"?
9. Why does Edna mimic Robert's answer?
10. Why does Robert say that Edna is cruel?

Answers

1. She wants to rest and talk about Robert.
2. Adèle makes Edna promise that she would go to her when she goes into labor, no matter what time of the day or night.
3. She warns her that Alcée has a bad reputation and that people might start talking about the two of them.

4. Edna expected that Robert would seek her out immediately after returning home.
5. He was having trouble with the Mexicans, and he was not making the money he thought he would.
6. She sees that he still loves her.
7. Edna doesn't like the person she was when she lived with Léonce.
8. He means that he has been thinking about Edna.
9. She wants him to understand that she feels the same way about him.
10. He thinks she is mocking him, because she is married and not free to love him.

Suggested Essay Topics

1. Explain from Robert's point of view why he hadn't called on Edna since his return. Compare this with the time they spent together at Grand Isle and explain why he felt freer then.
2. How is Edna different in her new house than in the old one? Why would she not have wanted Robert to know her in the old house?

Chapter XXXIV (pages 100–103)

Summary

The dining room is small and intimate, but dinner makes them both more formal. They talk about what they have been doing since they last met. After dinner Robert goes out to get cigarette paper. Edna notices that his tobacco pouch is new, and Robert admits that a girl gave it to him. Edna asks him lots of jealous questions, but he says the woman wasn't important.

Robert says Edna can throw him out any time, but Edna reminds him of all the time they spent together in Grand Isle. Robert responds that he remembers everything from Grand Isle.

Then Alcée drops in, and Robert takes that as a cue to leave.

Edna tells Alcée to leave. Alcée does not want to leave but compiles with Edna' request. After Alcée leaves, Edna falls into a stupor thinking about the hours she has just spent with Robert. She feels that they had actually been closer when he was still in Mexico.

Analysis

Edna is desperately trying to win Robert over, and Robert is just as desperately trying to remain aloof, although he makes his feelings clear when he says, without looking at her, "I have forgotten nothing about Grand Isle." Still he leaves at the first opportunity, which is when Alcée arrives.

Edna wants to be alone to think about Robert so she sends Alcée away. Alcée has always been a womanizer so it is ironic when he says to Edna of his stated devotion, "I have said it before, but I don't think I ever came so near meaning it." Alcée feels no more for Edna than she does for him. It is physical, nothing more.

Edna falls into a stupor when they leave. Her stupors are contrasted throughout the novel with her feelings of intoxication. She feels intoxicated when she feels powerful, and she goes into a stupor when she feels hopeless or powerless. She feels powerless with Robert now because their reunion had not been all she had hoped for, and all she can do now is wait.

Study Questions

1. What happens when Robert and Edna sit down to eat dinner?
2. Why does Celestine spend time talking to Robert?
3. Why does Robert go out during dinner?
4. Why is Robert looking to leave when he says perhaps he shouldn't have come back?
5. What does Robert say in response to Edna's remembrance of all the time they spent together at Grand Isle?
6. Why does Edna pick up Robert's tobacco pouch?
7. How does Alcée's appearance affect the evening?
8. Why does Edna send Alcée away to mail a letter?

9. How does Edna feel after Alcée leaves?
10. How does Edna feel about Robert being home?

Answers

1. A degree of ceremony settles in during dinner, and they make small talk that has nothing to do with their feelings for each other.
2. Celestine knew Robert when he was a child, and besides, she is very interested in what is going on.
3. He goes out to get cigarette papers.
4. Robert is uncomfortable because of his feelings for Edna and feels safer when he is not with her.
5. He says that he has forgotten nothing about Grand Isle.
6. She picks up his tobacco pouch because it is new, and she is jealous of whomever gave it to him.
7. Robert leaves after Alcée arrives.
8. Edna wants to be alone with her thoughts of Robert.
9. She feels as if she is in a stupor.
10. She feels that in some ways she was closer to him when he was in Mexico.

Suggested Essay Topics

1. Why does Edna feel further away from Robert now that he is home?
2. Why does Edna send Alcée away? What is different this night than the night in Chapter XXXI?

Chapter XXXV (pages 103–105)

Summary

Edna wakes up filled with hope. She believes that Robert's love for her will surmount his reserve, whatever his reasons for it. She imagines him coming over that evening.

She receives letters from her children and from Léonce. Léonce writes that when he comes back they would take a trip abroad, as he had recently made a lot of money on Wall Street. She also receives a letter from Alcée saying good morning and assuring her of his devotion.

Edna writes back to the children and to Léonce. In Léonce's letter she is evasive, not on purpose, but because she had lost a sense of reality. She feels she has abandoned herself to Fate. She does not answer Alcée's letter.

Robert does not come that day, and Edna is very disappointed. Nor does he come either of the next two days. She would awake with hope and go to sleep despondent. However she does not seek him out; in fact she avoids places where he might be.

She goes out with Alcée one night, and they come back to Edna's to eat. It is late when he leaves. Since their relationship has become sexual, it has become a habit for him to spend time with her. That night she does not feel despondent when she goes to sleep, but neither does she wake up with any hope.

Analysis

Edna has completely lost sight of reality in the beginning of this chapter. She wakes up filled with hope and sees before her no denial; she still believes she will get everything she wants with no consequences.

She is also still being completely selfish. She doesn't care why Robert is being reserved. She is only interested in how she can break down that reserve.

After Robert does not come for a few days, Edna is willing to settle for Alcée and spends the night with him. That is when she gives up both despondency and hope, feeling nothing.

Study Questions

1. How does Edna feel when she wakes up?
2. How does she plan to melt Robert's reserve?
3. What does she daydream about?
4. From whom does Edna receive letters that morning?

5. How does Edna answer Léonce's letter?
6. What does Edna do with Alcée's letter?
7. How does Edna's next few days pass?
8. What does Edna do to try to see Robert?
9. Why does Edna enjoy the fastness of her ride with Alcée?
10. How do Edna's feelings change after not seeing Robert for a few days?

Answers

1. The morning is filled with sunlight and hope, and she imagines having everything she wants come true.
2. She believes that her passion will win him over.
3. She imagines Robert's day, from his walk to work, to the evening when he would come to see her.
4. She receives letters from Raoul, Léonce, and Alcée.
5. She answers it evasively because she is living in her fantasy world now and feels she is being driven along by Fate. Therefore she can't answer any of Léonce's questions about the future.
6. She doesn't respond to Alcée's letter.
7. She wakes up hopeful about seeing Robert and goes to sleep despondent over not having seen him.
8. She does nothing and in fact avoids places where she might run into him accidentally.
9. It is important to Edna to feel something and that feeling of recklessness would be a good temporary substitute for what she wants to feel.
10. She no longer feels despondency or hope.

Suggested Essay Topics

1. How do we know Edna is no longer living in the real world? Give examples from earlier in the book that show her lack of understanding or thought about reality.

2. Why have both despondency and hope left Edna after not seeing Robert?

Chapter XXXVI (pages 105–109)

Summary

When Edna is out walking, she often stops in a small quiet garden in the suburbs, where the proprietress sells and serves excellent food. It is not a place that is known to many people, and she never expects to see anyone she knows.

One afternoon, when she is eating dinner there, Robert walks in; he is uneasy and embarrassed when he sees Edna. Edna had intended to be reserved if she saw Robert but her reserve melts when she sees him. She asks him why he is staying away from her. Robert becomes almost angry and begs her to leave him alone.

Edna tells him he is selfish, not caring how she feels. Robert replies that she is being cruel, trying to force him into a disclosure that will result in nothing for him. They chat a bit about impersonal things; Robert tells Edna the end of the book she is reading so she won't have to finish it.

When they are finished, Robert walks Edna home. She goes into her room to wash up, and when she comes back to the living room, Robert is leaning back in a chair as if in a reverie. She leans over and kisses him, then moves away. Robert follows her and takes her in his arms. She touches his face with love and tenderness, and they kiss again.

Robert finally admits that he loves her. He says he has been fighting it because she was not free, but he had been dreaming of marrying her and that Léonce would set her free. Edna kisses him again and tells him he is being silly. She tells him she is not a possession of Léonce's and that he could not set her free if he wanted to. She makes it clear that she gives herself as she chooses.

Robert turns white; he does not understand. Just then Adèle's servant comes to the door to say that Adèle is ready to have her baby and wants Edna to come. Robert kisses Edna good-bye with more passion than before. Edna tells him she loves him, and they can be together now. She asks him to wait for her until she returns from Adèle's. Robert pleads with her not to go, but she leaves, promising to be back soon.

Analysis

Again Edna refuses to let Robert be. She presses until she gets a response. She tells Robert that he is being selfish, without thinking for a minute about how selfish she is being or how uncaring.

Edna is determined that her passion will win Robert over, and she is right at first. When she kisses him, he loses his senses and he kisses her back. Chopin lets us know that this is very different from the way she kisses Alcée. When she touches his face and presses his cheek against hers, "the action was full of love and tenderness." There's no question that Edna truly loves Robert; she has just blinded herself to the consequences of that love.

Robert finally admits that he loves her, but that he held back because she was not free to marry him, although he had dreamed of Léonce setting her free. Edna laughs at this because she has already set herself free. Robert, however, doesn't understand. He is a traditional Creole man and has no more understanding of Edna than Léonce or Alcée.

Robert begs Edna not to go to Adèle's because he knows that without her there he will come to his senses and have to do the honorable thing. However, Edna, self-absorbed as ever, doesn't understand Robert any more than he understands her. She believes if they love each other, everything else will work out. As we have seen already, Edna lacks forethought. She prefers to live in her fantasy world.

Study Questions

1. Why does Robert call Edna "Mrs. Pontellier"?
2. Why is Edna being selfish when she calls Robert selfish?
3. Why is walking so important to Edna?
4. In what way does Robert show himself to be just like Léonce and Alcée?
5. What makes Robert finally tell Edna that he loves her?
6. Why was Robert fighting against his feelings?

7. What does Edna tell Robert about the state of her marriage?
8. Why does Robert turn white when he hears Edna's statement?
9. Why does Robert plead with Edna not to go to Adèle's?
10. How do we know that Edna is living in her fantasy world?

Answers

1. He is trying to keep some distance between them.
2. All Edna thinks about anymore is her own pleasure and her own desires; she never stops to think of the turmoil Robert must feel being in love with a married woman.
3. Walking gives Edna a sense of independence and allows her to explore parts of life she would not ordinarily see.
4. Robert tells Edna the end of the book she is reading so she won't have to bother herself with finishing it; it's a very paternalistic attitude.
5. Edna kisses him and then moves away, and Robert follows her, takes her in his arms, and kisses her again. Then he finally has to tell her the truth.
6. Robert wanted Edna to be his wife, but he knew that she was not free and so he decided he better stay away.
7. She tells him that she is no longer one of Léonce's possessions and that she gives herself where she chooses. She says that she would laugh if Léonce offered to give her to Robert.
8. Robert is a traditional Creole man, and he doesn't understand Edna's attitude. If he did, he would disapprove.
9. Robert doesn't want the moment to end, because he knows that if he has time alone to come to his senses, he will have to do the honorable thing and leave.
10. Edna tells Robert that as long as they love each other nothing else is of consequence. She still doesn't understand that there would be severe consequences to their union.

Suggested Essay Topics

1. How does Robert's attitude doom Edna's plans? Knowing what you know about Robert, would he allow Edna the independence she craves?
2. What would be the likely consequences if Edna decided to openly love Robert?

Chapter XXXVII (pages 109–111)

Summary

Edna arrives at the Ratignolles and finds Adèle on a sofa in the salon, clearly in pain. She is berating Dr. Mandelet to her servant for being late. She is getting a little hysterical.

Finally Dr. Mandelet arrives, and Adèle goes into her room. Edna stays with her, but she feels uneasy. She is recalling her own experiences with a feeling of dread. She begins to wish she had not come, but she stays. Although she is in agony, she stays to witness the birth that she considers a torture.

She is stunned and speechless when she says goodbye to Adèle later. Adèle is exhausted but whispers to Edna to think of her children.

Analysis

Adèle is in obvious pain; her beautiful face is drawn and pinched, and her eyes are haggard and unnatural. We are clearly not supposed to look on this as a pleasant experience.

Edna begins to feel uneasy and afraid. There is a part of her that knows this childbirth will have some major impact on her. She doesn't remember much about her own childbirths because she was a different woman then. She remembers the stupor, which we know means that she felt hopeless and powerless when she gave birth.

Edna was in agony watching what she considered to be a scene of torture; she has deep resentment against Mother Nature for forcing women to bear children.

The last words Adèle says to Edna are a plea to think of her children. Although she didn't know it, this is what Edna had been dreading. She couldn't witness a childbirth without thinking of her own children, whom she had been trying very hard to forget.

Study Questions

1. What is Monsieur Ratignolle doing when Edna enters the drugstore?
2. How are the pains of childbirth first described as Edna sees Adèle?
3. Why isn't Dr. Mandelet upset at Adèle's "upraidings"?
4. What is the vague dread Edna began to feel?
5. Why do Edna's childbirths seem unreal and far away?
6. How would Edna explain the need for chloroform?
7. Why doesn't Edna leave when she wants to?
8. Why does Edna revolt against nature?
9. What are Adèle's final words to Edna?
10. Does Edna think of her children that night?

Answers

1. He is mixing a painkiller for Adèle.
2. Adèle's face is drawn and pinched, and her eyes are haggard and unnatural.
3. Dr. Mandelet is used to women being hysterical right before they give birth.
4. Possibly, it was a foreshadowing of how this childbirth would affect her life.
5. Her children were born to her in her old life when she was a different woman; the woman she is today would not have children.
6. It is necessary to deaden both the physical and emotional pain of such a traumatic experience.
7. Edna is loyal to Adèle.

8. Nature forced women to become mothers, whether they were emotionally equipped or not.
9. She pleads with her to think of the children.
10. No. She decides to postpone thinking about them until the following day.

Suggested Essay Topics

1. How would Edna and Adèle differently describe childbirth?
2. Why is Adèle so worried about Edna's children? What has she seen, heard or felt that would cause her to question Edna's commitment to her children?

Chapter XXXVIII (pages 111–113)

Summary

When Edna gets outside, she still feels dazed. Dr. Mandelet offers her a ride home, but she says she wants to walk. Dr. Mandelet decides to walk her home. He tells her that she shouldn't have been with Adèle.

Edna responds that Adèle was right, that she has to think of the children some time, preferably sooner than later. She tells Dr. Mandelet, in response to his question, that she will not be going abroad with Léonce when he returns. She tells him she just wants to be left alone and that nobody has the right to force her to do things, except children, maybe.

Dr. Mandelet seems to understand her. He says that youth is given to illusions, the illusions being the way to trap women into motherhood no matter what the consequences.

Edna agrees with Dr. Mandelet. She says her life had been a dream, but now she has awakened. She hints that she doesn't like what she found but thinks it is still probably better to wake up than to live with illusion all her life.

Dr. Mandelet offers his help if Edna feels like confiding in him, but she declines. She says the only thing she wants is her own way, which she realizes could cause pain to others. She also says she doesn't want to hurt her children.

When Edna returns home, she sits outside for a while, remembering her scene with Robert before she was called away. She acknowledges that tomorrow she will have to think of the children, but for tonight she just wants to be with Robert.

When Edna goes inside, Robert is not there. He left a note, saying he left because he loved her. Edna grows faint and lays down on the sofa. She remains there, not sleeping, all night.

Analysis

Edna is stung by Adèle's words, and, against her will, she finally begins to think about the children. She had talked herself into believing that nobody, including her children, should have a claim on her, but now she's questioning that with regard to her children.

Dr. Mandelet seems to have some understanding of Edna's problem. He acknowledges that Nature secures mothers by allowing young girls to be swayed by illusion. He also acknowledges that not every woman is cut out for motherhood, or marriage, but that there is no escape once it has begun.

Edna agrees that her life was based on illusion before, and she says that even though she doesn't like reality, especially the fact that her children have to be considered, it's still better to know the truth than to live with illusion. Edna has awakened not to freedom but to limitation. She admits her selfishness, saying that she wants her own way and doesn't care who gets hurt—except that she doesn't want to hurt her children. This, as we know, is her central dilemma. How can she have Robert without hurting her children?

As upset as she is, all thoughts of the children leave Edna when she thinks about Robert waiting for her at her house. She is ready to put off thinking about them for one more day.

When Edna returns, Robert is gone. He cannot live the "free" life that Edna wants. He cannot live in sin or with scandal. Robert is an honorable Creole man and wants a traditional marriage.

Edna turned her "affair" with Robert into a fairy tale (see, for example, Chapter XIII). However in true fairy tales, the woman is awakened and worthy of love because she is pure, for example, Snow White, Cinderella, Rapunzel. In this case, Edna is not pure and is not worthy of Robert's love.

Study Questions

1. Why doesn't Edna want to go in Dr. Mandelet's car?
2. How do we know Edna is thinking about Robert?
3. Why are Edna's thoughts racing ahead of her?
4. Why does Dr. Mandelet think it was cruel of Adèle to have had Edna there?
5. Why is Edna so confused?
6. How do we know that Dr. Mandelet has some understanding of Edna's problem?
7. How does Edna feel about her awakening?
8. How does Edna state the crux of her dilemma?
9. What happens when Edna begins to think about Robert again?
10. Why does Robert leave?

Answers

1. She wants to be alone with her thoughts.
2. The language is romantic: "the air was mild and caressing, but cool with the breath of spring and the night."
3. Edna is finally beginning to think about her children.
4. Dr. Mandelet believes that Edna is impressionable and not very stable, and he worries how she will be affected by what she saw and heard.
5. Edna had thought that even her children shouldn't affect what she wanted to do, but now she's beginning to wonder about that.
6. Dr. Mandelet acknowledges that not every woman is meant to be a mother.
7. Edna believes that even though she doesn't like what she discovered about life, it is still better to know the truth than to be blinded by illusion.

8. Edna says that all she wants is her own way, even if she has to hurt some people, but she doesn't want to hurt her children.
9. She pushes the children out of her mind again and says she will think about them tomorrow.
10. Robert is an honorable man and cannot live the kind of life that Edna is suggesting; he wants a traditional marriage.

Suggested Essay Questions

1. How does Nature dupe women into becoming mothers?
2. Describe the central conflict in Edna's life, and how it would be different if it were the 1990s instead of the 1890s.

Chapter XXXIX (pages 113–116)

Summary

Back in Grand Isle, Victor is working and Mariequita is watching him. He is talking about the dinner at Edna's exaggerating every detail. Mariequita thinks he is in love with Edna, and she becomes jealous and sullen but then lets Victor reassure her.

To their surprise Edna appears before them, looking tired from her trip. She tells them she is just here for a rest and that any room will do. Then she asks what time dinner would be served.

Edna tells them her intention to go to the beach and take a swim. They warn her that the water is too cold, but she says she would dip her toes at least.

Edna walks down to the beach without thinking about anything in particular. She had thought all night, long after Robert left. She acknowledges that after Alcée she would find another lover, and she understood how this would affect Raoul and Etienne. She also understood clearly what she meant the day she told Adèle she would never sacrifice herself for her children.

Edna became filled with despondence, realizing there was nothing and nobody she wanted except for Robert. She also realized that one day even that thought would fade, and she would be totally alone. Her children appeared before her like antagonists who were trying to enslave her, but she knew how to elude them.

All these things Edna thought about during her night on the couch. She isn't thinking of anything on her way to the beach. The voice of the sea is, as always, seductive. She sees a bird with a broken wing falling to the water.

Edna puts on her bathing suit but then takes it off, standing naked by the sea, feeling like a newborn creature. She walks into the water, into its sensuous touch. She keeps going, growing more tired. She thinks of Léonce and the children and how they thought they could possess her. She thinks that Mademoiselle Reisz would sneer, saying she is not a true artist because she does not possess a courageous soul.

Edna knows that Robert did not, and would not, understand her. She is far out now and feels that old moment of terror but it passes. She hears her father and sister's voices, and she hears the clanging spurs of the cavalry officer she had been infatuated with; finally she hears the hum of bees and smells the musty odor of pinks.

Analysis

This chapter opens with Victor exaggerating Edna's dinner party and her charms to the extent that Mariequita thinks of her as the "grand dame" of New Orleans. This is contrasted with the tired, defeated Edna who shows up at Grand Isle.

Critics debate over whether Edna's suicide was an act of passive defeat, an act of supreme courage, an acknowledgment that a woman seeking independence and selfhood has no viable alternatives in that society, or an acknowledgment that she doesn't have the psychological resources to resist the life society wants to foster on her. This is up to the reader to decide for him or herself.

Edna wasn't thinking on her way down to the beach because she was probably already in a hopeless stupor. She had been up all night thinking about what her life would be like if she stayed married for her children. She could have one affair after another, but she understood the effect that would have upon her children. She could end up married and alone, right back where she started. She refuses to give up what she had worked so hard for—her passion and independence.

If she didn't have children, she could just leave Léonce and do as she pleased. She knew there was no way to escape the "soul's slavery" her children put her into, except one.

Even if Edna were to leave Léonce, though, there is no other man out there who is any better. Both Alcée and Robert deny her independence as much as Léonce does. This contributes to Edna's feeling that she has no choice but to kill herself.

As Edna reaches the shore, she sees a bird with a broken wing heading back down to the water. This broken bird symbolizes her defeat. She has been broken by society and does not have the courage to fight anymore. And the seductive sea, as it has throughout the book, is calling her, offering rebirth and sensual pleasure. It is still the symbol of romantic possibility.

When Edna first thought about solitude and pictured the naked man on the beach, it was a sad picture. However, Edna feels "delicious" standing alone and naked by the sea. She is defeated, but there is some sense of power and freedom in the choice she is making. Nobody owns her anymore.

Of course it is questionable whether suicide is ever a true choice or just a passive giving up. Again it is up to the reader to decide.

Study Questions

1. What are Victor and Mariequita talking about when Edna shows up at Grand Isle?
2. Why, according to Mariequita, would it have been easy for her to run off with somebody's husband?
3. Why do Victor and Mariequita think Edna is an apparition when she first appears?
4. How does Edna seem when she first arrives?
5. Why isn't Edna thinking about anything as she walks down to the beach?
6. What has Edna concluded about her life?

7. What way has Edna devised to elude the slavery her children have planned for her?
8. What is the symbolism of the bird?
9. Why does Edna take her clothes off?
10. Why does Edna's old terror sink as quickly as it rises?

Answers

1. Victor is telling Mariequita, in exaggerated detail, about Edna's dinner party.
2. According to Mariequita it is the fashion to be in love with married people.
3. It is the middle of March, and there are never visitors to the island at that time.
4. She seems tired and indifferent. She doesn't care what room she has, all she asks for is some food.
5. Edna has been up all night thinking about her situation and deciding what to do.
6. Edna realizes that if she stayed married, she would continue to have affairs. She doesn't care about the scandal to herself or Léonce, but she realizes the effect it would have on her children and that she wouldn't be able to hurt them. She also realizes that she cannot live that way.
7. The only way Edna could avoid her fate was to kill herself.
8. The bird shows Edna's defeat; her wings are not strong enough to continue to fight, and the children are the reason.
9. She wants to feel completely free before she kills herself.
10. Edna is no longer afraid to die.

Suggested Essay Topics

1. Speaking as Edna, describe why you felt you had no choice but to kill yourself.
2. Was Edna's suicide an act of courage or defeat?

SECTION THREE

Bibliography

Other Sources:

Dyer, Joyce. *The Awakening—A Novel of Beginnings*. New York: Twayne Publishers, 1993.

Koloski, Bernard, ed. *Approaches to Teaching Chopin's The Awakening*. New York: Modern Language Association of America, 1988.

Martin, Wendy, ed. *New Essays on The Awakening*. Cambridge: Cambridge University Press, 1988.

Skaggs, Peggy. *Kate Chopin*. Boston: Twayne Publishers, 1985.

Toth, Emily. *Kate Chopin*. New York: William Morrow & Co., Inc., 1990.

DOVER · THRIFT · EDITIONS

FICTION

ADVENTURES OF HUCKLEBERRY FINN, Mark Twain. (0-486-28061-6)

THE AWAKENING, Kate Chopin. (0-486-27786-0)

A CHRISTMAS CAROL, Charles Dickens. (0-486-26865-9)

FRANKENSTEIN, Mary Shelley. (0-486-28211-2)

HEART OF DARKNESS, Joseph Conrad. (0-486-26464-5)

PRIDE AND PREJUDICE, Jane Austen. (0-486-28473-5)

THE SCARLET LETTER, Nathaniel Hawthorne. (0-486-28048-9)

THE ADVENTURES OF TOM SAWYER, Mark Twain. (0-486-40077-8)

ALICE'S ADVENTURES IN WONDERLAND, Lewis Carroll. (0-486-27543-4)

THE CALL OF THE WILD, Jack London. (0-486-26472-6)

CRIME AND PUNISHMENT, Fyodor Dostoyevsky. Translated by Constance Garnett. (0-486-41587-2)

DRACULA, Bram Stoker. (0-486-41109-5)

ETHAN FROME, Edith Wharton. (0-486-26690-7)

FLATLAND, Edwin A. Abbott. (0-486-27263-X)

GREAT AMERICAN SHORT STORIES, Edited by Paul Negri. (0-486-42119-8)

GREAT EXPECTATIONS, Charles Dickens. (0-486-41586-4)

JANE EYRE, Charlotte Brontë. (0-486-42449-9)

THE JUNGLE, Upton Sinclair. (0-486-41923-1)

THE METAMORPHOSIS AND OTHER STORIES, Franz Kafka. (0-486-29030-1)

THE ODYSSEY, Homer. (0-486-40654-7)

THE PICTURE OF DORIAN GRAY, Oscar Wilde. (0-486-27807-7)

SIDDHARTHA, Hermann Hesse. (0-486-40653-9)

THE STRANGE CASE OF DR. JEKYLL AND MR. HYDE, Robert Louis Stevenson. (0-486-26688-5)

A TALE OF TWO CITIES, Charles Dickens. (0-486-40651-2)

WUTHERING HEIGHTS, Emily Brontë. (0-486-29256-8)

ANNA KARENINA, Leo Tolstoy. Translated by Louise and Aylmer Maude. (0-486-43796-5)

AROUND THE WORLD IN EIGHTY DAYS, Jules Verne. (0-486-41111-7)

THE BROTHERS KARAMAZOV, Fyodor Dostoyevsky. Translated by Constance Garnett. (0-486-43791-4)

CANDIDE, Voltaire. Edited by Francois-Marie Arouet. (0-486-26689-3)

DOVER · THRIFT · EDITIONS

FICTION

DAISY MILLER, Henry James. (0-486-28773-4)

DAVID COPPERFIELD, Charles Dickens. (0-486-43665-9)

DUBLINERS, James Joyce. (0-486-26870-5)

EMMA, Jane Austen. (0-486-40648-2)

THE GIFT OF THE MAGI AND OTHER SHORT STORIES, O. Henry. (0-486-27061-0)

THE GOLD-BUG AND OTHER TALES, Edgar Allan Poe. (0-486-26875-6)

GREAT SHORT SHORT STORIES, Edited by Paul Negri. (0-486-44098-2)

GULLIVER'S TRAVELS, Jonathan Swift. (0-486-29273-8)

HARD TIMES, Charles Dickens. (0-486-41920-7)

THE HOUND OF THE BASKERVILLES, Arthur Conan Doyle. (0-486-28214-7)

THE ILIAD, Homer. (0-486-40883-3)

MOBY-DICK, Herman Melville. (0-486-43215-7)

MY ÁNTONIA, Willa Cather. (0-486-28240-6)

NORTHANGER ABBEY, Jane Austen. (0-486-41412-4)

NOT WITHOUT LAUGHTER, Langston Hughes. (0-486-45448-7)

OLIVER TWIST, Charles Dickens. (0-486-42453-7)

PERSUASION, Jane Austen. (0-486-29555-9)

THE PHANTOM OF THE OPERA, Gaston Leroux. (0-486-43458-3)

A PORTRAIT OF THE ARTIST AS A YOUNG MAN, James Joyce. (0-486-28050-0)

PUDD'NHEAD WILSON, Mark Twain. (0-486-40885-X)

THE RED BADGE OF COURAGE, Stephen Crane. (0-486-26465-3)

THE SCARLET PIMPERNEL, Baroness Orczy. (0-486-42122-8)

SENSE AND SENSIBILITY, Jane Austen. (0-486-29049-2)

SILAS MARNER, George Eliot. (0-486-29246-0)

TESS OF THE D'URBERVILLES, Thomas Hardy. (0-486-41589-9)

THE TIME MACHINE, H. G. Wells. (0-486-28472-7)

TREASURE ISLAND, Robert Louis Stevenson. (0-486-27559-0)

THE TURN OF THE SCREW, Henry James. (0-486-26684-2)

UNCLE TOM'S CABIN, Harriet Beecher Stowe. (0-486-44028-1)

THE WAR OF THE WORLDS, H. G. Wells. (0-486-29506-0)

THE WORLD'S GREATEST SHORT STORIES, Edited by James Daley. (0-486-44716-2)

THE AGE OF INNOCENCE, Edith Wharton. (0-486-29803-5)

DOVER · THRIFT · EDITIONS

FICTION

AGNES GREY, Anne Brontë. (0-486-45121-6)

AT FAULT, Kate Chopin. (0-486-46133-5)

THE AUTOBIOGRAPHY OF AN EX-COLORED MAN, James Weldon Johnson. (0-486-28512-X)

BARTLEBY AND BENITO CERENO, Herman Melville. (0-486-26473-4)

BEOWULF, Translated by R. K. Gordon. (0-486-27264-8)

CIVIL WAR STORIES, Ambrose Bierce. (0-486-28038-1)

A CONNECTICUT YANKEE IN KING ARTHUR'S COURT, Mark Twain. (0-486-41591-0)

THE DEERSLAYER, James Fenimore Cooper. (0-486-46136-X)

DEMIAN, Hermann Hesse. (0-486-41413-2)

FAR FROM THE MADDING CROWD, Thomas Hardy. (0-486-45684-6)

FAVORITE FATHER BROWN STORIES, G. K. Chesterton. (0-486-27545-0)

GREAT HORROR STORIES, Edited by John Grafton. Introduction by Mike Ashley. (0-486-46143-2)

GREAT RUSSIAN SHORT STORIES, Edited by Paul Negri. (0-486-42992-X)

GREAT SHORT STORIES BY AMERICAN WOMEN, Edited by Candace Ward. (0-486-28776-9)

GRIMM'S FAIRY TALES, Jacob and Wilhelm Grimm. (0-486-45656-0)

HUMOROUS STORIES AND SKETCHES, Mark Twain. (0-486-29279-7)

THE HUNCHBACK OF NOTRE DAME, Victor Hugo. Translated by A. L. Alger. (0-486-45242-5)

THE INVISIBLE MAN, H. G. Wells. (0-486-27071-8)

THE ISLAND OF DR. MOREAU, H. G. Wells. (0-486-29027-1)

A JOURNAL OF THE PLAGUE YEAR, Daniel Defoe. (0-486-41919-3)

JOURNEY TO THE CENTER OF THE EARTH, Jules Verne. (0-486-44088-5)

KIM, Rudyard Kipling. (0-486-44508-9)

THE LAST OF THE MOHICANS, James Fenimore Cooper. (0-486-42678-5)

THE LEGEND OF SLEEPY HOLLOW AND OTHER STORIES, Washington Irving. (0-486-46658-2)

LILACS AND OTHER STORIES, Kate Chopin. (0-486-44095-8)

MANSFIELD PARK, Jane Austen. (0-486-41585-6)

THE MAYOR OF CASTERBRIDGE, Thomas Hardy. (0-486-43749-3)

THE MYSTERIOUS STRANGER AND OTHER STORIES, Mark Twain. (0-486-27069-6)

NOTES FROM THE UNDERGROUND, Fyodor Dostoyevsky. (0-486-27053-X)

DOVER · THRIFT · EDITIONS

FICTION

O PIONEERS!, Willa Cather. (0-486-27785-2)

AN OCCURRENCE AT OWL CREEK BRIDGE AND OTHER STORIES, Ambrose Bierce. (0-486-46657-4)

THE OLD CURIOSITY SHOP, Charles Dickens. (0-486-42679-3)

THE OPEN BOAT AND OTHER STORIES, Stephen Crane. (0-486-27547-7)

ROBINSON CRUSOE, Daniel Defoe. (0-486-40427-7)

THIS SIDE OF PARADISE, F. Scott Fitzgerald. (0-486-28999-0)

THE THREE MUSKETEERS, Alexandre Dumas. (0-486-45681-1)

TWENTY THOUSAND LEAGUES UNDER THE SEA, Jules Verne. (0-486-44849-5)

WHITE FANG, Jack London. (0-486-26968-X)

WHITE NIGHTS AND OTHER STORIES, Fyodor Dostoyevsky. (0-486-46948-4)

NONFICTION

GREAT SPEECHES, Abraham Lincoln. (0-486-26872-1)

WISDOM OF THE BUDDHA, Edited by F. Max Müller. (0-486-41120-6)

NARRATIVE OF SOJOURNER TRUTH, Sojourner Truth. (0-486-29899-X)

THE TRIAL AND DEATH OF SOCRATES, Plato. (0-486-27066-1)

WIT AND WISDOM OF THE AMERICAN PRESIDENTS, Edited by Joslyn Pine. (0-486-41427-2)

GREAT SPEECHES BY AFRICAN AMERICANS, Edited by James Daley. (0-486-44761-8)

INTERIOR CASTLE, St. Teresa of Avila. Edited and Translated by E. Allison Peers. (0-486-46145-9)

GREAT SPEECHES BY AMERICAN WOMEN, Edited by James Daley. (0-486-46141-6)

ON LIBERTY, John Stuart Mill. (0-486-42130-9)

MEDITATIONS, Marcus Aurelius. (0-486-29823-X)

THE SOULS OF BLACK FOLK, W.E.B. DuBois. (0-486-28041-1)

GREAT SPEECHES BY NATIVE AMERICANS, Edited by Bob Blaisdell. (0-486-41122-2)

WIT AND WISDOM FROM POOR RICHARD'S ALMANACK, Benjamin Franklin. (0-486-40891-4)

THE AUTOBIOGRAPHY OF BENJAMIN FRANKLIN, Benjamin Franklin. (0-486-29073-5)

OSCAR WILDE'S WIT AND WISDOM, Oscar Wilde. (0-486-40146-4)

THE WIT AND WISDOM OF ABRAHAM LINCOLN, Abraham Lincoln. Edited by Bob Blaisdell. (0-486-44097-4)

DOVER · THRIFT · EDITIONS

NONFICTION

ON THE ORIGIN OF SPECIES, Charles Darwin. (0-486-45006-6)

SIX GREAT DIALOGUES, Plato. Translated by Benjamin Jowett. (0-486-45465-7)

NATURE AND OTHER ESSAYS, Ralph Waldo Emerson. (0-486-46947-6)

THE COMMUNIST MANIFESTO AND OTHER REVOLUTIONARY WRITINGS, Edited by Bob Blaisdell. (0-486-42465-0)

THE CONFESSIONS OF ST. AUGUSTINE, St. Augustine. (0-486-42466-9)

THE WIT AND WISDOM OF MARK TWAIN, Mark Twain. (0-486-40664-4)

LIFE ON THE MISSISSIPPI, Mark Twain. (0-486-41426-4)

BEYOND GOOD AND EVIL, Friedrich Nietzsche. (0-486-29868-X)

CIVIL DISOBEDIENCE AND OTHER ESSAYS, Henry David Thoreau. (0-486-27563-9)

A MODEST PROPOSAL AND OTHER SATIRICAL WORKS, Jonathan Swift. (0-486-28759-9)

UTOPIA, Sir Thomas More. (0-486-29583-4)

GREAT SPEECHES, Franklin Delano Roosevelt. (0-486-40894-9)

WALDEN; OR, LIFE IN THE WOODS, Henry David Thoreau. (0-486-28495-6)

UP FROM SLAVERY, Booker T. Washington. (0-486-28738-6)

DARK NIGHT OF THE SOUL, St. John of the Cross. (0-486-42693-9)

GREEK AND ROMAN LIVES, Plutarch. Translated by John Dryden. Revised and Edited by Arthur Hugh Clough. (0-486-44576-3)

WOMEN'S WIT AND WISDOM, Edited by Susan L. Rattiner. (0-486-41123-0)

MUSIC, Edited by Herb Galewitz. (0-486-41596-1)

INCIDENTS IN THE LIFE OF A SLAVE GIRL, Harriet Jacobs. (0-486-41931-2)

THE LIFE OF OLAUDAH EQUIANO, Olaudah Equiano. (0-486-40661-X)

THE DECLARATION OF INDEPENDENCE AND OTHER GREAT DOCUMENTS OF AMERICAN HISTORY, Edited by John Grafton. (0-486-41124-9)

THE PRINCE, Niccolò Machiavelli. (0-486-27274-5)

WOMAN IN THE NINETEENTH CENTURY, Margaret Fuller. (0-486-40662-8)

SELF-RELIANCE AND OTHER ESSAYS, Ralph Waldo Emerson. (0-486-27790-9)

COMMON SENSE, Thomas Paine. (0-486-29602-4)

THE REPUBLIC, Plato. (0-486-41121-4)

POETICS, Aristotle. (0-486-29577-X)

THE DEVIL'S DICTIONARY, Ambrose Bierce. (0-486-27542-6)

NARRATIVE OF THE LIFE OF FREDERICK DOUGLASS, Frederick Douglass. (0-486-28499-9)

DOVER · THRIFT · EDITIONS

NONFICTION

GREAT ENGLISH ESSAYS, Edited by Bob Blaisdell. (0-486-44082-6)

THE KORAN, Translated by J. M. Rodwell. (0-486-44569-0)

28 GREAT INAUGURAL ADDRESSES, Edited by John Grafton and James Daley. (0-486-44621-2)

WHEN I WAS A SLAVE, Edited by Norman R. Yetman. (0-486-42070-1)

THE IMITATION OF CHRIST, Thomas à Kempis. Translated by Aloysius Croft and Harold Bolton. (0-486-43185-1)

PLAYS

ANTIGONE, Sophocles. (0-486-27804-2)

AS YOU LIKE IT, William Shakespeare. (0-486-40432-3)

CYRANO DE BERGERAC, Edmond Rostand. (0-486-41119-2)

A DOLL'S HOUSE, Henrik Ibsen. (0-486-27062-9)

DR. FAUSTUS, Christopher Marlowe. (0-486-28208-2)

HAMLET, William Shakespeare. (0-486-27278-8)

HENRY V, William Shakespeare. (0-486-42887-7)

THE IMPORTANCE OF BEING EARNEST, Oscar Wilde. (0-486-26478-5)

JULIUS CAESAR, William Shakespeare. (0-486-26876-4)

KING LEAR, William Shakespeare. (0-486-28058-6)

MACBETH, William Shakespeare. (0-486-27802-6)

MEDEA, Euripides. (0-486-27548-5)

THE MERCHANT OF VENICE, William Shakespeare. (0-486-28492-1)

A MIDSUMMER NIGHT'S DREAM, William Shakespeare. (0-486-27067-X)

MUCH ADO ABOUT NOTHING, William Shakespeare. (0-486-28272-4)

OEDIPUS REX, Sophocles. (0-486-26877-2)

OTHELLO, William Shakespeare. (0-486-29097-2)

PYGMALION, George Bernard Shaw. (0-486-28222-8)

ROMEO AND JULIET, William Shakespeare. (0-486-27557-4)

THE TAMING OF THE SHREW, William Shakespeare. (0-486-29765-9)

THE TEMPEST, William Shakespeare. (0-486-40658-X)

TWELFTH NIGHT; OR, WHAT YOU WILL, William Shakespeare. (0-486-29290-8)